Tinna's Reign

More about the Author:
www.mirandamayer.com

The Trilogy of Tinna

Tinna's Promise
Tinna's Might
Tinna's Reign

Other titles by Miranda:

The Wizard King
Blackroot
The Belletrist (Anthology)

Character art for the cover design created by Abigail Larson
www.abigaillarson.com

Tinna's Reign

A fantasy by
Miranda Mayer

FOX DEN

OREGON

MIRANDA MAYER

Tinna's Promise

Copyright © 2015 by Miranda Mayer

Fox Den Publishing may be ordered through booksellers or by contacting

Fox Den Books
PO Box 39
Brightwood, OR 97011

Fox Den Publishing rev. date 2/10/2015

To my first uber-fan, Jathia. Thank you for your beautiful enthusiasm. It is the sort of thing that makes writing worthwhile.

To Alex, Dan, Nee, Hellie, S2, Molly, No-no, Charlie, Heather & Aelfgyva. You guys are lifeblood.

And to Wendy Pamay—as always.

CHAPTER ONE – MARRIAGE

Offrin gazed up at his bride and he could barely contain his joy. He could not believe his fortune. He wanted the ceremony to be completed immediately, so nothing could disrupt the union. Two years of solid longing, hoping and striving to earn her affections all culminated into this moment, where she stood beside him as his bride. The ceremony seemed to go on forever, but it proceeded uninterrupted, and Offrin's fast-beating heart swelled when she said "I take him to me," and he saw her slender arm reach out to receive the binding bracelet.

She was resplendent, a good head and a half taller than he, Avria wore a gown of snowy white; of fine, sheer, wispy fabric over an emerald green under-dress with a high waist and elegant draping skirts. The short train of the white over-dress fanned out gracefully behind her. Her long sleeves, sheer white and fitted to her arms had gathered lace cuffs that flared slightly out over her knuckles. Her hair was a shock of black curls decorated with a circlet of stylized silver knots of the Adrei style; and freshwater pearls nested in woven bands of silver adorned her neck and ears. She knelt beside Offrin at the altar of the great temple, where Master Baruld stood in his ceremonial robes, shorter by far than Offrin, but still powerful and grave in presence.

Offrin knew Avria did not love him as he loved her. She cared for him deeply; she did love him, but not in the way she loved Eleran. Her love for Offrin was sweet, and sedate, trusting and gentle; her love for Eleran was one of burning passion that would remain locked away inside her heart. Eleran was gone—time had softened her grief, and Offrin's doting attentions soon won her heart; at least most of it.

He was content to have that much; he loved her so. When her fingers slid into his, and Baruld sealed the binding bracelets, he thought his heart would explode it was so full. He looked up at her beautiful, serene face, her dark eyes taking in his happiness, and he kissed her tender lips, still unbelieving that he had been so lucky as to be wed to her.

He had loved her the moment he first set eyes upon her. She had led her horse into the Taruttee village square, Eleran was hunched, pale and weak on the graceful equine and as soon as the she stopped, he keeled sideways and fell from the horse. Offrin recalled seeing her, kneeling with terrified eyes over the still form of his rival when he'd slid out of the saddle, and crumpled to the ground. He'd been called to her side then, and had remained there since. Through the war, and after, he was there, comforting her when she wept for Eleran, cheering her up when she was moping, following her between Taruttee and Thamatoc, and helping her as much as he could in her work with Master Gavorre. It was inevitable that she would come to love Offrin. Now here she was leaning down to kiss him for the first time as his wife.

The spectators exploded into applause when they kissed, and Baruld gestured for them to stand and to face their community and family as a wedded couple. And with that, the ceremony was over and the celebration would begin.

It was a mixed crowd; people of Taruttee, quite short in stature, mingled in with the taller Araki people, all jubilant and merry. They stood from the long stone benches facing the grand altar, and flowed into the aisle behind the newly married couple. The ceremony was being held at old human settlement of Klatna so that they could make use of the restored temple there. It was big enough to hold the extraordinary number of guests that expressed a wish to be present for this binding.

Klatna was a second home for Avria's family now—the city had become such a gathering place for the regional peoples, it was inevitable that they choose it as a venue for this momentous occasion. The crowd poured out onto the street, cascading from the forest of columns of the temple, and following the new couple up the hill in a euphoric procession, throwing handfuls of pine nuts up the road towards the couple, and showering them in blessings, and on several occasions, with stinging pain from particularly fast flying pine-nut projectiles. The crowd moved with festive purpose towards an old manor where a banquet and musicians awaited them.

Above them, the stones of the academy were being replaced, the broken walls being resurrected, the towers under reconstruction. The old academy of Hildercross had once dominated the crest of Mt. Klatna like a crenellated crown, the town once spiraling up the hillside towards it. However the destruction had decimated the better part of the small city, and killed nearly all of its human inhabitants, rendering this ancient academy into rubble, leaving only a few walls standing. It was a long time coming for this academy to receive such special attention. Klatna's placement on a crucial trade-road made the town important, so the Araki took it over and went about rebuilding the things they thought necessary for the city to thrive. The Academy was never high on the list, but after the One-Day War, priorities were shifted. The balance of the decisions now rested largely on the will of two people alone; Taneth; Avria's father, and Tinna; Avria's mother.

Both of Avria's parents were trailing quietly behind the wedding crowd, holding hands. On Tinna's free arm, propped on her hip was a little baby boy of just shy of a year of age who was avidly chewing on his little fist. He was a wide-eyed, handsome little creature with silver-grey eyes and a thick thatch of dark hair. This was Avria's new sibling Istvan; an already well-established personality even at so young an age. He was also already attempting to toddle about and was most curious by nature, much like his father.

Tinna smiled when Avria looked down the hill for her, breaking into a brilliant grin and waving when she finally caught her mother's gaze. Tinna marveled at how beautiful her daughter was, and what a wonderful person she had become. Both she and Taneth adored Offrin, and thought them to be an excellent match. They loved him greatly, and cared only that he make their daughter happy after all the trauma she'd endured.

It took Drashun and a few of Avria's closest friends at home to get used to the idea that she was marrying a little person, but since the war, the auberge communities opened up to the Araki, and they had begun to function more like a single community; both little people and the irrevocably average Araki horse-worshippers. In fact,

Taneth, who was a highly ranked Wiseman, had become particularly close to the Adrei apothecary with whom Avria had lived and trained with for some time. He was known as Master Gavorre. Both he and Taneth now traveled often together to the archive town of Lemoram, and Master Gavorre contributed a great number of ideas to the reformation of the educational academies, including Hildercross, working to include a place for his people in the plan. It had been a busy time since they returned from the One-Day War.

The couple climbed the wide steps to the old-style brown-brick manor house, and threw open the doors. The wedding attendees flowed in behind them, the last to enter; the manor's actual residents. Once but a shell of masonry walls, the manor that was to host them was a home away from home of sorts for Tinna and her family. Tinna had refused to move north and leave the forests as the Keepers had requested. She was however, the Ashru of the Araki, the chosen Queen of sorts for the largest group of people in the world now—and the Keepers were pushing her to become more than that. The human leadership was laughable at best; non-effective and not even useful as an inspirational figurehead. The High King, a young man recently crowned in place of his aging father, was an insolent, useless youth, and he represented a population that was dwindling into insignificance instead of growing strong again.

The manor was a compromise. She would take residence here for some times during the year, and then return to the humbler abode at her clan village of Thamatoc when she'd had enough. Being a new mother after forty was taxing as it was; adding the responsibility of a struggling empire was another matter altogether. Mix in the marriage of her daughter and the planning for a wedding, and Tinna was looking forward to leaving Klatna in the morning and spending a good, long, quiet winter at Thamatoc. Taneth predicted that the bright sun and crisp dry skies would abate, and the snows were soon to arrive. So soon, she could smell the sharp scent of it in the air before she entered the manor. Winters in the forestlands were known to be harsh. She hoped it would be a such a heinous, snowy, icy winter; that it would hinder travel even for dragons and give her some peace.

This day it was cold, but it was clear and bright, and the afternoon was giving way to a raw night of flawless skies filled with myriad stars. The manor sported fires in its recently restored hearths that bellowed out warmth and welcome into its two connected assembly rooms. The whole manor still smelled of the new wood and fresh lacquer they'd used to treat the new paneling on the walls.

The guests gathered around two great tables stacked with platters containing a variety of foods. Each table had a mountain of tiers topped by an elegant hart of made of bronze. The tiers boasted platters of foods, from freshly roasted slices of venison heaped into a cone to tiny cakes in snow-white icing topped with sweet winterberries of salmon pink. The spaces between the platters were decorated with evergreen boughs and sprigs of holly bright with berries, and fragrant branches of juniper with their subtle blue berries. The tall ceilings were hung with a row of swags made of conifer sprigs, evergreens and berries, filling the rooms with the scent of pine. Between each window, massive standing candelabras brandishing branches full of thick candles shed warm light into the darkening space as the afternoon gave way to evening. Behind these were mirrors hung to reflect even more of that light back into the festive space.

Draperies of rich fabrics, and portraits both new and salvaged adorned the newly paneled walls—one particular portrait of Tinna and Taneth in stately pose and costume dominated the wall above the main hearth in the great hall. Tinna hated it, Taneth couldn't help but puff his chest out and smirk when he saw the image of himself in his fine formal robes of office standing over his wife, who was seated in a stylish chair in a gown of midnight-blue velvet with silver embroidered hems. They looked downright royal, and Taneth thought the depiction of his wife was masterful, and marveled at how her black eyes seemed to follow the viewer wherever they went in the room. Whenever he had the chance, he would boast of this, and make visitors join him in his experiment, navigating about the room and exclaiming: "See? She's still got you in her sights!"

This evening, Tinna was dressed like royalty again; a true lady. Like her daughter, she wore a trained gown, hers a sapphire blue silk as light as air, her hair up, jewelry on and dainty silken slippers. She removed her heavy black cloak and a servant seemed to materialize out of the ether and took it. She switched carrying arms for the boy, glanced at her husband, who smiled down at her from his lofty height, and entered the great hall at her side. The baby was immediately yanked from her arms by his elder sister, who twirled him and made him squeal in delight. She hugged him to her chest and kissed his nose and cheeks, lifting his little tunic to blow raspberries on his belly. His laughter rang out in peals of enchantment.

"Well then, little brother, what think you of all of this?" she asked. "What think you of your new brother? He cuts a fine figure does he not?" Avria danced around Offrin who laughed merrily. All the while, the child produced the most brilliant dimpled smiles he could muster; simply tickled to see his sister he adored so. His face always lit up when he saw her. Tinna laughed gently and found a free seat. In the back of the second hall, the musicians were plucking their instruments and tuning them up; passively summoning the dancers to the floor. Offrin grasped his wife's hand and dragged her away, baby and all. Taneth went to retrieve the boy so they could head the dance as a proper couple. He returned toting his young son, and sat next to his wife, plopping the child on his knee. Istvan was entranced by all the people in their bright and sparkling clothing. The music made him squeal again and he kicked his feet as if dancing himself. The dancing began and immediately, the noise level escalated, and the festive mood intensified.

Couples wove about the space as the dance began, gowns flaring out, smiles flashing while the vaulted ceiling was filled with music. Rigerd danced with his wife; even Rhoa had come from the north to join them for the wedding, guiding her gruff ungainly Duke through the steps. "You mock me now," he shouted, "but in my day, I was quite light of foot, with the grace of a buck!" he shouted over the music, a smile looking odd on his badly scarred face. Tinna laughed, and Taneth chuckled. Avria was radiant, her husband even more so, his face aglow. Offrin looked fine in his elegant blue frock coat and snow-white stockings. Master Gavorre appeared quietly at Tinna's side, and he glanced up at her.

"They are good together."

"Indeed," she sighed. Master Gavorre had become a sort of uncle to Avria. When she was at Taruttee, she stayed with him. She studied what he did in his apothecary shop. It was a good enough reason for her to stay at Taruttee. With Jestin; a young man who could potentially bring her to harm; still theoretically about and dangerous, they thought it would be good for her to remain at the Adrei community, in spite of the fact that the person she'd returned there to be with was no longer present. Eleran had been taken away before the war ended, but Avria remained on the most part. At first she remained in the hopes that Eleran would return, but eventually, she stayed simply because she had grown to love it there and to love Offrin too.

"Offrin; he has a curative effect on her. She has forgotten her loss, it seems."

"Oh, Tinna, do not be fooled by her smile, that girl's heart is still broken. But she put that part of it away for now. She is living a life that isn't entirely hers. She plays a role," the apothecary muttered gravely. Tinna's brows rose in concern.

"Is that what you believe? That she is unhappy?" Her eyes wandered back to her daughter, who at that moment danced around Offrin, and stole as kiss as she passed him by, her grey eyes sparkling.

"No, I do not doubt her happiness; but her complete happiness is forever lost. She isn't whole anymore. She never will be." Tinna frowned deeply and she turned to look at Taneth. Her eyes looked worried. Before Taneth could open his mouth, another person joined the conversation.

"Sorry I'm so late." Tinna looked up to take in a tall, lanky gentleman of later years, with hauntingly light blue eyes, a shaved head and a pointed, meticulously trimmed beard of grey. He was dashingly handsome and he never seemed to get older in the years she'd known him.

"I won't brook excuses, Phenmal, Avria looks to you like a second father. You should have been here for the ceremony," Tinna immediately admonished, quite serious in her dressing-down.

"I apologize with all my soul, I…"

"You chose to travel by coach, when Leya offered to fly you here herself in place of Igro!" Tinna snapped.

"I am not comfortable with dragons. Mind you it's not always on a personal level—they're mostly tolerably kind and affable as individuals. Igro and I, we tolerate one another well enough, and I've come to trust his flight over time, and we can partake in reasonable discussions about reasonable things. Other dragons? No. Igro can be trusted not to purposefully shake me about or drop like a stone from the sky without warning for laughs. The others seem to delight in doing things like this to me for their amusement. What bothers me *most* is the whole being suspended in the sky thing. Being huddled behind a head-shield does nothing to protect a rider from the gusts

13

of wind and the cold. I do not like being at the mercy of these beasts." Taneth nodded emphatically in agreement beside his wife, he was no great fan of flying on dragons himself.

"The dragons offer to take me hither and thither, yes. They do. But truth be told, they don't really like me because I am Chaiva. They make sport of playing with my apprehensions about flight and torment me. With Igro, we've come to a sort of mutual respect; he is decent and does not do stupid things like his brethren. If I am to travel on wing, it is with Igro alone," he retorted with more animation than any of them had seen out of this gentleman in a long time.

"Not to mention that Igro and I share many hours on the wing as it is, so when I have the opportunity for respite from the blowing, cold air in exchange for the comfort of a plush, upholstered coach, I will take it. And Igro gets a rest to boot." They listened to him with amused expressions, taking in the impassioned light in his remarkably clear and strikingly blue eyes.

It was good to see Phenmal, and unusual to see him in a city. He didn't like the voices of a thousand people filling his head and avoided it as much as he could. However Tinna had to concede that he was here, facing a houseful of people after all; a huge sacrifice for a sensitive mind-reader.

"If Rhoa could swallow her fear and pride, so could you," she snorted, half smiling. "Now go and apologize to Avria, she was disappointed not to see you before the ceremony," Tinna grumbled. Taneth looked to his friend and shrugged as if to say: *what are you going to do? Argue with her?* Phenmal knew better, and bowed curtly, striding elegantly towards the dance area, where the quickstepping jig was just ending and the introductory notes of a more sedate dance were being played.

Phenmal caught Avria's hand before she was claimed by anyone else, and led her onto the floor, bowing elegantly to her. Everyone could see the reverence and adoration in her eyes at seeing Phenmal. She once feared this icy man, now; her respect for him was unmatchable. The couples lined up, and the music began in earnest, and away they went, into spins and turns, bows and curtsies, setting and casting in stylish figures. Phenmal moved with liquid grace, one hand clutched formally behind his back, the other handing her off and turning her, his chest out, his steps smooth. He did cut a fine, dignified figure, Tinna could not deny it. He seemed even more handsome every time she saw him.

Offrin came to Tinna to ask her to dance, but she declined before he had a chance to open his mouth.

"Don't even bother, Offrin, I do not dance," she said good-humouredly, waving her hand. "Even Taneth must go and find a partnerless woman when he desires to dance, for he knows I will refuse him." Tinna's Thran accent was still quite evident, and Offrin found it pleasant.

"There is still plenty of time to join the bottom of the set, Lady Tinna. I wish you would…"

"Offrin, I thank you, but no, truly no. I do not plan to dance at all this evening. Please go and choose a willing partner, it would be a waste to spend the entire dance trying to convince me to do something I am most certain to refuse." Offrin gave up and bowed in concession, offering her a smile as he turned to find someone else to pester.

They rarely danced at Thamatoc. Just making room in the main hall was such a task; moving the massive tables and the benches, it just wasn't much worth it. They did dance in the summer sometimes, out in the village common under the founder's tree. At the annual clan meetings, they performed dances almost every night. Everyone knew these individual dances by heart. They were old dances. In the few remaining human settlements, these dances had gone out of fashion long ago; however, since human fashions and pastimes were no longer the trend, these old dances were enjoying a new life as the markedly old-fashioned Araki influence spread out from the isolation of the forests.

It was a glorious sound; the music. The festive colours and food was also delightful. Tinna was beside herself simply sitting with Istvan in her lap, and taking in the ambience. In the past two decades, she had yet to experience a celebration this lavish and grand, but here she was, acting like a true blue-blood, lording over a crowd of her beloved villagers from Thamatoc, a large group of Avria's friends, Offrin's family from Taruttee, and some of the closer clan chieftains and their families from other Araki towns. It was a great affair by Araki standards, and extremely high-brow; servants and manors were not the norm. But with the shift of power between

15

peoples, things were gradually altering, and so was the lifestyle the Araki were accustomed to. Everything was changing.

Towns were being taken over by Araki clans. Chieftains were becoming mayors and governors. The trends were changing from insular communities to more human-like settlements infused with Araki culture.

Tinna took a moment to hover about the table to find some choice treats to sate her mild hunger, and then wandered back to the area where she'd been sitting before. The men still sat in discussion in the circle of settees and chairs. Tinna sank down next to her husband who scarce noticed she'd left in the first place.

"How do they plan to do that?"

"I am not sure, truth be told. Those sorts of mechanics are not my specialty, but it is a good way to start including the dragons into things; making things accessible to them," Taneth replied to Master Gavorre, who held the baby's arms while he stomped about in circles and then used the chair to sidle to his mother. Tinna scooped him right up and propped him on her lap again. They were discussing the dragon rookeries that Taneth wanted to install at the various new and restored towns and settlements, including here at Klatna. "Towers with narrow bases, no great footprint is required if it's built and balanced well. They're proposing a byre of sorts to top the towers; with high, vaulted ceilings and doors to close out the cold. They are also discussing some sort of oven below-floors that can heat the byre, for when they come in winter..." Tinna's mind faded out immediately. Since the war it was nothing but talk about building this or changing that. She was exhausted by it all. Her husband was either gone on some trip to plan these projects, or at home rattling on and on incessantly about them. With a subtle sigh, she turned her attention to the dancing; but the realization crept up on her that she was extremely tired.

All the talking and activity, as exhilarating and sophisticated as it felt, exhausted Tinna; and Istvan grew weary as well as babies do when the hour grows late. When he began to fuss, Tinna excused herself and climbed the great stairway, carrying the boy to the private apartments; which were ten times the size of their apartments at home. Here, she lived like true royalty. The rooms were all tall ceilings, detailed woodwork, delicate architecture of the human style, towering windows, paneled walls and woven rugs of rich colours.

Istvan's room by comparison was small, but it was cozy, snug against the back of the fireplace chimney, which generated a nice passive heat. She changed him into his night-clothes and tucked him into his cradle, and sat with him; rocking his ornate cradle until he went to sleep. He was an even tempered, calm child, not restless and endlessly active like Avria had been. When he finally dozed off, Tinna shucked her formal gown, and dressed in something more appropriate for Thamatoc; loose floor-length skirts with a slight train, and a wide V-neck fitted tunic sweater that ended at her thighs.

She sank down into the comfortable chair and stared at her baby boy. With a sigh, she leaned back into the tall seat, and within a few moments, Tinna was sleeping soundly.

It was well past the midnight hour when the last of the guests exited the house. Taneth had retired for the evening hours before—rousing his wife from her chair to guide her to her sleeping clothes and bed. Phenmal was snoring lightly in one of the soft chairs in the private drawing room where he'd retreated to smoke his pipe and escape the chatter of the guests. As close to a member of their family as one could be, Phenmal had his own rooms set aside upstairs, but he hadn't quite made it that far. Offrin was eager to go to bed, and went upstairs ahead of Avria to stoke the fire in their apartments.

"Are you sure you won't stay?" Avria took her cousin's arm and gave him a worried look. "It's so late already, and you will be riding in the dark. It's really quite cold out here..."

"We will be fine. We have a room at The Saddle. It's only a short ride down the hill. We won't leave for Thamatoc until morning, I promise," he assured her. "It's likely we will be ahead of your party well before sunrise," he said.

Avria bade her cousin Drashun and his young wife Ynn goodnight, and watched them climb onto their horses, which had been saddled and brought forth from the manor's stable and tethered to the gate only moments before they left the house. Ynn mounted sideways on her traditional astride saddle, grinning awkwardly at Avria. She was Araki; she would be fine with a knee crossed over the flat pommel of the thin Araki saddle. With the fine gown she had made for this occasion, she did not want to tear its delicate seams by riding astride, nor did she want to gather it up and ride with her stockings and pantaloons exposed. Araki women did not generally

17

own sidesaddles, they rode astride with split skirts and under-breeches; although Avria and Tinna did own sidesaddles for their jaunts to Loshan and points north into the human settlements, where sidesaddle was considered proper and more practical for the long-skirted, voluminous habits that were the fashion.

Ynn waved at Avria, as did her husband, whose endearing smile warmed Avria's heart. "Goodnight, Drashe, bye Ynn. See you two soon." She watched them fade into the darkness until they were nothing more but the retreating rhythm of hooves on cobbles.

Below her, the lights of the small city sparkled between the swaying branches of the young evergreens that grew where many of the old buildings used to be. Klatna had once been a densely packed city with hardly any greenery. Now, much of what grew in after the destruction was left undisturbed, and new construction was built around most of the new trees. Most Araki felt comfortable where there were trees. It was only natural.

It was exceedingly cold. Avria clasped her elbows and watched her breath turn into steam. She could see yellow glow of lamplight behind some windows in the houses below, and the many arcs of chimney smoke rising up into the darkness at the same slow angle from the rooftops of the houses. Some lanterns had been placed on the curbs to shed light onto darkened streets for the late-night revelers like her cousin and the remaining guests who'd left only moments before. Most of the guests chose to travel through the night to avoid the possibility of being caught in bad weather. Rhoa and her husband for instance left on dragon hours ago, flying north towards Zadrudas. Neither Avria nor her mother had spent much time with them. Avria felt bad. Others chose to lodge at Klatna, betting the weather would hold out long enough for their trip home. It was their bet too. The prospect of a warm bed seemed much more appealing than the idea of saddling up and leaving at that moment.

Avria sighed, standing on the wide stairway alone, the double doors wide-open behind her. She clutched a shawl around her shoulders, and looked out into the night with sad eyes. Her head snapped in the direction of the uphill road for a moment, for she thought she heard something stir. But the wind blew and hissed through the evergreens, and nothing moved that she could see; except a single, minuscule snowflake that meandered down from the sky. It gusted before her, catching the light from the doorway. With a little sigh, a passing shadow of sorrow and resignation crossed her eyes. Avria turned back into the house, and closed the night behind her.

Eleran took her in. His beauty. His love. He'd watched through the tall windows all night, as she twirled and danced the evening through, until the curls around her face sagged and clung from perspiration, and she could dance no more. He watched her chat spiritedly to old friends, throw her head back and laugh heartily at a joke. She drank dark wine, and bent down to kiss her new husband now and again, who stood beside her as much as possible, his arm possessively draped around her waist.

How beautiful she was in those gowns, they flattered her form. He recalled the first moment he saw her, upon entering the small village common. She was a lily in white amid a garden of muted nothings. She wore a gown like the one she wore tonight. She was fully innocent then, wide-eyed and idealistic, barely more than a girl. Now, she looked like a woman. She looked tired, and he felt her sense of... he paused for a moment, trying to place it. *Resignation, perhaps*, he was not certain. *None of that matters now*, thought he. He moved but a shade, but she sensed it and for a moment he thought he was discovered. He felt his heart swell at the idea of seeing her face to face. Alas, she did not see him. *It is for the better. For now.* He watched her go back inside, and tried not to think about the fact that she was going upstairs to another man. The trees suddenly began to shiver all around him, as his eyes turned baleful.

Two hours before dawn, Offrin was awoken by the movement of the bed. He turned to see his new wife bathed in sweat, squirming and twitching in the throes of a nightmare. He reached out and touched her face. Her eyes shot open, she pulled away and screamed. It seemed to take her a moment to recognize that she was looking at Offrin and she then collapsed back onto her side, plopping her head on her pillow. In the waning light of the fire, she looked weary and frightened.

"What is it, Avria?" Offrin asked, patting down her wild hair and soothing her. She sighed heavily, her bare shoulder rising and falling, and she shook her head clumsily on her pillow.

"Nothing but a silly dream; I can barely remember it," she lied— her voice broken and groggy. She scooted closer to him, and huddled against his body. She was still trembling. He wrapped his arms around her and kissed the top of her head. Soon, she was sleeping again.

That little snowflake had been the first of many, for come morning, there was a layer of snow eight fingers thick blanketing the mountain. It thinned out significantly as the group of riders descended Mt. Klatna and left the city, but the snow showed no sign of stopping. They turned onto the main trade road, and followed it south for a bit before turning onto the gypsy roads towards Thamatoc.

"I had a strange dream last night, mother," Avria muttered this as the two women rode ahead of the group. "I can't get it out of my head." Tinna huddled around Istvan, who was propped in front of her on the saddle, held fast to her torso by a sling. He didn't seem much bothered by the snow that still fell, and waved his chubby fingers about and grasped hunks of Beast's mane. Avria did not respond to his giggles of delight as he took in all these things. Offrin mentioned her little nightmare to Tinna that morning while they breakfasted, and pointed out how morose Avria seemed. She told Offrin that it would pass, and thought nothing more of it. Tinna glanced at her and frowned with thought, waiting for Avria to elaborate.

"It was strange and horrible," she continued. "I was walking... or maybe riding, I don't remember. And it's dark, and out of the darkness comes Eleran. I think it's Eleran at least, but he's so disfigured I can hardly recognize him. He is different," Tinna saw Avria shudder and her brows furrowed deeply.

"How do you mean, different, Avie?"

"He's all wrong. He's still there, I can feel him in here..." she clutched her hand to her heart, "but there's something deeply wrong. He is chasing me. I am afraid of him and I am running. He finds me and then he comes for me, but my response is terror, not happiness... that's when Offrin woke me."

"And you don't think it's just a bad dream?" Tinna asked without admonishment. Avria shook her head, her eyes glassy, and her throat tight.

"How often do your dreams stay with you? Less than an hour after you're awake, you normally don't remember them..."

"That's true," Tinna conceded, "but still, what do you think it could be otherwise? Eleran is gone. He may not be dead, but Gavorre said his essence was no longer connected to his body. What remains of Eleran is a shell, Avria, and wherever that shell is, it cannot harm you."

"It didn't feel like a dream, mother," Avria said, her eyes wide and scared. "It felt like... him." There was a stony silence as Tinna took in what Avria was saying.

"You think Eleran could return? That his essence has been reunited with his body?"

"I'm not sure..."

"Why would you feel fear of that, Avria? He loved you beyond measure. Surely this dream is connected to your feelings for Eleran; perhaps you sense that you somehow betray him by moving on with your life? You should not feel guilty for finding love again. I am certain, if Eleran could, he would wish this for you as well. He would not wish you to continue on pining for his existence until your death,"

"No. It's not guilt. I know what I have chosen is right, I love Offrin. Eleran is gone. But this dream, it was different. Eleran was something other than what he was. He felt... evil."

"Eleran loved you so much. So much so, he sacrificed his soul to save you," Tinna said, her eyes filled with concern. "He would never harm you. He loved you."

"And I, he. But again... I don't know," she whispered. She was stricken, her eyes sunken and her lips a hard, tight line of worry. In her mind, she thought of Eleran's tale; of his people's beliefs that people only carried half a soul and that the other half was always out there inside someone else. He said if they were lucky enough to meet during a lifetime, that there was no mistaking that connection. He could see it because he was gifted with powers. She only knew that the moment she saw him she was drawn to him like a moth to a flame. She wondered if that same connection was what caused her nightmare. She shifted in her saddle and smiled wanly at her mother, who still gazed at her with worry. Snow drifted down and settled into her curls. "It's nothing I'm sure, mother. I am probably still suffering some residual stress from the wedding. I'm looking forward to wintering at Thamatoc. It will be good to feel truly at home."

Chapter two – Foreshadowing

Tinna sighed in contentment and reached for the kettle with a rag protecting her hand. She lifted it off the hook and carried it to the table where a pot full of tea leaves awaited. She poured it into the pot and then took the kettle back, where she put it in one of the many nooks built into the façade of the hearth. She turned to look at Avria, who was wearing informal Araki style skirts of dark brown with a droopy black tunic. Tinna was dressed just as casually, a similar long set of layered skirts of black and grey, an ivory undershirt, and the most threadbare, shapeless sweater made of knitted wool. It had once been a vibrant orangey-red colour, but most of the dye had faded away. The colour wasn't even, leaving it looking less than fashionable. The shape it once held was now gone, and the neckline barely caught Tinna's shoulders, one side sliding down onto her arm. The sleeves were too long now, and Tinna bunched them up on her arm to keep the cuffs from dipping into the tea.

No matter how old and ugly that sweater had become, it was still the most valued piece of clothing amid the immediate family. It was the only artifact of Tinna's past that she held onto—it had belonged to her father. She knew nothing of him at all, except that he was a gypsy; but somehow when Tinna needed comfort and peace, she found it wearing his sweater. Avria loved it because it was soothing to be in, because she saw how much comfort it gave her mother. They treated it like it was spun of gold. Tinna knew how to knit and fixed it as best she could when a piece of the yarn snapped, but its days were nearing an end, and soon it would be too fragile, too spindly to wear anymore. It was irreplaceable, but Tinna could not keep from wrapping herself in it.

Tinna sank down in her chair, and poured the tea into the tiny cups, looking at Avria with a motherly glance. She handed Avria a cup and she took it. The girl smirked and said: "Gods, it's good to be home."

"I second that declaration my dear. No offense against you my sweet girl, but I am glad your wedding is done. I'm glad you chose to come here instead of going back to Taruttee. It's nice to have you home."

"Staying with Master Gavorre with a new husband isn't appropriate, and Offrin lived at the barracks, so we were want for a place to go. I confess only to you how strange it would be to continue to live and work in a home where everything is scaled to the uses of the Adrei… I'm no giant of a woman, but it's still close quarters for me much of the time. It's good to walk through wide doorways and sit in reasonably sized chairs," she smiled easily.

Tinna had never heard of the Adrei until the One Day War. She learned that human communities sent babies and children born with small bodies to what were called Auberge communities; places of shelter, where they could be among their own 'kind'. The humans believed that the little people that were born to them were something other than human.

They were misguided, but she imagined it was far more humane than what she knew her own people, the Thran would do to imperfect babies. Her being a half-blood gypsy alone nearly marked her for death. The only reason she still lived is because her mother was nobility, and had the favour of the ruler. But surviving this still exposed her to a childhood of abuse and cruelty far beyond the norm for Thran girls.

The practice of sending imperfect, small-statured children to the Auberges had mostly ended since the war, Taneth made sure of that. The law was now that the little children would remain at home until they are old enough to choose their own way; and the Adrei, the little people of this northern world, would remain in their communities as they pleased; always offering an option to those who wished to live in a world built to suit them. Many humans still resisted this edict, still holding on to the idea that their child was not human and not meant for their world. The Adrei were always there to receive the unwanted and to make them welcome—and the adoptees still arrived with a fair regularity. Master Gavorre's daughter had just taken in a new baby only a few months before. It would be a difficult task, to educate the ignorant on the matter, Taneth declared to Master Gavorre on the subject. "There are so few humans remaining the practice will surely fade anyway."

Avria explained to Tinna that sometimes the Adrei couples would produce a child of average size. But they did not send them away, most did stay but some children would go off to seek out the greater world. Most of them stayed at the auberges with their families, married and lived their lives, hunching under doorways and squatting in tiny chairs.

"Almost two years I've been in and out of there, and I still hit my head on Master Gavorre's door frame in the kitchen," she shook her head laughing. There was a light rap on the door, and Taneth poked his head in.

"Snow's getting hideous out there. We have a small band of visitors asking for shelter..." he added, looking concerned. Taneth was a lanky, awkardish sort of fellow with a unique handsomeness that Tinna found quite appealing. He had a long face with strong angles softened by a trimmed goatee and a thick mat of short hair that was graying at the temples. His whiskers also had a silver dusting. He looked at his women with his stormy grey eyes and rubbed his nose with the back of his hand, sniffling a bit. He wore a pair of tiny spectacles pinched to the bridge of his nose, something he'd just acquired from the city of Lemoram only a few weeks ago to help him see things close to him—but he often forgot he had them on and looked at everyone else over the top of them. He was dressed quite informally this day. Taneth was a high-ranked Wiseman, one of consequence, and had the robes to suit his office, however, whenever at home on the most part, he stuck to comfortable clothes and bare feet as much as he could get away with it. He was bundled up against the snow this day, and his cheeks and nose were rosy from the chill. He plucked his spectacles off of his nose and put them carefully on a small table in a box where he usually stored them.

"Visitors?" Tinna asked, wondering who in their right mind would be traveling in this weather voluntarily. For a moment she dreaded it would be someone from the Keepers; but she knew Taneth would mention this if it were.

"Gypsies," he elaborated. It wasn't unusual to have a band pass through. They had a network of circuitous routes through the forests that they traveled on, constantly moving along in and out of the forests, to the far north and then south again. The Araki used and often helped maintain the roads when they cut through clan territory. The nomads passed through once or twice a year, traded their unusual goods collected from around the land, and then were on their way fairly quickly. It was unusual to have them at winter, and even more unusual for them to seek shelter. Their caravans were well equipped and they were set up to survive the hard seasons unaided. The snow had been coming down quite hard when they got home that afternoon. They were relieved upon entering the lodges, which were comfortably underground and warm from constant fires. After two and a half solid days of riding, it was a welcoming feeling. This storm was particularly wicked; with powerful winds that brought limbs and branches down, and hurled the snow into stinging projectiles, even underneath the canopy where the winds were usually more subdued by the protection of trees.

"Well… They can go into the worship lodge, without a doubt. It's not as cozy as the residences, but it's a nice series of broad spaces and the open hearths ought to serve them well. They can stable their horses and draught animals in the back," Tinna replied. She stood and so did Avria, and they both tugged on their soft hide fur-lined boots. It took only a moment for them to grasp cloaks, and they followed Taneth out of the apartments and down the long corridor to the entrance hall, where he opened the door and was pushed back by a powerful wind that showered the floor of the antechamber in tiny crystals of snow. The women stepped into the gusting wind, and the flakes of snow felt like needles on their faces. They all three forged out into the common after Taneth pulled the door closed with all his might.

"By Arak, this is awful," Tinna shouted over the whistling wind. She had no idea it had gotten this bad in only a few hours. "Some of the wedding guests are probably traveling in this … I hope they're alright. Perhaps I should ask Ledroran to send out a dragon or two to scout them out and see if they need help…" she yelled. Taneth shook his head, picking up most of what she said.

"I can't imagine even dragons would fly in this."

"Or see anything…" she added. Most of her words were eaten up by gusts of wind and buffered by the volume of snow blowing around them. "They can only fly above it."

He led them to a figure against the curtains of blowing flakes and gestured for him to follow. Tinna then noticed several other figures behind the first one, all clutching fur-lined hoods closed around their faces, she sensed more people, but they were obscured by the snow. Taneth led them to the rarely-used temple hall, one of the smaller lodges but still sizable enough to accommodate the travelers. "You can probably bring your caravans right in if you need to. The door here opens wide enough," he shouted at the man-but he gestured that he couldn't hear. Taneth opened the man-door that was nested into the larger door, and they all stepped in out of the storm. Suddenly, as the heavy door was shut, the silence became as deafening as the din of the storm. The gypsies threw back their hoods and looked to Taneth and then Tinna. There were eight men and six women. Five children clung to various adults… Tinna hadn't seen them all because of the horrible visibility. Two mid-sized dogs also accompanied them.

"Get your animals in here. We can open the main door and you can have them drive your caravans inside. They can snug them up against the side wall here and fit nicely. This storm is terrible… they should not be out there in it any longer than they need to," Taneth instructed the swarthy, severe-looking people.

"We only have three caravans… six pullers; two draught horses, four Moropus. We normally don't do this…"

"This isn't normal. This storm is the worst I've seen since I've been here. Please… I will help you."

Taneth and the men went out and Tinna and Avria closed the inset door and then lifted the bars that kept the larger door secured against the weather. They heaved it open and snow blew right into the large space. Tinna took off her cloak and draped it on a half wall, and then went back to light torches and brighten the darkened, little-used lodge. A few minutes later, the shadow of the first caravan filled the opening, and the two moropus pulling it widened their sheep-like nostrils and warily stepped inside, pulling the rumbling house behind them. The man that led the animals pulled them deep into the lodge, and soon the second and third of the caravans arrived. The men shoved the great door closed. The gypsies set to removing the harness from the pulling beasts, and then led them to the stall enclosures in the back of the lodge where newborn foals were kept with the mares for the first few weeks of their lives. Here the stalls were spacious and comfortable. There was already a good stock of bedding moss and hay stored there taken fresh from the fields in the waning days of summer. The animals were settled in and fires were lit in the three central hearths.

Tinna and Avria stood by watching the gypsies going about their work, both curious and waiting for Taneth to finish up his business. As they did, one of the gypsy women passed close to Tinna and stopped, tilting her head as she looked at her. She boldly reached out and picked up the hem of Tinna's old, ugly sweater. "Lathlo," she smiled. "Old, but unmistakable. The knit pattern is Garev Clan. When did they come through here? It's not their normal route. They prefer more southerly trails…"

"Pardon?" Tinna asked.

"Gypsy clans, madam. This is the colour and knit pattern of the Lathlo Garev clan. It's worse for wear, but their workmanship has probably made it last a lot longer than any ordinary knit garment would, I'll wager." Her accent was thick and luscious, and her eyes dark and full of kindness.

Tinna's eyes took in the woman's clothes; she wore a shawl; a triangle of knit wool dyed a vibrant but dark blue, barely discernible in the weak light of the lodge. The pattern was pretty, a scaling of V shapes in the knit. She never noticed that before, that they wore the same type of knit wear. The pattern was the same on all the pieces she could see. The men wore similar sweaters to hers, much less damaged, much less stretched, adorned in the same pattern as the woman's shawl. They wore clan colours—it was a revelation. She did not know this of the gypsies. Few probably did.

Tinna's throat tightened and she clutched the sleeves of her sweater to her chest.

"Then my father must have been of this clan," she said to Avria, who looked on with wide eyes. She saw joy in Tinna's face—such a delightful discovery for a woman who always wished to know more about her father.

"So you are of us," the gypsy woman surmised. Avria glanced at her with an arched brow while the woman appraised Tinna carefully. "You are of the Lathlo-Garev, your tunic speaks of this, but now that

I look, your features are distinct, I can see the Lathlo family in them; the way your brows are angled, serious it looks; the tilt of your eyes. You look strongly of that family, despite the mix of Thran blood. Your father must have been strongly connected to the Lathlo line to produce such distinctions in a mixed blood. Your Lathlo features are more powerful than your Thran ones. Any of the six Lathlo family clans would know you as one of their own by looking at you. Any one of them."

"I know nothing of my father's family or his clan..." Tinna muttered.

"I know little myself of the Lathlo besides my sister's marriage into that particular clan. It is a large clan, with eleven bands in it alone."

"First family, then clan, then bands," Taneth whispered, appearing as if out of nowhere beside his wife. Anything new, anything interesting, he wanted to be part of it. This was exactly the sort of conversation that would attract Tinna's husband. Tinna's brows rose up and she pursed her lips.

"So you or anyone else, would not know of who my father could be?"

"No. If you must know, you should go to the family gatherings." Tinna nodded, and clutched the front of her tunic. The woman picked up the droopy hem again and shook her head.

"This is so old. It isn't quite dead yet though. If you pass it to me, perhaps I can fix it; re-knit it with some of our wool to give it strength. I can try to match the colour and dye it afresh, and tighten the knit perhaps... give it new life. It looks as if we are to be snowed in a few days. I think I can do this in that time. A small gift for your hospitality." Tinna looked at her apprehensively, and the woman stuck out her hand. "I will return it, I promise."

"She needs to go out in the snow... This is the only lodge that isn't connected," Avria interjected. The woman nodded and took her blue shawl from her shoulders, and proffered it to Tinna.

"A fair trade... we can exchange them again when I am finished. We will not leave until it is finished to your liking. I will respect your heirloom with my soul; I see what it means to you." Tinna lifted the heavy knit work over her head, fully exposing the wide-necked white shirt she wore beneath. The woman took the bundle of yarn, and Tinna lifted the shawl from her hand, and draped it over her shoulders. Avria handed her the cloak she'd left draping on the wall and Tinna put it on over that.

"There. You will see how well I can give this old thing new life and do its first owner justice."

"She is the most skilled artisan among us," a dignified looking elderly gentleman interjected, arriving behind the ladies. Tinna had seen him helping set up the horses for the night and assisting in lighting the fires in the open hearths. He bowed deeply to Tinna, studying her closely, and then looking at Avria.

"I see it as well, your heritage. It is good to know the leader of this village is of our kind. It makes us feel welcomed when most of the time we are not. We know this village has been much welcoming to other bands, they speak well of Thamatoc."

"You are too kind, Elder."

"I am Azrash... the seer of this band."

"Like our holyman?" Avria asked. It was the first time in all her life they actually truly engaged the gypsy passers-by. They usually kept a respectful distance from one another and spoke only in transactions and trade. Rhoa was the only one who had any long-term experience with the gypsies, and she now lived far north.

"In essence, yes," he replied. He then turned to look at Tinna. "We are glad to find shelter among welcoming people. It has not been awfully welcoming anywhere else. The non-Araki settlements outside of the forest have been especially unkind to our people of late," the Azrash told them. Tinna's brow furrowed.

"You mean the human settlements?" He nodded with a regretful look on his face. She turned to Taneth, her brow furrowed. "I can't imagine why they'd act cruelly against them all of a sudden?"

"They have always been leery of us, we are used to that. But we were never completely unwelcome. We bring things to trade, and stories of different places, so we have always found some place to stay near their towns and cities. But there is definitely some tension these past few months; some towns have taken to chasing our caravans off their lands, and refusing to trade with us. This is the reason why we come to you now for shelter. We would have already been at our wintering region by now, but we had to travel farther during summer and autumn to trade for the supplies we needed to bridge the coldest months. We don't understand the sudden change of heart, but we suspect it might have something to do with the war—because it seems to have begun shortly after that." Tinna nodded and sighed in agitation.

"Or perhaps with the coronation," Taneth said knowingly. Tinna huffed again through her nose and shook her head.

"There have been some tidings from the north of the King and his kind making declarations that might incite the human settlements to resentment. They are few and far between to begin with, their world has been shattered nigh twenty years and they have not recovered at all in all that time, in spite of our efforts to assist them. They tried to protect their land from invasion with an army so small; every last soldier would have been massacred. They have much to be sorrowful for. But still... I don't understand. The people of Arak saved them from the Thran. Our armies stood up to keep theirs from being obliterated, and yet they still are able to harbor anger against anyone remotely connected to us," Tinna grumbled.

The understanding of the connection between the wandering people and the horse people had become common knowledge since the war—as did everything else Taneth learned about the shape of the world. He believed it was important that humanity understand who walked among them, so they could be more understanding of them. It had apparently taken the opposite effect and given reason for humanity to further isolate themselves from the other races. Taneth's brow was furrowed, his lips pursed. "There's no good reason for that. I am greatly sorry for that, kind Elder."

"You do not need to apologize for the human race, good man. It is a challenge we've known before, even when we once believed we all shared the same race; and it will be something we can endure and overcome as we always have." There was a lull as they pondered all this, and Tinna clutched the shawl closed at her neck. Avria's eyes were wide and curious.

"Well then," Tinna said, feeling suddenly quite awkward, "we'll be on our way. We'll leave you to your lodge..."

"There is another matter I wish to discuss before you return to your lodge, although I am hesitant to bring it up." The Azrash smiled gently, and then paused. The expression on his face was one that indicated he had something important to say but didn't know how to say it. He looked at Tinna pointedly and cleared his throat. "On the matter of my being Azrash... I wish to tell of something that has raised my concern since my arrival," he paused again, looking as if he was having difficulty putting it into words.

"Please, do feel free to share your concerns, Azrash," Tinna said. He looked uncomfortable, as if he would be mocked for his exertion, but he nodded and spoke.

"I have, since my arrival in your village, been overcome with a sense of something... I don't know..." he sighed, gritting his teeth in frustration. Avria's eyes widened and she clutched her elbows, looking to her mother, who frowned.

"Sir, I beg you not hesitate to speak to us of your concern," Tinna urged him.

"You do not have a spiritual guide here?" he suddenly asked. "Do you have a holy man, as your settlements normally do, or any kind of spiritual leader who uses or senses magic?"

"No. At present we have no such person here," Avria muttered, her voice cracking. Tinna's hand fell on her daughter's shoulder reassuringly, and she glanced at her and then the gypsy seer.

"I suspected as much. There is an absence of something intangible. If you did have such a man present, they would tell you the same as I would say to you Madame. Since our arrival, I've sensed it. I do not like the way it feels. It feels..." his pause was lengthy.

"Wrong," Avria finished. She bit her lip and Tinna glowered. Taneth merely looked confused by the whole discussion but didn't interrupt.

"Yes. Something is amiss. It is difficult to describe without sounding half-mad. But I do sense this, and it looms heavily."

"I have no idea what that could be," Tinna admitted. The gypsy's eyes wandered away from Tinna and onto Avria. The girl's face seemed to drain of colour.

"Nor can I identify what the thing is." He looked at Tinna again, and shrugged his shoulders. "However, I assure you, for as long as I am here, I will keep my senses keen Madame Leader, kind Wiseman. This I promise. If anything changes, I will surely let you know the moment it does." Tinna nodded silently and clutched the front of her cloak together. She led her daughter into the snow, leaving her puzzled husband behind. They returned to Tinna's apartments to sit and drink cold tea in a strained silence. Even when Istvan was returned from Jenyk's home, his innocent antics did little to lift the strange quiet gloom.

The gypsies did not take Taneth up on the invitation to share general meal with the tenants of the main lodge. Instead, they kept inside their lodge, avoiding the short but harrowing trek across the village common to the summer lodge. The blizzard was not abating, for a day it continued to howl and blow. The sunken common and the tree cover kept the bulk of the snow from accumulating in the circle where the lodges faced, but the wind made it impossible to see where one was going, and the snow that was accumulating was drifting up against the doors of the lodges.

People traveled through the various connecting tunnels that linked lodge to lodge underground rather than cross the common. The worship hall was the only unconnected lodge, and the gypsies seemed content to remain isolated in there from the curious Araki community. Taneth could not resist making the trip to check in on them here and again during the day, always fascinated with unusual things.

"I'm glad you decided to get married when you did, Avria," her father declared, shaking snow off his shoulders and stamping his feet on the floor of the entrance hall. Avria happened to be passing through the entrance hall in search of Offrin, who'd gone to the library an hour ago and had yet to return. "This is the worst storm I've ever seen in my twenty odd years here. The worst. I'm sure Rigerd would say the same. By Arak, it's hideous out there. We missed that storm by the skin of our teeth coming home. Let's hope the rest of the guests made it to shelter, because this is the kind of winter that kills wisemen and holymen." He traipsed through to the second corridor and left Avria with an odd smirk on her face. He was referring to the village 'curse'. They'd lost a Wiseman and a holyman that way; each had gone out before a storm, never to return. Taneth was the one to replace the lost Wiseman many years ago. The Holyman was lost before the war a little over two years before. Each one was found frozen to death and those winter storms were not half as terrible as this one by far.

Avria moved towards her father's private library and knocked twice and then entered without leave, finding Offrin, Phenmal and Master Gavorre all seated around the central table, feet up on the table-top, smoking pipes and laughing. The fact that they were here without Taneth was astonishing. There was a strict rule when Avria was growing up that nobody was to enter the library without supervision from either Taneth or his senior student adept. But here they were, treating it like their own personal public house; drinking and carousing. What was worse, they were smoking their pipes, something Taneth would normally fly off the handle about in defense of his books against yellowing. The laughter stopped the moment she pushed open the door, and by the time she was able to fully look into the room, they had all managed to drop their feet down and straighten up in their seats. She smirked.

The fire was high and bright in the hearth and a bottle of wine hunkered on the table by an old tome they'd apparently been looking at. It was open, and the cover rested in a way that implied something was hidden beneath it. Avria suspected a deck of cards and some gambling chits. Three thick glass goblets were distributed 'round the table, a fourth one was waiting for the mysterious fourth accomplice on a sideboard under the window.

Offrin looked downright guilty. "Eh, Avria, sorry, I sort of became distracted," he muttered. Avria smiled and shook her head. There was something that delighted her in this scene. All these men she loved in different ways came from different worlds, and they were hanging about together like chums, gambling and drinking; including her new husband who had fretted terribly about truly integrating with her clan. Here he was, right in the thick of them with Gavorre as if it were the way things ought to be. It warmed her heart.

"It's nothing, really. I'm glad to see you've found the sanctuary of this library; my father spends much time in here when not abroad," she said in an overly sweet manner, giving Phenmal a quick narrow-eyed glare as he chewed his pipe and gazed at her smugly. "Does he *know* you're here?"

"Yes," Master Gavorre grunted. "He will be joining us again once he's back from wherever he traipsed off to." Avria's brows rose in mild shock. Perhaps her father was becoming mellower as he aged. She addressed her husband:

"I was going to go and sit with mother and Istvan, if that's alright with you. You needn't get up; I just wanted to let you know where I'd be."

"Of course, that's fine my dear," the young man retorted. He wore a knitted hat that hugged his bald head, and was clothed in far commoner clothing than he'd worn at Klatna; a heavy tunic, some thick breeches and a pair of leather lodge slippers. All three of them were dressed for relaxation. The other two looked on in amusement. Avria ducked out of the room. She heard the conversation and laughter resume as soon as the latch closed, and she laughed through her nose. She then heard the unmistakable snap of the cover of a book being closed. She stayed long enough to hear the whir of cards being shuffled and the click of chits being thrown onto the table. *The brats*, she thought. With a smile she went to find her mother.

She poked her head in the door of the family apartment. The lamps were lit, a fire was burning, but there was nobody there. Tinna couldn't be far. She thought perhaps to check Jenyk's apartment. She crossed the corridor and knocked on the door. Jenyk opened it, her round face changing from a look of annoyance to happiness when she saw who was at her door. "Avria, good you're here… Could you give me a hand with something?" She opened her door and stepped aside so the girl could enter. Jenyk's apartment was always in disarray. She had two children, and often watched the smaller children for other families in the clan. Istvan was not present. Instead, her children were happily occupied in playing a game of Enemies, but since both of them were too young to understand the complex rules of the board game, they merely took the multitude of beautifully carved pieces and acted out a battle on the inlaid wood board. They ignored Avria completely.

The large table where Jenyk often did her work was covered in a hefty swath of lovely snow-white fabric as sheer as a fading mist. She would probably make a garment from it, and then dye it. White was not always an easy colour to maintain in an Araki village. "For the life of me, I've been trying to get an even fold on this to start cutting the skirts for Tinna's summer gowns for Klatna… It's so wide I can't manage it, and there's no way I'd lay it on the floor with those little gremlins running about with sticky hands and grimy feet." Avria laughed. "Help me fold this?" she asked. Avria nodded, and did exactly as she was asked, matching the corners, and stretching the long piece of fabric all the way across the apartment, and then doubling it up and folding it so it could be managed better from her work table.

"Have you seen my mother and Istvan today, Jenyk?"

"I had Istvan for a few hours this morning while she met with the elders, but she came and got him just before luncheon. I have no idea where she is if she isn't in her apartments. She could be in any of the lodges." Avria gave Jenyk her end of the fabric, and sighed. She waved farewell to Jenyk and set out again in search of her mother.

She looked in the main hall, and saw nobody. It occurred to Avria that her mother would likely be at the new lodge, where Tinna was setting up a special work room for crafts which would solve problems like Jenyk's—it was a large space with huge work tables and the carpenter was making a bank of shelves to rival the archives at Lemoram. Thamatoc relied a great deal on goods trading; they did not farm much, they bought the majority of their flours and grains and fresh vegetables from clans with large agricultural land areas. Instead, Thamatoc traded hunted meats when they could, furniture and hand-crafted goods. The village was peppered with a variety of artisans that created a plethora of marketable goods, but there was one common complaint; the lack of workspace and light. So Tinna's solution was to assign a huge segment of the newest lodge to the artisans. She was excited about this project and spent a good deal of time overseeing the construction of it. She was having larger window-slots put in and an array of hanging chandeliers in addition to other wonderful things.

The newest lodge was finished only this summer, and because it was new, it was the one on the farthest end of the arc around the common. Avria sighed with annoyed resignation and walked to the corridor that connected to the autumn lodge. With a groan, she forged into the darkness, making the long circuit to where her mother and brother only *might* be.

Chapter Three - Devastation

The spring lodge was the last of the old lodges, and the two new corridors to the new lodge were still freshly excavated and dark, they both took a bit of a strange circuitous route around some massive boulders that were found beneath the earth. The front corridor was shorter simply because of the angle at which the lodges were placed, but it was under repair, as one of the newly excavated ceilings had collapsed to create a bit of a sinkhole in the forest floor above. The shortest route was off limits for now, blocked by several lengths of wood, and Avria was most irritated to have to walk the length of the Spring Lodge to the back, where the longer corridor was. Avria made her way without a torch or a lamp, by feel alone.

Her hand slipped along the freshly laid stone walls lining the way. The masonry gave way to the grittier surface of the first of the two massive boulders, both of which were each as big as a human house. She slid along, resuming the wall between the two boulders, when she came to a sudden stop. Her fingers had come up against a something soft that radiated warmth, something wearing a smooth, yielding fabric. Whoever it was, they were leaning on the wall, not moving, not speaking. She held her breath and squinted as if to see in the pitch black.

"Who's there?" she asked, "this isn't really very funny whoever you are. It's not a funny joke," she muttered in annoyance. Then she sighed intolerantly. "Drashe, if that's you I'm going to kill you." In the darkness, something brushed her cheek; cool fingers. Avria jumped back, out of reach of the wall. She turned a few times, feeling frantically about in the pitch black for a wall to guide her. "This is not funny at all." There was an edge of fear in her voice.

"Avria..." the voice froze her. Her breath was locked inside her lungs; she felt heaviness in her stomach and a pain in her heart like she hadn't felt in ages. She blinked in the darkness, listening, her head moving like a bird. She listened hard—in spite of the whooshing in her ears. For a moment she thought someone was playing a game with her; perhaps using some sort of spell to make her think she was hearing him. She could not think of a single person besides Jestin who would be so cruel—but Jestin did not have a proclivity for magic that she knew of and had no means to fool her with this voice she knew all too well. Her mind raced, her heart beat so loudly the blood was rushing in her ears, which seemed deafening in the silence and pitch darkness around her. If it wasn't Jestin, then perhaps it *was* him...

"Eleran?" she whispered, the incredulity raw and keenly evident in her voice. She remained alert, backing away from any small noise that might indicate his approach. She didn't know why fear filled her instead of abject joy at the possibility of reuniting with her lost love, but she could not control her instincts. She backed into the opposite wall, and clung to it. "Eleran?" she called again, needing to know where he was, or if she had dreamt his voice calling her name. It was unmistakably Eleran's voice. The memory of it was burned irrevocably into her heart. When she heard nothing, she immediately began to feel her way with a frantic air towards the spring lodge again until his voice stopped her cold again.

"My lovely Avria, I could not keep myself from you any longer." All that came in reply to this was a strangled gasp and then a sob. Whoever it was, it moved towards her. Avria was sidling away along the farthest wall.

"Where are you going?" Apparently her attempt to flee upset him, he sounded angry.

"Where have you been?" she whispered accusingly, her throat tight. The tears were palpable in her voice. "Where were you?" she sobbed. She stood with her back to the wall, her hands flat on the surface. Her instincts told her she should run, but her heart needed to know.

"I was lost; out there in the place beyond this world. But the Hevra brought me back, and here I am." She could hear his voice grow louder as he approached her. She imagined his face as she saw it in her dream, misshapen and twisted, and her stomach turned to ice.

Suddenly she felt an arm encircling her waist and she stiffened in terror, trying to pull away but his grip was tight.

"Why do you fear me, my Avria," he asked; his breath hot on her face; the disappointment clear in his words. Avria's trepidation compelled her to reach up and lay her hands on his face—to know he was not the monster her dreams had painted him to be. There were no scars or ridges, no hideous deformations as her dream had implied; it felt as it always had, strong and beautiful, and her tears came harder. He bent down and she felt his lips fall upon her tear-soaked mouth, and for a moment, she was lost in his kiss, lost in the man she had loved so surely. But then her instincts started to prickle at her again, and she pushed away, unable to extricate herself from his grip. He pinned up against the wall.

"You were gone... You were..." she stammered. "I am married now, Eleran. Let me go. Things are different now. You should go back to wherever you've been." There was a moment of quiet, and he pressed against her. She felt his shoulders stiffen and her anxiety flared.

"What does a ridiculous gesture of commitment, this empty binding matter in the greater scheme?" He snarled in her face suddenly, his anger raw and powerful. She felt the spittle on her face when he hissed out the words, "our souls are one; marriage in this existence means *nothing* at all." His words took an edge to them that was feral and wild. "That *half*-man you chose to give yourself to is nothing at all to me, to existence itself. You will come with me. We will be together. You belong with me." He said the last phrase between gritted teeth. He was bordering on rage. He *was* all wrong, twisted, deformed. Not his physical form, but his essence, his soul. It was wrong. Her dread turned to panic and she struggled violently against him.

"I will scream!" she yelled. "Scream until someone hears me... and Phenmal will feel you, you are probably discovered already!" she bellowed out hoarsely.

"That Chaiva is easy to block, my dear," his words suddenly chillingly calm, his body barely moving as she writhed and bucked to escape his grasp. "You are with me now. You are my soul, Avria. I will not let you go." She continued to weep and squirm, and the more she resisted the harder he leaned against her, the more firmly he pressed her against the wall. He knew Avria wasn't the wilting flower she seemed to be. He was aware of the training her mother had given her, and he knew the best way to hold her in place to render her helpless. She cried out for help, and screamed for her mother, but the long rough-walled corridor did little to carry her pleas. The Druid had chosen the place well. She felt him lean forward and bury his face in her tumbles of curls, taking a deep breath.

"I have missed your scent," his voice became deeper, and he ground against her. "You have no idea how much I have missed you, my precious Avria," he breathed, the heat of his excitement pouring into her hair and onto her neck. "I have thought of this moment for months, touching you again." His hand slid up and he squeezed each breast in turn. In a move that surprised and terrified Avria, he leaned back enough to grasp the collar of her tunic and in a powerful yank, he tore her tunic open. He grunted to himself as he felt her bare breasts his hand. Then, his free hand started to fumble with the drawstring of her skirts, sliding his fingers against her belly. She blanched, her screams growing increasingly sharp. Her movement made it impossible for him to untie her skirts with one hand, so he simply bent only enough to catch the hem, and he hiked her skirts up. Avria trembled and whimpered now.

"Why are you doing this, Eleran?" she sobbed. "Please! Eleran don't do this!" He did not answer. His mind was focused elsewhere; on the softness of her body, the scent he adored so which hung in his nostrils and fueled his desire, the fire of her resistance. When he'd shimmied up her skirts, his hands found the low-slung waistline of her winter leggings, which did not resist being pulled down. He used his feet to kick them away, tearing off Avria's lodge slippers as he did. Avria's high-pitched whining increased tenfold when he then freed himself from his breeches by opening the flap of his fall-fronts, and breathed heavily upon her as he moved to position her, gripping one of her thighs and yanking one of her legs up against his side.

He covered her screams with his mouth, and with a powerful thrust, he bore into her. With a groan of ecstasy, he buried himself in, and lingered there for a second, his skin trembling. "Ah, yes, this is the Avria I missed..." he breathed onto her face. He kissed her savagely and then began to move again. At first gently, but that faded almost immediately into brutal, unchecked thrusts. No matter how she kicked, no matter how she screamed, he did not cease. Instead, he was fed by her horror, and more determined to do what he wished the more she struggled, to show her who was in control. He forced himself into her with a cruelty Avria had never known, gripping a handful of her hair and pulling it hard to keep her pinned, causing her pain and injury as he repeatedly ground her onto the rough stone. Tears flowed down her face, and her child-like crying was muffled by his vicious kisses. She wrenched her face away from his, hitting her temple hard on the wall, not feeling the hot sticky blood as it coursed down the side of her face.

Avria cried and begged for him to stop, to let her go, pleading to the man that she thought she knew. He only continued until he reached climax, his huge frame dwarfing hers, rendering her helpless against his attack. He drove himself deep into her and then released, pressing her onto the wall with his chest, and shuddering, his breath searing the side of her face. "You will always be mine, Avria," he whispered hoarsely, victoriously; sated by her, his sweaty chest soaking the tatters of her torn tunic and chilling her bare front. "It is not in our power to change what is destined. You will always be mine," he hissed into her ear. She squirmed away, still sobbing, and then he stepped back and she fell into a heap on the ground. "You need to remember that," he added. She heard him fiddling with the fabric of his breeches and then he stooped in front of her.

"This only served to teach you your place, Avria. This is what happens when you defy the fates."

"What happened to you?" she sobbed. "Who are you? The Eleran I loved would never have done this."

"The Eleran you loved was weak... laughable," he spat in disgust. "He was not strong enough to bear the powers that he possessed, and he paid the price. But now, I am stronger than he ever was, and I have returned to claim what was his; to claim the half of my soul that is rightfully mine," he spat. "You will see it in time, Avria. I have been kind, and I have let you live on thinking you have not betrayed me—but now you know the truth. You *have* betrayed me. But I can no longer bear to see you giving yourself to anyone else. We were fixed for one another; I nearly died to save you. You are obligated to me—you *will* stand beside me again. You will come now." He reached down to take her arm.

"*Onithoth Teghed!*" a new voice shouted, and the darkness was suddenly filled with blinding light. For a fleeting second, Avria saw him, the man she'd felt such love for, the man who'd just taken her dignity so barbarically; lit up by the flash of brightness; his hair long and silky, loose against his back, black as night, still wavy from the braiding he often kept it in. His face was still angled and beautiful, not disfigured as she'd dreamt, but the expression was foreign to Avria. She'd never seen such hatred in anyone before, even with his sockets cast into shadows by the hot light, she could see his evil. She weakly lifted her trembling hand to cover her eyes, for the light was searing, and she saw Eleran fly off the ground and fall into a heap meters away before the light faded into blackness.

Eleran could be heard getting immediately back onto his feet, and he hissed an unintelligible word, and a blast of lightning exploded from his chest. The Gypsy Azrash responded with words of power and spread his arms to receive the bolt, absorbing it into him as if it was nothing, and his body glowed from the gift, casting a soft light about the bend of the corridor. He bellowed out two more words, but no sooner than the magic was cast, Eleran vanished in an explosion of light, and just before he disappeared, he looked at Avria and flashed a cold and haunting smile.

Avria, slumped to the ground, bruised and bleeding, tears flowing in a grief and pain she'd never experienced before. She heard boot heels approaching, and she saw the familiar and welcome image of Phenmal's face as he entered the reach of the gypsy's glowing light. She fell into fresh tears, and let the older man stoop before her and cover her with his banyan.

CHAPTER FOUR – CONCEALMENT

Phenmal carried the Avria's huddled form discreetly into her apartments and placed her on the bed. He was visibly upset and shaken, his eyes glassed over and his mouth tight. He kept whispering "I'm sorry, Avria, I'm sorry. I didn't feel it until it was too late." He tucked her under the blankets and sat on the edge of the bed next to her, pressing his hand on her cheek. She winced and he withdrew. The mind-reader was beside himself. "I didn't feel it until it was too late," he told her. She sobbed quietly and she took his hand and rolled onto her side, tucking it under her chin and constricting herself into the fetal position as if to wrap her body around it. He looked at this girl and his anger flared. She was scraped badly; one side of her face there was blood still seeping from cuts, one on the edge of her brow, another the back of her arms, and several on her back and her spine, blood stains peppered what was left of her garments.

He'd sent Offrin to find Tinna immediately simply to give the frantic man some occupation for he was almost out of control at the sight of his wife in the state she was in. The only other person in the room was the Gypsy wizard, who looked so much older and benign than he had when he was in the corridor. He sat down in a chair by the fire, his eyes focused somewhere else. He hummed something under his breath.

Phenmal was rusty at the arts he once performed in his younger days when he was a minion of the Keepers in earnest, and not just a means of supervision and manipulation of the Keepers' new obsession; Tinna. He was once a ruthless invader. But he had not practiced those arts in a long time. It was easy enough to just read someone's thoughts; they were as intrusive and loud to him in his head as they would be if people were holding conversations all around him. But to enter someone's inner mind, to affect healing or inject false memories, or erase the contents of a lifetime, these are things he had not done in some time—and he did not want to damage the mind of a girl he looked upon quite as his own—nor was he willing to erase what just happened to save her the pain, as appealing as the idea was. It was too invasive and with what had just happened to her, he did not want to do that to her. Everyone around her would know—and they would treat her differently, she would always wonder why. He thought about it once more, and then his brow wrinkled in sadness. He had to let her keep the memories, but he would have to find a way to help her live with them.

He loved Avria and Tinna like no one else in his entire life, and he was pained to see what destruction had been done by this horrible rape of her body and her soul. He bent low over her and with his free hand; he cupped the back of her head. She was no longer weeping, but still trembling. His gaze bored into her eyes and her trembling ceased as if someone had shut the door on it. She fell into a strange trance as he looked into her.

"Retreat, Avria. I am there with you. Where you go to when things are hard." He knew that place; it was a fabrication of her past, but with her own improvements to create comfort. The place had evolved over the years to include or exclude things. For a while, it was a hillside overlooking the oak cemeteries, where Eleran awaited her with a loving smile. Phenmal knew she retreated here even during her betrothal period with Offrin. When she was a child, Avria would retreat to her special place when she was upset. It was different when she was little. He would see it when he was visiting, when she thought she'd escaped her parents and was sulking. Today, her retreat world was the one of her childhood, not the hillside. The childhood place was her parent's apartments. They seemed slightly bigger, but Avria was as she always was in this secret place, innocent and small, a little girl, sitting by the fire on the soft sheepskin carpet, leaning on the body of a large male dog. She turned to look at him, her eyes red and puffy.

"*Phen…*" she whispered, her grown-up mouth never moving in the quiet room of reality. The tall, lanky man, younger in her image of him, stooped beside her and lifted her to her feet. She wrapped her child-like arms around him and nuzzled her face into his neck.

Phenmal stood and carried her to the chair, where he sat down and let her cry into his shoulder. He sat there, rubbing her back, feeling her misery and her pain course through him like a river. He always knew the intimate crime like this was one that scarred its victims with a permanence nobody could understand; but he never knew such humiliation or horror, such violation; he never understood that it was such an invasive way to cut into someone's soul. Eleran had stolen her power; he'd stolen her dignity, her control, her sense of self. He had rocked her wellbeing into oblivion. She was a child again, vulnerable to anything, unable to fight back; rendered helpless. If she could not have control of her own being, then over what did she have dominion at all? She was nothing.

He huddled her to his imagined self, and remained with her while the world outside her head went on.

Phenmal heard Tinna long before he saw her; he'd focused almost every part of his essence into Avria's retreat, and was stunted in his awareness of reality—which in terms of a Chaiva, meant he could only see and hear things; he could not read anyone else's thoughts. He could project thoughts and power, but not take in any more, since his head was full of Avria's sorrow. He heard her first with his ears, a cry of such fury; it could be heard by the whole lodge. Her screams of rage grew louder and louder until Tinna exploded into the room with Offrin, Taneth and Master Gavorre at her heels. Phenmal lifted his hand flat and formed a mental barrier between them. Tinna's rage was cut short by the painful twinge in her brain, and she cried out and turned away, gripping her temples. Offrin was the only other one who'd run against it and he roared out in anger.

"Phenmal, find that monster so I can kill him!" Tinna spat between gritted teeth. "The gypsy warned us he felt it. I should have known. I should have known Avria's instincts were spot-on. He was and is here. We need to find him. he needs to die!" Offrin flared up as well.

"Old man, Avria is my wife; you cannot dare to tell me I cannot..." Phenmal turned and glared at him, the force of his gaze silencing him.

"She has been violated, Offrin. By someone she once trusted beyond measure. Her heart is broken. Besides, I've taken her outside of this room right now. I have retreated her."

"Phenmal, where is he? Where is Eleran?" Taneth barked.

"He is nearby," the gypsy spoke. "The displacement spells never bring you too far unless you are a mage of tremendous power, or you are carried by the power of other mages. I did not sense that he has anyone assisting him. I sense him alone. He is powerful, but not so much so that he cannot be stopped. The Zsathri fled me. He sensed imminent defeat if he'd stayed to fight on. But do not take his cowardice for granted. The Zsathri are particularly cunning wielders; they have the power of the Hevra behind them. This one is a true danger. He was a trespasser; he broke sacred bonds, and instead of enduring the punishment in the voids, he was retrieved and freed. To retrieve a punished wielder from the voids is a terrible gamble. Returning them from the voids, the emptiness spawns madness; there are things in there that no soul should see..." he paused as if stricken by the idea. "The only way we will stop this wielder is to kill him or force him to kill with his magic, the latter I would prefer not to do."

"He will return," Tinna flared.

"Not as long as I am here beside her," the gypsy replied. "I sense him. He is distanced now; but I sense his nearness. I felt him when he came. I could not pinpoint him as fast as I would have liked. He was blocking as well, Chaiva. He was casting a spell to keep us blind; it was not your doing that you did not feel him. He only became vulnerable to you when I cast him down the first time; separating him from his spell. It was nothing you did not do that made you unable to sense him."

"I wish to see my daughter, Phenmal," Tinna interrupted. Phenmal shook his head.

"In a while. Let her retreat. I'm in there with her. She is wounded, and humiliated. She feels as if she invited this, and she is afraid that Offrin will no longer love her. She feels like she is no longer the custodian of her own being; that its ownership has been relegated to someone who aims only to harm her; someone who had once meant everything to her. She needs time in there, and I will help her through it."

"You are *not* her father! Who are you to... to... to just take over like this? She's *our* daughter! Ours!" Taneth snarled. Tinna put her arm out to block her husband who felt it necessary to advance on Phenmal. Considering that Taneth was the most non-violent man in the world, this was a clear indication to Tinna that he was deeply,

deeply upset by this situation. She'd never seen him like this, his rage just boiling under the surface. He looked at her in vehemence and betrayal, pushing against her arm. Tinna locked her eyes on his, and he calmed almost immediately. She shook her head coolly and told him to stand down with just a look. Phenmal watched this with little reaction. When Taneth's anger was marginally under control, he looked at each of them gravely.

"You must go. Everyone must go, except the soothsayer."

Taneth with a jaw set hard and furious, mandibles rippling, guided his wife towards the door and Offrin followed reluctantly. Before they were to the door, the mind-reader called out: "Tinna... in a few hours, can you send a tub with hot water please, and soap too?" *She will want to wash him off of her when she awakes.* "Pick some of her favorite clothing for her and prepare her some comforting food as well. Taneth, you should make her your sweetcakes. Those always make her happy. She will be feeling hollow and lost; we need to create an arsenal to tempt her back to some normality. Offrin, you will welcome her with love and gentleness. Until you can look at her without that mask of rage on your face, I recommend you stay away. She is already overcome with self-reproach. Keep your wrath and your revenge to yourself. Now is not the time for that." Phenmal then turned back to Avria, who lay still in her fetal coil, her eyes open, but unreadable.

"I will not be here forever, Mind-Reader," the gypsy sorcerer said when the others had retreated. "What then?" Phenmal turned and looked at the old man, and then back to Avria. *Indeed*, thought he, *what then?*

Avria opened her eyes and she thought she was alone in her humble apartment. A bit of white daylight was coming in the narrow window. The apartment was still fairly dark, no lamps were lit—only the strong fire in her hearth poured its yellow light into the room, flickering on the folds of Avria's pillow. For a moment she was disoriented, but then it all came flooding back, and she felt an instant hollowness in her chest, and all she wanted to do was sleep it all away. Her eyes felt dry and sandy, and her limbs listless.

She then remembered the quiet bath where she sat, water dripping from her face, staring at the cloudy surface of the water. Her body hurt. Her mother was there. She had lifted her arms and washed them gently with a cloth, her touch as light and feathery as she could manage. Tinna's face was waxen, but she kept offering Avria's distant gaze a wan smile in an attempt to offer comfort. She did not speak; she only focused on helping wash Avria's bruised and battered body.

Phenmal sat with his back to her by the fire next to the sorcerer. Neither of them had left her side at all since the attack. She remembered Phenmal's once-frightening eyes so full of concern and kindness, it nearly made her cry thinking of it. She loved the old man, more than she knew, and she realized that he loved her far more deeply; as if she were his own child and her throat tightened. She thought of how he felt, to see her pained, to feel her pain, she could sense his feelings when he was with her. He hated that he'd been powerless to stop what happened to her. He had been so gentle, and so caring; the memories of his being there felt more like a strange dream—but it somehow had helped. It had blunted the edges of the knives that cut into her heart; it brought her from the deepest of despair and wretchedness to an odd fugue where her feelings, although still keenly present, were not as sharp and prickling. He had given her the ability to function. Had he not helped, she knew she would be in much, much worse pain.

Her mother's ache was another matter altogether. Tinna, always the bastion of strength was barely holding herself together. Avria knew first-hand how much her mother invested in Avria's sense of security and happiness; she knew how much her mother valued the idea of Avria never suffering the indignities and sorrow of her own youth. "You can't save me from everything mother," Avria whispered to Tinna when she was standing and letting her mother wrap her in a towel. Tinna's lips tightened and she shook the words off, helping her daughter step from the tub. Tinna listlessly combed her hair and plaited it in two braids, one over each shoulder. She wordlessly helped Avria dress in her nightgown and robe and sat with her until she fell asleep.

"My little baby girl," she heard Tinna whisper just before she drifted off.

She had no idea how long she'd slept. She merely awoke with a snap of the eyes. She heard something, a subtle noise and lifted her head to see the elderly gypsy squatting by the fire, feeding the flames fresh wood, and gazing at the hungry blaze pensively. She sat up and put her legs over the side of the large bed. She clutched the neck of her robe tightly closed and padded towards the wizard, the rustling train of it following her. Her body was so sore. Every muscle. The skinned patches on her skin were already scabbing over, the cut on her temple felt tight and itchy. He turned his head to look at her and offered her a weak smile.

"It has been a difficult time for you," he said. She sat down next to him in Offrin's chair and hunched forward, wedging her elbows against her belly and leaning on them, staring at the fire. "You are fortunate to have the friendship of the Chaiva. They have many special skills." She took a long, silent pause before saying anything to him.

"I used to be so afraid of him; but I realized it wasn't fear, it was respect." Her voice was groggy and faint, and she rocked a bit in the chair. "How long have I been asleep since when I last woke?"

"Two days."

"Two days?" she repeated, incredulous. She rubbed her face, and then toyed with her braids, which were frayed and tight.

"The storm has abated. My people prepare to leave. You will be leaving as well," the old man informed her. Avria looked at him warily and then shook her head incredulously. The old man simply resumed tending to the fire. Avria didn't ask any more questions. She merely hunched forward and continued to watch the fire, her expression one of detachment and disappointment. Avria only then noticed that her small mantel clock was dreadfully loud. It had taken her some time to get used to it when Taneth brought it for her a few months ago when he came to Taruttee. Then she got used to its sound, and eventually found comfort in it. When it stopped and needed winding, her little room seemed too quiet. Now it sounded like a mallet striking an anvil. She glowered at nothing and then flopped back into her chair. She remained there unmoving.

About an hour later, Tinna entered the room. She carried a packet wrapped in rough linen, and laid it on Avria's little dining table. Avria stood and went to her mother and the woman wrapped her in a deep embrace. She felt her daughter trembling in her hold. Tinna's heart hurt for Avria, the idea of what she was suffering was too painful to bear. Tinna allowed herself to weep for her daughter. Avria's tears were dried it seemed. She was depressed and faded—somewhere distant and detached.

"Where is Offrin? Is he disgusted by me now?" Avria asked. Tinna wiped away her tears and shook her head, reaching out to touch Avria's pale, tired face.

"Not at all, Avria, he is so worried. We've sent him to Klatna with Haneet to fetch some herbs and medicines your father requested for your care. It's a fool's errand, but he has been distracted so by his fear for you. Giving him a purpose has kept him focused on helping rather than dwelling and festering on his rage."

"Mother..." Avria suddenly started to cry. She moved back to the fire and flopped into the chair and Tinna knelt in front of her. "What happened to Eleran?" her hoarse voice cracked when she asked this, and her tears ran down her nose. "What happened to him?"

"The sorcerer knows. It's not his fault." Tinna turned to the gypsy man, who was snoring in the chair. "He says it has to do with Eleran's punishment for killing using his powers; being cast out of his body into what is called the voids. It drove him to madness, and when he was retrieved by whatever power, he returned as someone other than the Eleran you knew." Avria wept harder, hunched forward on herself.

"I loved him so much. He has broken me into bits."

"I know. And he can hurt you again, Avria. His protection spell that saved you before is no more. When it was taken we do not know, but the gypsy says you have no spells over you now. I was hoping you'd be awake, Avria because I've something to tell you."

"I'm going away?" Avria guessed. She looked with purpose onto the sleeping sorcerer to indicate that he'd told her something of the like. Tinna nodded ruefully and stood up, clutching her elbows. She paced the open space in the center of the room.

"Phenmal told us he knows of a place of safety where you will be shielded from Eleran—so that he would not be able to find you using his magic."

"*Why must it be like this? First Jestin, now Eleran... why?*" Avria suddenly screamed, rocketing to her feet. The old man was startled into wakefulness just in time to see Avria pick up the sorcerer's clay mug of hot cider, now tepid, and hurl it across the room where it shattered into a mess over her bookshelf. "Why must I be subject to the whims of people like Jestin and Eleran, Mother? Why?" She started crying again. "I don't want to run any more. I want to be happy with my husband," she sobbed. "I just want to be happy—but how can I now with the memory so sharp of Eleran causing me pain?" Avria bawled, "How can I when he stole everything away?"

"It will heal, Avria, this I promise you. Enough so you can find some measure of peace with yourself and with Eleran. Phenmal will help you. And where you are going, you can find help there too, Phenmal says. You will not be gone forever; it's for now, until Phenmal can get to the bottom of this; to find out who retrieved him, and try to track Eleran down somehow. Please, Avria. Just for now…" Tinna approached and took Avria's hands. They were cold, and her fingers hung limp in hers.

"What of Offrin? Does he know of this?" Tinna's eyes dropped and a wash of shame moved over her.

"No. We will tell him when he's returned and you are gone. We do not want to risk him following you and leading Eleran to you. Not even we know where you are going; Phenmal wants to avoid the chance of our knowledge being stolen to find you."

"Such deceit, he will be devastated."

"He will come to understand it and accept it for the sake of your wellbeing. He loves you so, he will understand. But you must prepare to leave now."

"Now?"

"Ledroran has sent Eritrix to take you."

"Mother I don't want to go…"

"I don't want you hurt again, Avria!" Tinna said a bit too forcefully. She stopped herself and swallowed her feelings, calming herself. Only then did she look up at her daughter and continue. "I don't want you taken away again." There was a pall and then Tinna added: "if it makes it any more appealing to you, Phenmal let it slip that it is an island in a sea." Tinna knew this would make her pause, even now in her distracted misery. The ocean, much like it had once been for Tinna, was a fantasy of sorts for Avria; something she dreamt of seeing. Her elder brother Hanru had missed her wedding because he was on his way to Wye, an Araki settlement by the ocean, where he would be the new Wiseman. She had lamented her disappointment in not seeing her brother but also her jealousy that he was to live by the sea. It was something she wanted to do all her life, and had yet had the opportunity. Tinna saw it at once; the immediate effect of this idea on her broken daughter—a silly, childhood fancy to hold onto when everything else seemed to be crumbling away. *Surrounded by the sea.*

"Only for now?"

"Yes my dear. Only for now." Tinna pulled her forward and embraced her again, resting her hand on the back of Avria's head. "I am sorry, my little one. I am so very sorry." Avria's head became heavy on Tinna's shoulder, and she fell into her mother in racking sobs. Tinna stood it through, gently rocking Avria as she wept away her horror. When Avria was wicked dry of her tears, she stood back, empty and waxen, and she took her mother's hands, this time clasping them tightly.

"It is probably best that Offrin is away. I love him, but I fear I could not bear any man close to me or touching me right now."

"Yes. You need time to heal," Tinna agreed. Avria stood silent for a second.

"I don't know how I will do that, mother," she confessed. Tinna could only purse her lips and look at her with sad eyes. Avria nodded and said: "I will dress then."

"Warmly," Tinna warned her. She then crossed the room to the table and opened up the package she'd brought in. She pulled out the contents and turned to show Avria. It was the old sweater. The faded pumpkin orange had been rejuvenated into a vibrant burnt umber-rust, the old, thin fibers were now twisted around fresh, newly spun and dyed yarn, the pattern now raised instead of stretched, the tunic sweater again shaped and blocked like new. She held it up to Avria's front and smiled; her eyes glassy at the sight of it.

"It's so beautiful, like it was when I was a little girl, and he put it on me when I was cold. That is my only memory of him, and I don't remember his face. I remember the warmth that still lingered in it from when he'd taken it off his frame and then put it on me. I remember the tender loving smile, and a gentle laugh at how large it was on my tiny body," Tinna whispered. Avria's pale hands slid up onto the sweater being draped on her front, and she touched it lightly. "I want you to feel that same love when you wear it, to know that I'm here with you—even if we are to be separated again by tragedy." Avria's eyes glassed over again watching her mother suffer through this moment with her. She gathered up her wits, however, and cleared her throat.

"It will keep you warm, until you come home," Tinna said with slightly forced optimism. Avria nodded, and hugged the sweater to her. Hands still clutched to her chest, she simply walked into her mother, and dropped her head on her shoulder again, sighing deeply. Tinna patted down her disheveled curls, and kissed her temple. "Pack up some clothes sweet girl. The dragon will be here soon."

She felt a subtle nod under her chin, and Avria withdrew, moving quietly to her chest of drawers. Tinna slipped out, leaving behind her shattered daughter and the sorcerer, who'd fallen back into his comfortable doze by the fire as if trying to soak up as much of the quiet and warmth before he would be back in the swaying caravan again.

Tinna wrung her hands and moved down the corridor, rapping softly on the door belonging to Cennik's apartments. The young man opened the door. He was looking a bit rough 'round the edges, as if she'd woken him after only just falling asleep. His eyes were puffy and small. He was bare-chested, wearing only a pair of loose legged drawstring pants that looked like they'd been tugged on in haste, for one of his cheeks was barely covered and the front hung tenuously low. His breath smelled of spirits, and behind him, she spied the unmistakable shock of red hair of a certain young Dara in his bed.

"It's a bit late in the morning for you to be just waking up," Tinna intoned with a touch of undue acidity. The extremely comely summoner blushed a bit, and scratched his head of wild hair, which stood up straight, slanted to one side, pillow creases still red on the other side of his face. Cennik had arrived a year ago to reluctantly become the first resident summoner for an Araki community. He was a rake and a sophisticate of the human city of Rida and he was not pleased to be asked by the powers-that-be to live in an isolated somewhat backward community. But when he arrived at Thamatoc, he discovered an entire village full of fresh, beautiful and naïve single ladies all fawning over his worldliness and noble good looks. Suddenly, his inclination to stay was increased. He'd already bruised two hearts in the past year. Tinna knew he'd have a harder time with Dara. She was as fiery and willful as one would imagine a red-haired creature to be, and Tinna knew it was only a matter of time before her rogue of a summoner would learn his first lesson of the heart. She doubted it would slow his roguery down at all; he was young and dashing and was still being led by something other than the brain in his head.

"It was a late night," he admitted groggily. Dara stirred and her arm flopped out of his bed. She continued to slumber deeply, unnoticing of the movements of her own limbs.

"Have you had a chance to...?"

"With all due respect, Madame chieftain; it's fairly obvious I've had no chance to do anything this morning since you know you've only just woken me; but I will do you the favour of calling for the status of the arriving dragon, for I am certain this is what you wish to know."

"A little more respect in your tone, Cennik. Mind yourself," she snapped. Any fondness for humor at this point was not to be found for Tinna. She was about to send her daughter away to some mysterious location, and her little girl had endured the most horrid of experiences and she would not be there to help her through it. Tinna glared at him. Clueless to the chieftain's grave mood, he gave Tinna a blatant appraisal with his golden brown eyes, conscious of how well formed his body was, and how attractive, even in this rumpled, hung-over state, he was. His flirtation was a taunt if anything and Tinna arched her brow and glared dourly up at his smug face, disinterest plain in her burning glare. "Just get hold of the dragon and find out already, so we can get Avria on her way." She sailed away in a rustle of linen skirts and vanished into the main hall. Cennik turned, reminded that he had finally gotten Dara into his bed. With a wry grin, he closed the door and went to wake her.

Eritrix was a young, graceful, swan-like dragon—still fresh from the cliffs of the west, but eager and full of wonder and idealism as most young people were. She seemed almost miniscule to Tinna. Tinna was used to the mass and presence of her dearest Ledroran; the leader of the dragons, and he dwarfed his little grand-daughter by at least ten times. He was the largest dragon Tinna knew of, and he could barely land at Thamatoc anymore because the pastures were barely enough to accommodate his takeoffs and landings. But this lithe, dexterous creature, her scales a mix of ruby red and creamy white moved like a dancer. She came in with the grace of an eagle, landing; hardly disturbing the soft layer of snow. She'd glided into the pasture area, one of the few spaces with open expanses, and then let the cold air balloon on her wings, she stalled upwards just long enough to catch the ground with her delicate talons, and then she let her weight follow them.

She turned her head on her graceful neck, and lowered it. From behind her short crown-like head shield, a person appeared. Tinna was stunned at the sight of her. Garbed entirely in black, in breeches no less; a golden beauty leapt down from the back of the dragon's neck. She wore a thick cloak of black as well, with the hood edged in grey wolf fur. She looked in all respects except her fairer features, like a Thran. She moved like a Thran, with a trained purpose, sinewy, with hidden power. She walked over the snow towards Tinna and Avria, her eyes taking in the mother with a calculated assessing gaze, and then to Avria. When her eyes fell upon the girl, her brow furrowed into a tight patch, and concern filled her azure eyes. When she reached Tinna and Avria, she curtsied, giving Tinna a look of reverence. Then she reached for Avria's hand.

"I am Adrenne. We must haste. I am hiding our arrival as best I can, but this is a Zsathri, from what I understand. They are cunning wielders. I would love to stay and make introductions, but we must go at once." Tinna nodded, her eyes misting over. Avria blankly assented with a nod, and looked to her mother one more time.

"Tell Offrin I am sorry and that I love him."

"I will. Go now, darling."

"Where's father?"

"He isn't happy about this, Avria. He isn't coping well with anything that's happened. I told him it would be best I see you off alone."

"And Phenmal?"

"He's gone already, to find ways to stop Eleran. Go, sweet girl." The sister put her hand on Avria's shoulder and guided her to the sweet, young dragon that lowered her head for them to climb up.

"It's going to be dreadfully cold, Avria. Put on your cloak, and cover your hands. Huddle in there." Tinna heard the sister instructing her. Avria's face appeared 'round the edge of the shining red shield of Eritrix's head and she was crying.

"It won't be forever, Avria. We will fix this." With that the dragon spread her wings and began to move them in graceful gusts, lifting herself with little difficulty, blowing snow over her freshly made tracks. In moments, they vanished into the low clouds of the early afternoon sky. And with that, Avria was gone. Tinna swallowed back her sorrow, and made her way back to the village.

Try to find her now, you savage, Tinna seethed, thinking of the creature that claimed to be the honorable and good Eleran. The woman who had come for her looked like a warrior. *Magic bearing too.* The moment she saw the woman, she felt that Avria was in good hands. In the meantime, she would do what she could with Phenmal to get Eleran out of the quotient so Avria could finally live some semblance of the life she wanted; the life that Tinna herself had wanted; a life of simplicity, of family, of belonging. She would do what she could to insure that for Avria despite recent events. She would do her best to make it work for Avria, despite being resigned that there was little chance of that happening for herself. Things were going to change. They always did.

As she walked down the road towards the gates of Thamatoc, the gypsy caravan was already moving southward towards her, the beasts dragging the tall, lumbering carriages through the thin layer of snow that remained on the roads. Grejnal and Ordran hitched up the heavy draught horses to drag the plough sledge along the main paths around Thamatoc to clear the roads somewhat. Once the Gypsies found the deep forest roads created and managed by their people, the heavier forest cover would hopefully have protected them from heaviest of snowfall, and would be moderately navigable for the caravan. At this point, Tinna did not concern herself about their wellbeing, she was sure they were well equipped to contend with all sorts of situations. She was, however, grateful for providence, which had brought them and their Soothsayer to them when he was needed the most. If they had not come, she had no idea where Avria would be.

She stood by the side of the road when the gypsies passed, and thanked the woman who repaired her sweater, and thanked the sorcerer, and told them that they should always feel welcomed at Thamatoc, and they would always have a place to stay if they wanted it. These were partly her people, after all. She shook their hands and watched them move away. So persecuted they were as a people; misunderstood, and feared for their differences; feared for their incredible bond of brotherhood among their own clans, and their unusual ways—because of this fear, they'd grown insular and shy. She wished she would have time to learn more of them; to go to the

Lathlo family gathering, to know relatives of her father. But she had other things to concern herself with. She hurried through the cold towards Thamatoc to soothe her distraught husband now. *Poor man, can't wrap his mind around what's happened to his little Avria.* Tinna frowned and walked through the crunching snow into the summer lodge. She was greeted by its warmth, but she didn't notice it. All she saw was her pale husband waiting for her with tears in his eyes

MIRANDA MAYER

Chapter Five – The Keepers

Phenmal stepped off the dragon before it had come to a full stop, and landed with a feline grace on the ground, falling immediately into a determined stride, his great-coat flaring out behind him. The dragon, his most frequent flying companion by the name of Igro was used to Phenmal's athletic and premature dismounts and didn't bother to stop. He moved directly into a takeoff while Phenmal strode from the open courtyard into a vaulted covered passageway. The heels of his tall boots clattered on the hard floor. He strode past stone arcs that supported a hefty ceiling. Between each arc stood a soldier, one on each side facing one another like mirror images. Each was clutching a polearm, and they had beautifully hewn feathered helms that closed over their faces. They looked almost like effigies.

Phenmal did not slow. He looked out from under the broad brim of his black hat, keeping his thick black woolen scarf wrapped around his lower-face. The man presented a different aura than he did when he was among his Araki, or haunting the halls of his large empty home on his own. Here, he stood tall and moved lithely without the appearance of age or infirmity. He approached a door flanked by two ornately uniformed soldiers of the human army. They did not impede him; one simply stepped aside and opened the door so he could stride through, bowing his head in respect.

Phenmal walked right into a gathering of elderly men. The room they occupied was rather large but still managed to evoke a welcoming coziness. The tall ceilings were covered elaborately in brilliantly colored frescoes depicting stylized images of the ever-changing calendar of prophesies. These images were animated and alive whenever the old men were in this room, which they were most of the day, every day. So each time Phenmal visited, the ceiling looked different.

Personages of past and future significance languorously moved in a band of graphics around the base of the long, smooth, rounded coffin-like space lofting above them. The images were cast in the golden light of a painted, gold-leafed, and intricately carved medallion of the sun, which dominated the center of the ceiling. The sun's painted rays radiated out to the wide ribbon of images of the events and people. As always, the distinctive black hair and olive skin of Tinna's figure never ceased to haunt Phenmal when he looked up at it. He remembered recognizing her in it the first time just over twenty years ago, when being summoned to see the old men shortly after the destruction of the human settlements by the dragons. Tinna's figure was shadowed by the shape of Ledroran, who now still glided over her image, but higher up into the rays of the sun. Tinna had moved forward since the last time he'd been here and she wore different clothes now; a formal-looking gown with a train that trailed behind her. Before her, an arm was extended and she was holding a sword by the hilt with the blade pointing downwards.

He paused to study this newer placement, his eyes cast upwards. He could never fail to notice the sudden and noticeable absence of images that followed Tinna's figure and circled 'round to connect again with the earliest events on the timeline. Instead of a collection of images showing what was to come, Tinna's figure stood before a band of tangled vines and leaves. It had been like that for years now, the tangle growing longer with each passing year, the older events vanishing one by one behind her, but no new prophesies appearing ahead of her. The vines had once acted as the marker to show where the prophesies began and ended, and the patch was never that large. Now it took up a full third of the whole ribbon of images and with every visit Phenmal made to the Citadel, it was growing larger.

This fresco was created by one of the ancient keepers, long ago. The magic that sustained it was provided by the mere presence of the other Keepers that occupied the great palace now. They paid little heed to the moving images. They seemed quite unconcerned about what could possibly be hidden behind the expanding tangle of greenery and they were quite determined to move forward on what they knew was the only possible course. Their prevailing thought was that the new prophesies would either reveal themselves when

Tinna's time passed, or that the fresco's creator's spell was meant to end there. All they knew was that her effigy now wore the crown. The armies she'd rallied marched behind her in their uniforms—two years ago, they were in front of her, and she was bedecked in armor and chain mail. The band of vines was smaller then, but the prophesies were running out, and Tinna had finally put the last of them behind her, except for the crown on her head. Such faith in the steadiness of the ceiling's imagery and their own powerful ability to see what was to come, the old men did not take any message from this tangle of leaves and vines except to look forward to what lay hidden beneath them. They believed that once Tinna wore the crown in earnest, that the vines would reveal what was to come. Phenmal did not see it in the same way they did. It could represent many things—but he had the sense that they weren't all good.

One of the old men looked up when Phenmal entered. He waited for Phenmal to take a moment to study the changes on the fresco and when Phenmal's cool blue eyes fell down upon his face, the old man exclaimed: "We were just talking about you, boy," alerting the others of his presence, all of whom seemed quite unconcerned with his arrival. Phenmal pulled his scarf down from his face, and tugged off his gloves, shoving them into the pocket of his heavy greatcoat.

The room was a simple rectangle with a fireplace centered on the wall directly across from the door. Both of these were placed on the mid-mark of each long wall. The short walls were both comprised mostly of five towering windows on each side. One side overlooked the wintry forest park that sprawled out from the face of the building; the other gave view to the more intimate, white-dusted courtyard around which this massive building was wrapped. There was only one more entrance to the space and that was the hidden servant's door that was blended into the dark paneling on the back wall near the corner.

This citadel was as old as the forest, if not older. Its walls protected the old men, just as they kept it from falling apart. They rarely left the security of the citadel's walls. What they had to fear, Phenmal did not know, but they lived like frightened little mice, puttering about their ancient edifice. They were strange characters, even from Phenmal's perspective. He'd been acquainted with them for many long years—and he still found them odd after all this time.

Some had come and some had gone, but they were all, strangely, the same—as if they were all born of the same source. Young or ancient, they were all the same.

Phenmal felt the room's warmth infuse him and the scent of burning wood filled his nostrils. The feel of the thick woolen rug beneath his cold feet was good after freezing himself on that long flight from Thamatoc. The austere portraits of past Keepers circled the room in an oddly ordered scattering on the long, tall paneled walls. There were a few intermittent shelf-nooks here and there, or a sideboard-style piece of furniture holding huge urns exploding with sprays of dried pussy willows, winter-berries, holly and evergreen branches. In the center of the room was the arc of chairs facing the door and on each end of the room, softer chaises and lounging sofas were set in intimate sitting areas along with a few small tables and some lamps. All of the room's occupants however were collected in front of Phenmal, but he only had the attention of one of them.

"I do not have much time, honorable Master. Please make your message quick," Phenmal barked. The other old men were huddled around a table that had been wheeled in by one of the elusive servants, holding a large silver urn, from which they were dispensing a steaming tea into diminutive cups. Next to the urn was a tiered platter holding a luxurious selection of little cakes. They all looked up when Phenmal spoke. Six doddering old men, all of them dressed richly in velvet frock coats in a variety of subdued colours, in sculpted soft leather slippers and the finest silks, seemed reluctant in giving the newcomer his due attention, more focused on securing themselves a cup of hot tea and one or two of the tiny cakes. The man Phenmal had addressed frowned.

"What could possibly be more important than a summons from the Keepers' high-seat, my boy?" he asked sternly. Phenmal glowered.

"I'm hunting a Zsathri and I don't have time to be distracted. I confess I was not happy to receive your summons."

"Hunting a Zsathri you say? Whatever for?" another asked.

"That is personal."

"There are no Zsathris to be seen," one of them muttered, gazing up at the mural.

"Zsathris are irrelevant," another replied. Phenmal took their mutterings in stride, he was used to them.

"So you say it's personal; I see. Well, perhaps, if you sit down and share some tea with us, I will send someone to help you find your Zsathri; someone to help you contain him. Come, come old friend, have some tea and a little cake. We are to be brought freshly roasted chestnuts, right from Gadrin's home. His granddaughter gathered them just before the snowfall; they should be ready soon."

"Your message," Phenmal growled. The old men straightened and then dispersed about the small room, moving to their chairs in a guileless, tottering sort of way. A cacophony of slurping sips followed as each one drank from his small cup, and one or two of them made appreciative little grunts of delight as they popped a cake into their mouths. Phenmal stood patiently and waited for them to settle in. There was no sense in hurrying them, he knew this. They would do as they wished—they did not change.

These seemingly ingenuous little old men were the most highly-ranked leaders of the Keepers. They seemed like dodderers, but Phenmal knew better. Each and every one of these long-lived old men was a force to be reckoned with. Each one wielded tremendous power in one form or another; it was a requisite to being a Keeper. How one became one was a mystery to Phenmal, but they continued to appear, the children's annex always seemed to have fresh young faces there.

The Keeper's control of the world's goings-on was paramount. In spite of their claiming they oversaw only the sacred lands of Oromoii, it was well known that they interfered elsewhere as well. They had a hand in everything in the known world. Their power superseded any throne. This group was overseen by one power alone, and that was the Trinity; a triumvirate of leaders from each most dominant race. The Trinity watched over these old men and their meddlings. The Trinity held court much farther north, in the icy wastelands but agents resided at the Citadel to keep the connection strong between these two ancient organizations.

These particular six old codgers were the top tier of the small army of Keepers, their collective arranged tidily into ranks over which the six ruled. Each of the five ranks had its own residence in the citadel, and its own purpose to follow, and they remained in their isolated groups on the most part. Some managed the pursuit of collecting knowledge, others were responsible for identifying children for tutelage in the academies, others tasked with finding the ones born to magic, and there was even a small group responsible for finding new Keepers as they arrived into the world as babies.

Phenmal dealt mostly with these six, and a few of the ones ranked directly below them. He occasionally saw the little boys slated to become like these old men being led about in neat files around the Citadel's great campus. But he did not interact with any others. The citadel housed many of the strongest bearers of power. Chaiva were not usually privileged to have a place at the citadel, but Phenmal was a special case since he was connected to Tinna.

"Gentlemen, please," Phenmal grunted. A few more sips and one of them muttered:

"Yes, yes, boy. Take your kettle off the fire, please. This is a matter of some importance; I do not believe you should be taking this information in any other way except with the gravity it deserves," Master Heln said in his booming, bass voice. Phenmal felt drained by their energy; he could not read any of them. He could feel the passive restorative powers working on him just by being near them. Anyone who worked closely with them could live an unusually long life. One particularly beloved servant Gadrin was hundreds of years old. His marriages and the families that branched from those over the years were many.

"Dearest boy, it is nice to see you. It's been two months. Last we spoke you said you were to attend a joyous occasion; the wedding of the Ashru's daughter. Has it occurred?" Phenmal did not answer. He did not wish to encourage the idle chatter these little old men lived for. So much time spent in limited company had made them act like a clutch of tittering old ladies sometimes. They seemed to get the point of Phenmal's silence, and one of them took a serious tone.

"You've put yourself in a place where you have become quite crucial to us, Master Phenmal," he said. "I know we say that often, but you must be reminded how important it is you continue your path. It's vital!"

"*I've* put myself in that place? No, gentlemen; *you* have put me there. It was naught but a chance encounter that brought me to her. You are the ones that tied me to her irrevocably,"

"Fate is to blame for that, my boy. Fate. However, now you advise the Ashru of the Araki, and she has had significant influence on the world. Even the Thran have dedicated their loyalty to her, to some degree. You must know this."

"I have not been living in a cave these past two years," Phenmal grunted. They ignored his insolence and continued.

"Her influence; it is affecting things among the humans. It is time now to move things forward, time to stop this before it becomes a problem."

"Stop what?"

"The High Throne has been restless since the coronation last year. The father left the son with little to rule, and the over-indulged boy regrets is lack of power most keenly. He is angry. Angry that the race of dragons has been returned to their trusted status among the Araki majority—his father's lingering hatred of them has been carried on in the new King. He is frantic that the greater part of Oromoii's people are Araki, Dragon kind and Adrei and that their armies are unrivaled now, even the Thran have proven no match, and lastly, he is furious about the Ashru. He knows we seek to put her in his place. He has been hard at work undermining the efforts made to bridge the gap between humanity and the Araki, to break down the trust that was created when the Araki came to humanity's salvation against the Thran.

"He does not want to give up the High Throne. He's been gathering people around him; people who do not want to relinquish rule to the majority race. Humanity is languishing but they are too proud to let go. There have been stirrings, Phenmal. He's been careful to keep the scent of revolt quite undetectable in Araki-strong settlements like your Lemoram, or the city of Loshan. But the remaining pure human communities from Suthervale to Gheraine have been infected with this angered entitlement, and people are being made to believe that the motives of the Araki people and their allies are no better than those of the Thran. The High King enjoys his privilege and his power. He is not content to leave well enough alone. The Trinity has asked that we move forward; that we act before there is more war. It is time, Phenmal. It is time to move her up. To establish her leadership, and neutralize the stirrings before they spread beyond our capacity to contain it. We worry it might be too late already. She must don the crown."

"She's not ready," Phenmal grunted. "Your sense of timing, like the last time, is questionable. Something terrible has happened to her daughter…"

"There's no time for these paltry things…" Master Ijka waved his hand dismissively.

"*Then make time!*" Phenmal barked. He glowered at the old men each in turn. "Why are you so worried if the humans are growing restless? They are so few, how much of a threat could they be? The Araki army could subdue any uprisings with ease; not to mention the how quickly a few of the sky borne dragons could stop something!" Phenmal snarled. The old men shifted about in their chairs. His question was a good one. It seemed simple enough. But their eyes cast upwards to the mural. What they saw there that Phenmal did not see, he did not know. They wanted Tinna at the Seat of High Power at Miranne and that was that.

"You propose to destroy the race your Ashru fought so hard to save? Twice in her lifetime she's come to the aid of these people. This race could easily disappear into oblivion if they become embroiled in war with the Araki. It would be their end."

"And Tinna could stop this?"

"Without a doubt. She has earned her credibility; she needs only supersede that of the sitting monarch to succeed. The people will respect her. But we need to get that pox of a King out now before his infection spreads and put a hero in place no one can question. He will not stand in the way of prophesy! Nothing stands in the way of the prophesies! You know all this, Phenmal. It is our lot to ensure things happen as they should!" He sighed intolerantly and shook his head, giving them all an impatient look.

"You may go and hunt your magic bearer, Phenmal, but only after you've put things in motion. The High King must be removed from the throne, and the Ashru *must* become Queen; and her strength, her army, her power must be elevated to the highest position so there is leadership. It is what must be. If there continues to be no leadership and this old-blood royal continues to create problems, we will have another war. Humanity is threatened; we must either unify them with the rest of the population or they will separate themselves. We will insure the transition is smooth with whatever resources she needs, as usual."

"How am I supposed to go about this?"

"We'll take care of the little king. You must get the Ashru to the Palace at Miranne just in the same way you got her to Iromi two years ago," the eldest of the Keepers said gruffly. He paused, looking at

Phenmal's angry face. "To make this easier for you, because I know even without personal problems, the Ashru is an obstinate, stubborn, strong-willed sort of creature; we will provide you with a Drathar to hunt your Zsathri." Phenmal's face blanched a bit, and his brow tightened. There was little that struck fear into the heart of a Chaiva; but the mention of this creature sent chills down his spine. He did not protest. If anything was capable of stopping a magic-bearing madman, it would be a Drathar. He nodded subtly and bowed his head in a rare outpouring of gratitude. It would be of tremendous help to him.

"Get some rest; you can fly out tomorrow morning."

"I bloody hate flying," Phenmal grumbled. He turned on his heel and walked out towards the private residences where he had his own small apartments. He did not like coming to the citadel. Although he held a high place in the ranks of Keepers, he was not at home here. He, like Tinna, wished for something simpler, but also like Tinna, he was given little choice for the past twenty or so years. He'd given these little old men over three hundred years of his life already. He'd brokered a deal some decades back with the old men; they would agree to set him free of service in exchange for one particularly questionable job they wanted done. He did it, and they had sent him adrift to age in peace. But then Tinna came along, and the dragons started destroying the world, and everything changed. He was thrown back into their clutches. Enough was enough. He wanted it to be finished; he wanted to age and to die like a normal person, to fade at peace, in the company of people he enjoyed, if any at all. Instead, his relationship with them persisted, and his youth was being returned to him bit by bit.

Phenmal's encounter with Tinna had indeed cut his retirement short and had prolonged his connection to the Keepers. It was a worthy sacrifice in the end, for Tinna and Avria were part of his life and he would not wish that away by any means. But he wanted to be the safe fatherly figure; to remain benign and non-threatening to women he loved; to putter around and grumble about the stupidity of people, and sit and smoke a pipe in the comfort of the lodge at Thamatoc while Tinna spoke in her velvety voice. But that was already changing, and he wouldn't be able to hide it much longer. Soon she would notice the years were taken from his face; no longer interpreting it as his being unchanged. The infirmities he'd worked so hard to acquire were all dissolved away and he spent most of his time pretending to be older than he felt. Tinna would eventually notice it. So would Avria. He couldn't think of a single person who would be so annoyed to be given his youth back.

He moved through the labyrinthine passages and walked through a garden courtyard covered in snow, where he found the door to his apartments. He climbed up a flight of stairs and entered the familiar space. He spent little time here, but it remained his private residence in spite of his frequent and extended absences. It was decorated to his preferences and his servant was always present to anticipate his needs. Fires had been lit, and a warm supper had been laid out at the small table by the window where the snow fell. His servant knew full well that Phenmal liked his privacy, and remained successfully unseen. He sat down and leaned back in his chair, sighing wearily. His eyes looked down through the window to the courtyard. The evergreens were weighed down with snow, the cobbles covered. A few tracks showed that people other than he had come through recently. He picked up a cup of steaming tea and sipped.

Suddenly, his skull began to throb. His eyes locked on the doorway across the courtyard. He squinted and fought the cringe of pain. "Stop…" he hissed through his teeth, spilling a bit of his tea. The pain suddenly subsided to a faint hum and Phenmal's shoulders relaxed a bit. A second later, the doorway opened to the courtyard and a dark shadow of a creature appeared.

Garbed entirely in black, including a sheer black veil over the face, the Drathar stepped out of the door, and paused. He moved with precision, and his face angled immediately upward towards Phenmal in the window. There was somewhere in this citadel where the Keepers housed a handful of these dark creatures. Phenmal was not privy to where. They were rare and excessively powerful—known to be the most powerful bearers of magic of all—rumored to be even more powerful than the magical Keepers themselves. How the Keepers kept them under such a tight rein, Phenmal did not know. But they served quietly, stoically and remained mostly elusive and secret. Phenmal had witnessed first-hand the devastating effects the unveiled gaze of a Drathar can have on a person. He knew their powers were vast and varied.

The older man nodded to the figure, and watched him continue along, crossing into the main building and vanishing under the archway. Phenmal's headache worsened with each approaching step. When he felt like his eyes were going to pop out of his head, the door opened without a knock or an invitation, and the shadow stepped into the room.

"You will take me to where this magician last was seen; where he cast magic." A young-sounding voice mumbled from behind his veil. Eerily white skin could be seen through the sheer fabric and the shine of almost-white irises. He wore a heavily draped black woolen cowl, a cloak of the same material and underneath, a dense, thick felted sweater, and a pair of loose black trousers that bagged down around some crumpled, rather shabby looking leather boots. He carried no weapons, nor did he boast any adornments.

"I will. In the morning. We leave at dawn. You will have to dress warmly—it's a cold ride up with the dragons," he mumbled. "Be forewarned," he said, "dragons do not take kindly to being read or having their heads invaded. They are telepathic, and speak to one another over great distances using it, and that means they are more sensitive to unsolicited invasions into their heads. If you want to stay in the air, I suggest you keep your mind to yourself." He drained his tea and then poured himself a fresh cup. "You did not need to pry about in *my* head, Drathar. I am trusted among the highest ranks of the Keepers."

"I *pry* everyone… even the old men," the shadow replied. "You would not suffer a headache if you weren't fighting me. You bring discomfort to yourself," he muttered in a strange, hollow voice. He then turned to walk out, pausing briefly to add: "You keep interesting thoughts, Chaiva. You hold people close; a great liability for one so high; but I can see why you cherish them," he stopped for a moment, as if relishing the images Phenmal's mind showed him. He then sighed, and said: "I will be here at dawn." Phenmal watched him slink like a wraith across the snow.

Drathar were few, and they operated all from this place where they could be closely monitored by the elderly men. Phenmal had worked with one or two in his time and was somewhat familiar with them. Among all their other powers, they also possessed capabilities as his, and he knew that the Drathar had scoured every corner of his mind and gotten clear, detailed images of everyone Phenmal cared about.

MIRANDA MAYER

Chapter Six – Pursuit

This time Tinna did meet Phenmal with defiance when he came bearing bad news. It was as if she knew that was what he was going to do, but she merely shook her head and looked across the room where the baby was napping in his bassinette. "I can't leave. I can't go to a palace where I am not welcome. I can't be expected to do all this, Phenmal. Not now, not ever..." she sighed. "It's already hard enough with just the visits to Klatna; it's already taxing to live this double life." Phenmal, still bundled up from the flight was stripping off his outer garments and looking at her regrettably.

"Then perhaps simplifying as much as you can; moving you and your family where leadership is supposed to be," he watched her shake her head and smirk at his lame attempt at persuasion and he succumbed to laughter too for a moment. "The Keepers are worried about the High King; he still keeps a circle of influence. He is propagating fear among his kind. There are rumours that he is decrying the idea that humanity should relinquish ruling power to the dominant race as they should. He will start a war, Tinna, and the humans will either fall at his side in fear of becoming irrelevant, or they will trust the woman who saved what was left of this empire. You need to step in before this little idea catches fire among a desperate race." At that moment, Taneth entered and seeing Phenmal, he gave him a terse smile and crossed to Tinna, kissing her before asking her what was going on.

Taneth had been focusing on his duties for his village to keep his mind off Avria's absence and the tragedy that had been beset upon her. He looked at Phenmal, his eyes pained.

"I thought you were hunting that *animal*..."

"I will be. I've brought some help. He is at this moment where…" he paused, surprised at the emotional response he felt speaking of it; "where it happened. I came to deliver a message to Tinna."

"I see," Taneth said tightly, quite keen on his wife's stressed look.

"I will be following the Drathar for a few days…"

"The Drathar? Those actually exist?" Taneth blurted. "Aren't they supposed to be some sort of demon?"

"Not necessarily…"

"You have brought a *demon* to Thamatoc?" Taneth was a skeptic by nature, but he'd become more open minded this past few years now that a good portion of the types magic bearers and creatures he'd previously believed non-existent had passed through his doors at some point or other. He still believed in the rational, and did not think there was anything unnatural about them, and that their powers or existence could eventually be explained. It was funny to Phenmal to hear him complain about bringing a demon into his community.

"They are *not* demons. They're not exactly human; but they are not the wild mythical things the books say they are, Taneth. They are powerful, the most powerful magic bearer known to the world; and they are rare, so we are privileged to have one assisting Avria. I do not find pleasure in much of my dealings with the Keepers, my friend, but this is a significant gift they've given me. They've all but guaranteed that Avria will be safe by giving us the service of this so-called demon," Phenmal said strongly. Taneth's mouth snapped shut and he scratched his head, shaking it incredulously.

"A bloody Drathar…" Poor Taneth. A staunch skeptic of the strictest kind, these past years had been difficult for him; an exercise of acceptance, a challenging puzzle. He was a man of facts and science, yet he was now faced with creatures that defied logic; and he spent many an hour trying to wrap his busy mind around it all, trying to find some way to explain it all with science and knowledge. Each time he felt he could explain something, or had a theory, he was presented with something more insane and incredible. Phenmal smirked at Taneth's bemused expression.

"Tinna, when I return, we need to speak in earnest of this. I hope you will think on this while I'm away." As he spoke, the Drathar slid into the room and Tinna and Taneth immediately grunted in pain as the creature invaded their minds.

"Get out of my head!" she roared, her eyes turning feral. The Drathar withdrew from her head, and then assaulted Taneth, who groaned from the discomfort.

"Enough, Drathar; these are *my* people.

"I seek traces of magic, Chaiva. They leave footprints, if spells had been cast to glean information…" Taneth shook his head,

"The Zsathri can't do that, they are natural wielders, and they can follow auras and…"

"A *normal* Zsathri respects the laws; this one is tainted. Much tainted. Not just by madness but by something else from the voids. This is no ordinary bearer here. His powers are not incredible; the other magic bearer that chased him off proved that," the Drathar muttered. He moved about the space, running his fingers along the spines of some books on the small shelf by the door, picking up and examining a small carved figurine of a horse; "The place your Chaiva here chose for the girl was an inspired choice, she will be protected there and untraceable using magic. But he already has an idea where she is—if he can read as clearly as I think. *Surrounded by the sea*, he took that from your head," he turned to Tinna, who frowned and her eyes glassed over.

"There are not too many places one can live fully protected, and magic bearers know them all to begin with; knowing that it is an isle narrows the options significantly. This Zsathri is no longer bound by any laws; something has given him freedom from those. The gypsy magician said he could be incapacitated if he used his magic to kill again; this is not true. He can do as he wishes. And he will. He *will* find her. For now, I have an impression of him. I have something to follow. Once I know his bearing, I will know if he has found the right place." The man's voice had a strange gentleness to it; which contradicted his appearance and his hidden face. Tinna wondered why he was dressed as he was and wondered what was underneath all the draping folds of black fabric.

"I must follow these signs now, before they fade." Phenmal nodded and turned to Tinna, tugging on his greatcoat and donning his gloves which he'd scarce stripped off. He picked up his scarf;

"I will accompany him for now. I will return in a while. After that, we need to have that talk." He looked at her gravely and then wound the scarf 'round his neck and face. "Come, Drathar; dragons do not like the cold and the snow; our friend must be less than pleased waiting upon us." The Drathar nodded and they both bowed to Tinna and her family. They exited the apartments, striding with single minded purpose down the long corridor to the front of the lodge.

"The Zsathri did not transport himself too far, but he is probably long-gone from there, but if we move quickly, the trail can be found," The Drathar muttered. Phenmal followed, watching the Drathar wrap himself further in a thicker coat, wondering what sort of person lay beneath the veil. If there was any benefit to traveling with a Drathar, it was that they were unreadable. It was strangely peaceful for Phenmal. They exited in silence and were soon on the wing.

Taneth and Tinna remained quiet for a while after the departure of the two men. Taneth helped himself to a late supper. "Phenmal had that grave look I do not like; it harkens back to before the little one was born."

"Yes, it's that sort of thing," Tinna agreed, taking some more tea. She walked to the fire and stood there. "It's so much and we have yet to face Offrin, who should be returning soon."

* * * *

It will be like it used to be, where she would welcome me, and wrap herself around me with love and bliss. She will moan with pleasure beneath me once more. She will kiss me and touch me in the way she once did. She will look at me as she used to, her eyes so hungry for the sight of me, her body drawn to me, her eyes always on me—as if I were true north and she was a compass. She will. Eleran's eyes were glassed over, the lower lids shining with tears. *She is all I see, she is the scent that fills my head. There will no longer be a need to show her, or punish her.* He froze, and swallowed, a tear falling onto his hard cheekbone. He bit down on his teeth with determination, and chewed his mandibles. *No. No need to punish her. She will understand.*

His hands moved quickly as stuffed his items back into his bag. With a strange, faraway look, he threw it over his shoulder. "An island in the sea..." he said to himself. "Dodderer forgets things sometimes when he's around the mother." *He is powerless to her. If I ever wanted to hurt that old man, I would just have to hurt Avria's mother. But I will not... because it would hurt Avria. I do not like to hurt my Avria. But sometimes I must be firm, sometimes it is necessary.*

The island in the sea. She awaits me there, and all will be as it was. She will be away from the half-man, away from the ones that persuaded her that I am the enemy. She will welcome me again, she will want me again. She will no longer fear me, for how could she fear me? She had loved me once as I loved her. She has to know I am only better than I was before, so she could only love me more. There is no reason for her to fear me. She would surely know this. She is mine. She is my Avria after all. My perfect little dark-haired siren, my love. The other half of my soul. He would go. He had an idea where she was going. It would not be easy, but he could use his powers to make the journey shorter. He would work out the challenges on the way. *She must be removed from the influences that harm her. She must be returned to me, where she belongs.* Bundled in wintry clothes, the Zsathri fastened his items to the stolen horse. With a smooth movement he swung up onto its back and yanked the rein harshly. His eyes focused forward onto the road ahead. With a flash of light, he gave himself and his mount a good head-start.

MIRANDA MAYER

Chapter Seven – The Core

Avria's way of contending with the wind, the cold and the pain in her ears was to sink further against the warmth of the dragon's head and into her cloak and hood. She'd heard the short introduction from the woman that had come to collect her. She was a member of the Dreff Sisterhood. That was all she shared for that moment. The sister's body was presently wedged up against hers, and the woman's face was not visible in profile, only the fur of her hood and a few locks of her wheaten hair that hung free and tossed about in the frigid winds. They did not speak. The dragon's short head-shield did not provide enough coverage to keep out the heavy winds, and if they wanted to speak, they had to scream. Avria was in no mind to do so, and she didn't quite know what to say to someone like the sister. She'd learn more about her soon enough. For now, she concentrated on keeping herself warm and keeping her hands and feet wrapped tightly in her thick cloak.

She managed to slip into a strange light sleep through the night, where dreams intermixed with glimpses of starry sky and moonlit cloud. For hours, the dragon carried them on the winds; her wings pumping occasionally, always level, always forward. At dawn, Avria's ears began to hurt horribly again and she felt as if her stomach was moving up into her throat. They entered clouds again, and all she saw was whiteness and grey. With a startling dip down, they broke out from the bottom of a rather thick layer of clouds and Avria found herself looking down at an expanse of water of the like she'd never seen before. For that second, she forgot all that was awful, all that horrified her and all she could see were the tall haystack rocks being pummeled by the white-capped waves. Down the back of the dragon, receding behind her, she could see the mainland; it was barely visible in the mists of early morning, the pink light of the rising sun tinting the faces of the cliff sides.

"Where are we?"

"En route to the Isle of Gales," the Sister replied loudly, her voice nearly lost to the wind. Avria was astonished. She immediately looked back at the cliffs that grew further and further away, and she thought of Hanru, and Wye so nearby.

The Dragon dove a bit more, and then banked slightly towards the south. Her speed was slowing, and the air seemed warmer. Avria looked 'round the edge of the head-shield to see where they were going and she gasped. Before them was what looked like a table of rock; the Isle of Gales. A platform of land rose high above the turbulent waters, it was surrounded entirely by cliffs of stone as black as soot; the land on the isle a thick, lush thatch of green, dense with trees with an undulating landscape. This greenery was currently flocked in a coat of sparkling snow and ice. As they descended in altitude, it grew large, so large she could not see the other end of it. There was a ridge of mountains down the center, the peaks rocky and covered in fresh snow. There were several steep fjords cutting into the island, the one before them massive beyond Avria's imagination. A forest of towering stone pillars carved to look like gods jutted out from the waters in tidy rows, taming the rough seas where they met the waterway, and someone, sometime in history, had sculpted the two rocky cliffs that opened into the fjord to look like a tangle of colossal tree trunks. The dragon dropped down low over the fjord, following the waterway from the thundering waves pummeling the impossible constructs of the pillars, to the place where the water swirled in a heavy, powerful battle with the river meeting the sea, and then inland, where it grew languorous.

A flock of wintry-white cliff-birds had caught the Dragon's tailwind and then began to overtake her, flying parallel to the elegant creature's body, some just over the wings, instinctively rising and falling along with their movement. Avria watched all this with a sense of awe. The sister stood gingerly on the dragon's neck, and holding the edge of the shield, looked out over it. "There is the abbey," she leaned down and shouted. "Take a look, you must. This is the first time a sister has seen it from above. They will all expect you to bear witness and describe it." Avria stood clumsily and moved next to the woman. She was much shorter and could barely see over the tall fan-like shield behind the dragon's head. The wind buffeted her and blew her hood off, but it wasn't so frigid that she couldn't bear it long enough to see the abbey for herself.

Two unimaginably large tapering spires rose up from the forest cover, between them, the angled, snow-covered roof of the stone abbey. The towers bookended the building where the roof gables would have been, and the edifice was covered in hundreds of windows without much order to their location. There were few rows, few columns, they seemed randomly scattered, with a variety of shapes and styles that spanned centuries of architectural trends. Off the back wall, what looked like a glass hot-house clung to its side, the bottom like an elaborate corbel holding a faceted jewel with a dollop of snow upon it. The walls themselves were a mottle of various masonry stones and styles, some areas covered in a smoothened plaster which was old and flaked away. The towers on the other hand each had a line of windows encircling them in lazy rising spirals, connecting fairly regularly spaced horizontal rows of windows. The tiny size and sheer number of the windows bespoke the tremendous mass and dimension of this building. It was bigger than anything Avria knew of; bigger than the palace at Miranne; bigger than Hildercross before it was reduced to rubble, and she realized the height of the towers when they approached them and was completely astonished by them. Avria ducked down, for the cold wind was making her lips blue.

Sister Adrenne followed, grinning. "What a rare gift I've been given in collecting you. To ride in the skies," she said loudly. The sister touched the soft skin of Eritrix's head underneath the shield that protected them from the violent winds. Avria smiled wanly and then squealed as the dragon dropped and banked at the same time, making her stomach lurch. The woman laughed in delight and then leaned out. Avria had ridden dragons before, and she often forgot that most others were not permitted this privilege. She had to take pause from her own thoughts to acknowledge this, and be amused by the Sister's wonder.

"Oh, there's the High Mother, I can see her in her red robes standing in the bailey to receive us," she smiled easily. The dragon had come between the towers and over the roof, and below them a round courtyard surrounded by a wall of smaller buildings hugged up against the face of the main building. The forest surrounded the entire installation. Avria would be comfortable here. The dragon turned sharply and dove again, and the rooftops came into view. Within a few seconds, there was a flap of the wings, and the lurch of her stomach, and they were down safe on the cobbles. The sister was already off the dragon, and reaching up to help Avria down.

Reality returned the moment her feet touched the ground. Standing there, her bag slumped on the thin layer of snow of the courtyard, her fatigue, being surrounded by strangers; she suddenly felt her exhaustion and perhaps a touch of defeat. She was in a place with wonders that she suspected even her father knew little of, but could not find the true wonder in it. She felt alone. A hand clasped her shoulder and she turned. Facing her was a woman almost as tall as Taneth with chestnut hair that fell well below her thighs. She wore a gown of the style Avria wore at her wedding in a soft rose red, and over that a deep red robe with a train that fanned out behind her. Six more women stood behind her, all dressed in black as her travel companion was, all wearing the same ankle-length cloak with the heavy hood with the fur lining. They were all tall, lithe, willowy creatures, all strikingly pretty, and all staring quite adoringly at Eritrix. All except the woman in red, who was focused on Avria's pale face and sunken eyes.

"The ladies wish to know if it is acceptable to greet the dragon with touch?" the High Mother asked. Avria shrugged.

"Ask Eritrix. She can speak for herself." The large creature looked on with dragon-bemusement. She nodded without speaking, comprehending the conversation for herself. Sister Adrenne reached out and touched Eritrix's cheek to show the other sisters, and the women immediately gravitated towards the large red dragon, their hands fanning out on her scales, sounds of wonder and delight mixed into their voices. The High Mother smiled at Avria.

"They've been waiting with great anticipation since Adrenne left us to see the dragon for themselves. We see them so rarely; these cliffs are not warm enough to tempt them here. The Chaiva's message was a great surprise to us, but I am glad you are here, young Avria and I am pleased to be here to assist you. Come." She lifted her hand palm-up, and waited for Avria to take it. Avria hiked her bag onto her shoulder and placed her hand in hers.

The High Mother was an elegant woman of Avria's mother's age, perhaps a few years more. Pretty would be too little a word to describe her mature elegance and grace—her presence was powerful, and overwhelming. They left the dragon and the sisters behind, and she led her towards the main building. "The great abbey is many thousands of years old. We are privileged to have use of it, to care for it. We have been stewards of this great isle for generations, and part of our work is to preserve the great works of the ancient ones who dwelled here long ago... the ones that built the spires and the gates of Dareen, and the sea-breaker gods. It is an ancient land," the woman explained. "It was once part of the greater land that is Oromoii, but the connecting land was washed away in the five floods during the age of Storms."

"I think my father would very much benefit from meeting you."

"Oh?"

"He is a Wiseman, and like my mother says, he wasn't just made a Wiseman by his school, he was born with it in his blood, for he wants to know everything about everything. I thought he knew everything about everything; but seeing this world; he has much more to see and learn."

"Everyone has much to see in learn, even those who have lived long in this world," the High Mother said. She paused by a colossal door and looked back. Avria followed her gaze. The Dragon had broken away from the women, and was following Avria.

"What is it Eritrix?" Avria asked. The dragon stopped several paces away and lowered her head.

"*I CANNOT STAY. THIS COLD IS NOT FOR ME. BUT I WILL RETURN WHEN IT IS YOUR TIME TO GO HOME,*" the dragon hissed between her teeth. Behind her, the sisters huddled together, still entranced by the vision of the beautiful creature among them.

"I understand," Avria replied. "I thank you, Eretrix." The dragon bowed her head.

"*I WILL GO NOW. I BID YOU AND YOUR FRIENDS FAREWELL.*" Eretrix then pivoted on her hind legs, and jumped over the line of women causing a titter of delight and excitement, bounding almost like an exuberant dog, flaring out her wings and leaping up into the air, catching the wind and lifting herself up in powerful pumps of her wings. She spiraled up and then cast herself west, following the river to the fjord, back to the sea-breakers, where she would head to warmer lands until she was needed again.

Meanwhile, the High Mother opened the great door, which swiveled inwards with astonishing ease and led Avria into the great hall. Avria was instantly cowed by a sense of smallness and inadequacy. The great hall was exactly as it was named. It was a chamber of impossible proportions; vaulted ceilings towered high above her, held aloft by great pillars and buttresses arching together to give the ceiling the appearance of a cage of ribs. The floor was a shining white marble. Swagged between the pillars were chains holding massive chandeliers with hundreds of candles shedding weak light into the cavernous space. There was no feature anywhere to be seen except for the pillars and the smooth floor. Three towering windows of leaded glass loomed over the end of the chamber, casting a soft, snowy light into three arched pools of brightness on the floor before them. The sound of heels clacking on marble resonated and then echoed high above Avria, making it impossible to determine where they were originating.

"What was this place, before it became your home?"

"Nobody knows. There were no temple statues, no glyphs, merely what you see. We think it was a palace, for there is indication that there was once a dais over in the head of the nave by the great windows... we think perhaps a throne sat there," she pointed towards the depths of the chamber. Far off, Avria could see two red-garbed figures crossing the main hall. It wasn't heated, it was cold and unwelcoming. The High Mother led her down the center and then turned left, leading her between columns that led to an archway into a vaulted, dark corridor.

"And your order; the Dreff," Avria began. The High Mother launched into a lengthy explanation as they moved down the long corridor, passing other arches into other spaces, and wide stairways spiraling into the darkness.

"We are much like the Zsathri your Chaiva described. We are stewards, but we are not children of the Hevra as the Zsathri Druids are. We are sisters to another higher-order of magic bearer, one that is often reviled and feared. But we possess many of the same qualities. The Drathar are our brothers. Like they, we are gifted with powers that we believe are a divine bequest, and should be used with discipline and discretion—our powers against our brothers' is tempered and much less dangerous, but it comes from the same source, an ancient source. We believe that our gifts and those others who possess them are a danger to others without proper training.

"The powers can regulate themselves to some measure. For example, as in the communication from your Chaiva friend implied, the Zsathri that pursues you was first rendered helpless; his spark and essence extracted into a place called the void where he might harm no one with the gifts he was given. No matter the intention, when powers are used against those without them, that is the price. Sometimes, depending on the situation, the punishment can be lightened; sometimes, when the crimes are too grave, the wielder is doomed to be banished out of his body until it dies," she paused at one of several spiral stairway columns rising up along the corridor, and gestured for Avria to precede her. Avria climbed, and the lady followed, resuming her explanation.

"Your Chaiva thought of us, because he knows our combined powers create a space of peace and restraint—your presence in this world is rendered invisible by your being inside the reach of what we call our *core*. Our core emanates a cloud of magic that removes the powers of those inside it for as long as they remain, it neutralizes any magic cast upon others and it keeps prying magical eyes from spying within the core. There are several places I can think of that have a similar effect in our world; but ours is the only one created from the powers of a collective," she was breathing a bit harder as they climbed. She continued on. Avria waited for an indication to stop, to veer off into one of the doorways or archways they passed, but she did not. So Avria continued climbing, listening, feeling her bag getting heavier and heavier with every step.

"This cloud does not affect us, but only others who come bearing powers; we are here to heal, to teach discipline; for those who are not raised among these walls find it difficult to control their powers, so our Core assists them and enables us to help them. We help those who sometimes are punished by the powers; but on the most part, our purpose is to be stewards of our gifts and of the gifts of others. Your Chaiva also knows that this core is connected to us; it is part of us; and once you are within our protection, we will know if anything happens to you. He chose the right place for you," The High Mother finally stopped at a doorway facing the wide flight Avria had just crossed. Avria turned back. The High Mother laid her hand on the latch of this heavy wooden door, and smiled kindly and sympathetically, "and if I might add at the risk of touching a sensitive subject… it is also a good place for you to heal from the injury that has been inflicted upon you." Avria blushed and felt a burn of tears almost at once. For a while, she'd forgotten, all this new information, these new sights, for a second, she'd let herself ignore the pain of her body, the humiliation of her memories.

High Mother lifted the latch and pushed the door open, letting Avria pass before she did. Avria found herself walking into another hallway, this one more reasonable in its proportions. The High Mother turned left and followed it, and Avria looked out the intermittent windows that lined the left wall of this corridor. They were above the tall trees, and the morning was rising bright and clear. The forest that grew up against this abbey was coated in ice, each branch, every pin, every tenacious leaf. Lone ravens kited into the sky, riding the icy currents, their grating calls barely audible behind the thick glass and stone mullions. The floor was carpeted in a single long woven rug of intricate design, a weaving pattern in ivory tones against a ruddy red background. There were portraits on the right wall between the occasional doors, portraits of sisters, portraits of elderly high mothers.

They walked the full length of the corridor to its end. There, a set of double doors was embedded in a large stone archway. She opened one side and ushered Avria in. Avria realized they were in one of the towers. A set of stairs landed just to the right of the doorway and rose up, hugging the curved wall of this large chamber. The stairway, open to one side with no railing, vanished into the ceiling. The wall to the left was straight, and it cut forward and then angled towards the curved wall some ways back. This appeared to be a large parlor of some sort. It was commodious and a warm fire burned in a hearth on the flat wall directly in front of the double doors. Shelves covered the wall to the right, crammed full of books. Avria smiled wanly, thinking of how Taneth would love this room. There were two work tables with work lamps on them, and a number of chairs of varying styles peppered around the room, including one particularly beautiful reclining settee that looked newly made, with beautiful silk upholstery.

"This is one of our many special reading rooms for tower guests. This room is shared by three sets of apartments, but you are the only guest here right now as we rarely get visitors in mid-winter. A fire has been lit in here for your use. Come with me, the High Mother crossed the room, and entered a short hallway through an arch that butted up against the tower wall. There were two doors and a window in this small space, a door directly ahead, one to the right and the window was on the outer wall. It was a larger window that went from the floor up to the ceiling, with large divided lights and wooden framing so it could be opened. It was shut fast and the panes were frosted in the corners. The priestess pointed to the door directly to the front of them; "that is another set of stairs to the other apartments," she said. "Here," High Mother opened the door to the right, and Avria found herself in a set of opulent apartments. Cut from a significant wedge of the tower's area, the space opened up into a welcoming sitting room with cozily appointed chairs and a warm fire sharing the same flue as the fire in the large parlor. There were no windows in this part of the room. A double door of paned glass separated this sitting room from the sleeping room, which was a massive space with a huge bed smack in the center of it facing the three widows looking out of the tower. To the right was an open wash chamber with a large bathing tub made of marble. Avria had never seen anything so beautiful as this room.

"This is much more than I need…"

"It is what you get, my dear. You are royalty, after all." Avria's brow furrowed and she shook her head, confused by the statement, but not quite bothered enough to argue with her about it. Bewildered, she put down her bag and turned to the High Mother.

"I thank you for your hospitality."

"You are welcome. You may go wherever you wish; but be sure to stay close to where there are others; it's easy to find yourself lost in this place. Just please don't walk outside the gates of the abbey; our *core* only extends as far as the abbey. You will have someone to assist you of course; she will bring you your meals and help you with whatever you require. I would like that you please dine with me the evening after next; I would like to have a nice talk with you. I must go to Nadeem today. The people are restless there and require guidance, but I will be back soon. Sister Adrenne is here, your assistant can help you find her if you need to find someone you know. I just ask that if you come upon the sisters and they are meditating, please do not disturb them."

"Of course. Thank you." With a smile and an elegant sweep of the red train of her robes and she was gone. Avria stood for a long moment in silence, unmoving. The fire was freshly stoked, and the sound of it gave her some comfort. She sighed deeply. She shucked her cloak and her other outer garments and threw them onto one of the chairs, and she sat on the edge of the bed, staring out at the forest below, which from this perspective looked like a silvery green ocean. She felt like someone else. As if she'd stepped out of her nightmare and into someone else's life. Perhaps that was what she needed. She flopped back onto the huge bed, and laughed bitterly to herself. Royalty indeed.

Chapter Eight – Admission

Offrin stormed out of the family apartments and slammed the door so hard, dirt sifted down from the rafters. Tinna looked at Taneth and shook her head. There was no arguing with him. He decided he would go to Master Gavorre for guidance; in what neither of Avria's parents were sure. They wondered if he was going after Eleran or going to find his wife, or going home; he was so angry, it was difficult to tell what he was communicating except his abject fury. It was unbelievable to Tinna that such a gentle soul could hold such a violent temper. He'd screamed non-stop for at least ten minutes and he punched the furniture, upset the tea table, smashing Tinna's favorite tea pot and the plate of sweet cakes that Taneth had made for his wife that morning. The baby was startled by the noise and crying at the top of his lungs. That instantly dissipated Offrin's violence and he stood there steaming for a moment as if utterly without thought. He then told Tinna that he would go to Gavorre to find the help she was so unwilling to offer, and accused her of being a terrible mother to Avria and then the door was slammed with bravado. Tinna stood stricken, her eyes filled with tears.

Tinna spent the better part of the day concentrating on getting things together for the trip north, arranging for a military Araki rider escort, finding a suitable coach, coming up with an appropriate wardrobe to stand in the presence of the High King. She also had to move Cennik north as well. He was her assigned summoner, and she knew it would be hard to tear him from Thamatoc now that he had grown so accustomed to life here. Phenmal had returned as promised only two days after his departure with the shadow-man and he looked tired and worried.

Phenmal arrived while Tinna was alone. She had just finished bathing the baby, and she was putting on his tiny clothes so he could crawl freely about the apartments while she packed and fussed. She looked up at Phenmal when he strode in, and didn't say anything to him as he stripped off his outer garments and made himself at home. Her eyes smiled at him. His heart melted. *If only she weren't married.* But she was and to a man he liked quite a bit, so he had to set aside his disappointment for a moment to give her some news.

"The Drathar found a trail. Eleran is cleverer than I gave him credit for. He is headed in the correct direction. But Eleran does not have the benefit of flight and his magic can only carry him so far. Only the most powerful of bearers could bridge great distances and he is not so powerful. It will take him time to travel, even with his powers. The Drathar says it will be impossible to shape out which route he will take at this point, so hunting him is a wasted effort. But the Drathar is certain he will ultimately end up where Avria is hidden. The shadow has gone to greet him there. I've instructed him to remain at Avria's side. As sorcerers and magic-bearers and the like go, there are none more powerful than the Drathar. They are barely human; the magic consumes so much of their being. They have abilities upon abilities. Avria will be safe."

"Then why bother keeping her where she is? Why not move her back?"

"Because if Eleran goes near her, he will have to stand in a place where his powers will be drained and blocked. Drathar is not subject to the effects of this spell that protects Avria. It is the best way."

"To use her as bait?" Tinna asked matter-of-factly, her brow arched. He'd dreaded this moment, because he knew Tinna's concern for her daughter was above all else. He'd already experienced her rage when delivering similar news to her before the war. In her mind, Avria's wellbeing should never be secondary to anything, and Phenmal seemed to always fall into a position where he had to force Tinna to put her concern for Avria aside for more pressing matters. She'd nearly choked him two years ago, he was waiting for her to explode again—and this time Taneth was not in the room to intercede as he had last time.

"In essence. We can waste time and resources hunting down the Zsathri in the forests between here and the coast, or we can just wait for him to come to us." Tinna remained collected and level-headed however, her shoulders tensing up and her jaw setting hard.

"You know it won't be that easy; just capture him as he arrives. You know he will have thought things through," Tinna reminded Phenmal with a hard glare. The older man nodded in resignation. She stooped and picked up little Istvan, who was looking drowsy after his hectic day of play, bathing and toddling about on his own. She put him in his cradle and gazed down at him with an expression of concern. The child merely turned his head towards the window and stuck his thumb in his mouth, his eyes drooping.

"We will do what we can, Tinna. We have been working on contingencies; she is surrounded by protection. Let it be." She sighed and rubbed her temples. Phenmal took in the stacks of clothes, the empty bags on the bed, the shuffle or papers on her desk.

"I see you've made up your mind..."

"As usual Phenmal, you pretend as if I actually have a choice to begin with." Tinna put her hand on her hip and shook her head. *Beautiful Tinna*. Like Avria, she had a magnetic presence; she was still ravishing at forty and post-baby; her body still toned to the point of perfection from her daily ritual of martial dances; which she practiced with other village women. She hadn't lifted a weapon since her battle with her mother, but she was always prepared to do so if needed. It was her nature as a Thran; a warrior born. Her softness had come to her over the past two decades; having raised her own daughter and an adopted son. She found a well of nurturing she didn't know she had, and she discovered satisfaction in it like nobody else.

She was happiest here, at Thamatoc with her awkward brainy husband, going about her daily duties as leader, resolving petty conflicts between villagers with an amused smile, planning trade runs with the new foals, appointing new elders, being the mother of an entire community in essence. Phenmal wanted the same for himself, to knock about back and forth between his quiet house and this bustling village of close lodges and tiny apartments; to sit at Tinna's fire with Taneth and discuss the variety of nonsense that interested the intellectual man that was Tinna's spouse; to tease Avria, and watch her grow as a human being and watch the newest one in the family grow up, such potential this dark-haired boy had. Phenmal knew on a personal level what Tinna was giving up as she packed away some of her common skirts he doubted she'd wear where she was going. It was trite, an act of cluelessness, or comfort, he didn't pry into her head to find out. She would hit him if she sensed him in there; that he knew. She hated it when he rummaged her brain.

"Well, my concubine; what other grim things do you bring?" she said, bringing up the private joke between she, Taneth and Phenmal. A discussion had come up when Avria was six or seven, as to what Phenmal truly was to their family. He spent an inordinate amount of time at Thamatoc, specifically in their apartments or with Taneth. He loved her children like his own. For Avria's sake, they appointed him honorary grandfather, since Avria had none. One evening, after a community supper, they retired to the family apartments for a sip of wine and some discussion. Phenmal had been away, and they wanted to catch up. After a few glasses of wine, the conversation strayed to personal things; namely, where Phenmal stood in the family hierarchy. Phenmal responded: "Grandfather, how insulting. I'm more like a second husband if anything.

"You *wish* you were a second husband," Taneth blurted into his glass, which was tipped up over his nose when Phenmal had spoken. Tinna laughed heartily and got up to get the bottle to pour some more. The wine oddly made her graceful, sensuous, and it made her more flirtatious. Phenmal knew that when she was young and free, she had been a terror to mankind; a temptress and a user. He often pictured her during those days in his imagination. It was the encounter with the strange and pragmatic character of Taneth that tamed her.

"Perhaps a concubine," she suggested, her curls framing her beautiful face, her dark lashes making her black eyes even more striking. "I can have as many of *those* as I please, is that right?" Phenmal, like every other man who knew her, even the dragon Ledroran, was hopelessly in love with Tinna. She had an almost supernatural attractiveness that Avria had inherited. In Tinna's case, her tough exterior prevented it being an issue; for Avria, it created monsters.

"Ahh, maybe, but I do not enjoy the benefits of that title," Phenmal lamented.

"*That's* all *mine*," Taneth said smugly, slapping Tinna's behind as she moved to sit beside him. She shook her head, and smiled at the older man, her eyes shining.

"I'll take the leavings, and that's good enough for me," Phenmal confessed. "As long as I am welcome."

"That you always are, no matter what a strange creature you can be." Tinna's gaze was hot, teasing and flirtatious. Phenmal felt that little minx's powerful affection for him; he even sensed some temptation on her part, which was torturous to know. It made his tired body heat up a bit, and he had to clear his throat and look away from her plump lips, stained with wine, and the cleft of her breasts. He loved Taneth like a brother, he was a good man, but he was the most bizarre match for the former Thran. Despite a vast chasm of differences standing between them, they managed to be quite disgustingly happy together. Phenmal still couldn't figure out what it was that made Tinna choose such a creature, but he'd given up trying.

"Except when he brings bad tidings. Then he's not welcome;" Taneth chimed in. Phenmal snorted and crossed his legs, his foot wagging with a touch of irritation. He loved Taneth, he reminded himself. Taneth was like a brother—*the simpleton.*

"Concubine indeed." One glance at her, and her gaze burned him to the core. He would have to make do with the leavings, he told himself, as he had so many times. He did know one thing; leadership would involve her with the Keepers. She would be around a long time. Perhaps long enough.

Now, her gaze was far from flirtatious, it was tired and confused. She was so comfortable with him, her eyes spoke more clearly than her mind or her mouth could say. Phenmal hated that he was the deliverer of this fate. He wanted more than anyone to free her of this unwanted responsibility; to help her escape the destiny of being someone she did not want to be. He wanted to let her stay here, at Thamatoc, and let her live here in simplicity as she wished until she was old and grey and he was only a warm memory. His selfish wishes aside, he did truly wish this for Tinna.

"Oh, Tinna," Phenmal said with more emotion than he normally expressed. She put her hands down from folding clothes, and looked up at him, her eyes wide and searching. He approached her and put his hands on her shoulders, "I am so sorry about all this. I know I had no control over what they chose for you; but perhaps I could have done something..."

"Phenmal, appointing blame and taking unnecessary responsibility is not going to change anything. You're here with me, and you always have been since the moment our paths crossed. I need you, and I need you to not feel bad for what is being imposed upon me. It's being imposed upon you too," she said, looking up at him. He studied her beautiful face, hardly showing her age since he first met her; a grey hair here and there wound into her curls. He reached up and pinched her chin, smiling at her. How he wanted to kiss her.

"Ah woman, you are everything. You and that maddening daughter of yours."

"I do love you Phenmal. I have for a long time."

"I know."

"Of course you know," she laughed easily. He gave in. He bent down and kissed her lips gently and then withdrew. This was the first time they'd ever shared that sort of affection in more than two decades in one another's company. She leaned against his chest, laying her ear on his heart. Her arms wrapped around his torso, and she let him envelope and comfort her.

Taneth strode into the apartments and took it all in with no concern. "Phen... when did you get back? How goes the hunt?" Phenmal didn't release Tinna, and Tinna did not step away from Phenmal; he simply retold the things he'd told Tinna only moments before, still soaking in her love; wishing to drown in it. Taneth knew this was no betrayal. It was just the way things were. It was family.

CHAPTER NINE - FAMILY

The Drathar watched her for a long time before he made his appearance. He knew there was something indefinable about this young woman that made so many men mad about her. She was singularly... something. She was with child, but she didn't know it yet. A spark of life started from the encounter of violence with a former lover. He felt the power of the little seed already radiating from her belly. It was a power of the likes he'd never seen. The Keepers should be made to know of this, he thought. He did not feel particularly compelled to share it. Especially after he'd assessed and read Avria.

He studied the new mother. He felt her unease with herself, her damaged sense of self and her broken sense of control. The Chaiva had given her a good head-start on healing, softened some of the more painful thoughts, given her a foundation of strength to draw from. But she was still brittle. She was shrunken. But her beauty was not easy to miss; it did not shrink with her. It wasn't just her appearance; it was the light she exuded, the goodness and the kindness; the decency and understanding, the capacity for love and acceptance and even forgiveness was only just beneath the surface, but she was fragile. Too fragile.

He was gentle as he explored her mind; shared her pain, wandered through her childhood, her broken heart over the betrayal by her childhood friend Jestin, her journey with the Zsathri that she still loved in spite of what he had done, and then her sweet affection for the man Offrin who she thought of much of late and feared she would lose. It was her capacity for love, her steadfastness, her hidden power... The Drathar felt it all. He understood why the Zsathri had loved her with his entire being; believing her to be his other half; he understood why Jestin had risked even his own sanity to insure he could keep her, he understood why Offrin had worked so hard to mean something more to her. What the Drathar found even more compelling, was that he sensed that despite all the heartbreak, the devastation, even the resignation, this woman was not defeated. She was floundering a bit, yes, but she was not completely damaged. He felt her healing even as he watched. He felt the influence of the powerful mother, her steadfast father; and the Chaiva who would give his life to keep her safe.

He understood. With a controlled sigh, he approached her. Avria was walking back to her reading room and apartments after having gotten lost several times. She finally found the right floor, the right stairwell, the right corridor, and now she was walking towards a shadow. It took her a moment to realize that it wasn't what she thought; that it had form and substance; that it breathed. She paused, terrified. Her scream was stifled however, it would not escape. She just froze in horror for but a second.

"Do not fear. Phenmal sent me," the figure said. Her face had gone waxen, but the mention of Phenmal's name gave her an immediate sense of security. She clutched the pages she'd gotten down in the scriptorium and nodded stiffly in greeting. The Drathar found that the sight of her eyes struck something deep inside his soul. Dark and wide, still possessing some element of idealism and innocence despite what she'd endured in her short life.

"I see," she muttered. "I need to go through that door you're blocking..." she said nervously. The Drathar stepped aside, and let her pass, following unbidden. She walked into the reading room, and set to lighting one of the table lamps. "One of my favorite things to do with my father is to help him copy texts. I've done it since I was little. I find it soothing," she explained. The Drathar stood in front of the door after closing it, watching her. "I thought, since I'm alone with my thoughts most every day here, I would do some of this work, copy a few books that I know my father would like but might not have; there are many books in here I know he would like," she rambled. She put her paper stack down on the table, and went and got a pot of ink and a stylus. She looked again at the Drathar.

"You should not be alone with your thoughts," he said.

"Why are you garbed so drearily, why do you have your face covered?"

"My gaze can be damaging to people," he replied, still not moving. "Our skin is sensitive to light. So this is our... uniform of sorts."

"Like the Dreff sisters? They wear black too, except the high-ranked ones. They wear red." Avria picked a book from the shelf and took it to the table.

"They are the counterparts of sorts, of my kind; a different order perhaps is the best way to describe it. They too have similar restrictions, but they are not so dangerous as to require a veil to shield the world from their gaze. And they are not afflicted with the same physical manifestations as we are; not all of them."

"Are you always so? Always looking through the fabric? Or do you get to take it off in company of each other?"

"There are only eleven of us in this world right now. We don't see one another much if at all after we reach adulthood."

"That's it? Only eleven?" Avria asked, both interested and not.

"More might be born someday, but we are a rare type of bearer. One that many ordinary people fear; one where babies born like us might be killed before they are given a chance. We are too different; too frightening." Avria pondered this as she sat down, holding her book.

"And does the core of the Dreff, does it neutralize you?" He smiled underneath the veil, finding her curiosity charming.

"No. We are the same. When we are here, our essence contributes to the core. We are always welcome among our sisters."

"Why are you here? Why did Phenmal send you?"

"I am here to find him. To stop him." Avria froze and her face grew pale again.

"Is he here?"

"He comes."

"Then I should run again? I do not want to run again," her throat tightened and her eyes immediately misted up. Raggedly, she added, "I'm so tired."

"No, Avria. You have an army of sorceresses here—my sisters; and you have me. You will be safe. But I must remain with you. He cannot perform magic in the core; but he might have tricks up his sleeve. So I am to stay and protect you at all costs."

* * * *

Phenmal was tired, but further exhausted by yet another trip through the icy winds on dragon to the citadel. But he was finally at Thamatoc, and for the moment he had no need to go anywhere yet. He found Tinna packed and irritable, but happy to find him at the door when she opened it. She ushered him in, sliding her arm around his waist and hugging him close.

"Have you any news of Avria?"

"No. The Drathar is with her by now. She is in good hands."

"If you say so," Tinna feigned a shudder and smiled tersely. She was in her usual attire of a trained skirt and long tunic. Her thick hair was tied back in a tail with a metal cuff. The apartment was in an unusual state of disarray. There were toys scattered by the hearth, the bed in the corner and the cradle were a tousle of blankets, clothes were piled high on a chair, the table a shuffle of papers. Tinna looked harassed.

"Where's the little one?"

"With Jenyk, of course. I just got back from a meeting with the elders. The elders are not too pleased that I am leaving this village. They refuse to appoint a new leader in my stead. They will only agree to someone as acting leader. It's simply ridiculous," She stopped and her shoulders sagged. "Phenmal…" she turned to look at him. "I don't want to leave. I don't want to."

"I'm sorry Tinna," he intoned, dropping his gloved hands. Tinna sighed and rolled her misted eyes up to his.

"I miss Avria. She's alone with all this pain and horror; she needs her mother."

"I know she does. It won't be long, Tinna. She will come to Miranne as soon as the situation with Eleran is resolved; and trust me Tinna, it will be resolved." Tinna gazed at Phenmal for a long, poignant moment, her eyes looking deep into his.

"I cannot live at Miranne without you," she said with finality. Phenmal sighed and took off his scarf and hat, shrugging off the capes of his greatcoat and throwing the whole lot on the back of a chair. He felt that was all he was doing of late, taking his damned greatcoat off and shrugging it back on over and over again.

"Taneth will be with you…"

"Taneth is more than a Wiseman. He is Artreth now. He will be traveling to the academy at Adremateen constantly and he disclosed to me today that he wants to start arranging conferences with all the Wisemen serving in Araki villages in addition to those at the human settlements. And all that aside; my husband is not built for the life at Miranne. He will come and he will go, but what I need is you. Your mind. Your support, your ideas, your presence."

"I don't know, Tinna." Phenmal picked up the pile of clothes and threw them on the bed. He sank down into his usual chair and rubbed his face. "I don't know…"

"I can isolate your living quarters so you are separated from the people. The palace at Miranne is not nestled in a great city…"

"I know. It's not that."

"You can escape just as you do now when things get too noisy for you, come back to your manor here…" she spread her hands in bewilderment.

"Tinna, please…" She stopped talking and dropped her hands, her dark, elegantly arched brows furrowing. He looked up at her, and the sight of her guileless expression and the natural beauty of her face just filled him with heartache. She would need him more. Even more than she had during the war; but that was only a brief period of time and he could run away to his home where he could take a break from the torture of being around her. Her expectant look turned to confusion and she faced him fully.

"What is it Phenmal?" He shook his head and sighed.

"I don't know if I can do it."

"Why not? Please, tell me why not? I don't want to be obstinate about it, but honestly, Phenmal, if you're not beside me at Miranne, I will not go." He groaned and put his face into his hands, the anger building at the position she was putting him in. "I won't go, Phenmal."

"How dare you blackmail me, Tinna?" Phenmal shot to his feet and shouted at her. She did not balk or cringe, she stood against it, her brow angry as well.

"Tell me why!" she shouted back at him.

"Because you drive me mad! I can't be around you all the time and not have you! It's hard enough here, but at least I can go, at least Taneth's presence tempers me and brings me back to the reality; but I cannot be at Miranne so close to you all the time, it's bloody torture," he barked. "I can't!" He realized he'd let it all slip and he exhaled in resignation, and let his eyes fall on Tinna's face.

"I love Taneth."

"I know."

"I love you."

"I know," he laughed sardonically, and shook his head. "But Taneth is your husband and he is a good man, and I respect and love him too much. I feel tremendous guilt for harboring these desires because I feel like I am betraying a brother." Tinna's gaze burned into his, and unexpectedly, Tinna moved forward, lifting her hands to grasp the sides of his face, and she pulled him down to her lips. The kiss was not the tender, gentle kiss they'd shared the a few days ago. This was a passionate, burning kiss that seared his lips and set his body ablaze.

They staggered backward towards the bed, lips and tongues entangled all the while. Tinna grappled to undo the front of his heavy woolen waistcoat, and then the removal of the cravat and the crisp white shirt beneath. She and pushed it up, tugging it over his head, interrupting the kiss only for the material to pass over his face. His hands did the same for her tunic. By the time they reached the bed, they were both bare from the waist, up. Phenmal reached around to Tinna's back and pulled the silver cuff from her thick hair, freeing the thick make of raven curls, tossing it to the floor with a clatter. Phenmal stepped back to look and groaned at the sight of her.

He did not live like a monk, by any means, but he did not sleep around too much either. He often simply found someone to bear the brunt of his frustration for Tinna, and then went weeks without. It had been awhile to begin with and now the woman he dreamt of stood before him bare breasted, with fire in her eyes. He was completely incapable of controlling himself. He tore at the lace of Tinna's skirts, shoved down her little winter leggings and the sight of her in the full glory of nudity made his mind reel. He picked her up by the waist and put her on the bed. With a smooth movement, he kicked off his long boots and breeches and under breeches, and crawled onto the bed over her. He could scarce believe he was about to make love to Tinna. He used his arm to swipe away the clothing and wads of blankets and he settled over her. One hand propped him over her, the other found her hip, and then slid up her waist to her breast.

"Gods, this is so wrong…"

"Hush…" Tinna replied huskily. Her eyes were glazed over with passion, her cheeks filled with a youthful pink glow. Her body was a marvel, still a perfectly honed weapon. How a woman who existed in a reasonably sedate life of deskwork, supervision and travel, she still looked like a warrior. He leaned down and kissed her deeply, his tongue twisting with hers. Her breath was heavy and hot, her soft moans sultry. He pulled away and looked down at her flushed face, her glazed, heavy-lidded eyes, and her lips plump and parted. He lowered his face between her breasts, following the subtle ripple of muscles to the flat of her tummy, which showed hardly any sign of her pregnancies. He could barely contain himself, he was painfully aroused, and Tinna was so, so beautiful. He lapped at her hard, erect nipples and then, his thighs trembling, he maneuvered himself fully between her legs. Tinna did not let him drag it out or hesitate; she was never the type to play games. She wanted him, so she reached down and guided him into her.

Phenmal's face dropped to the hollow of her neck and he licked her there, his breath cooling the moisture and making her skin rise into goose bumps. She moaned as he began to stroke into her. "God I've wanted this for twenty years," he groaned, thrusting into her more ardently. Tinna's fingers raked across his shoulders and back, and she writhed sensuously beneath him.

"I love you Phenmal," Tinna said hoarsely, wrapping her powerful legs around him. Phenmal's well-hidden youthful vigor, the gift of the Keepers, surged through him, and any attempt to look his age abandoned him. He brought her to a screaming climax, and then let his own needs satisfy themselves inside the woman he had loved for two decades. When he collapsed, sweating on top of her, she wrapped her arms around him and kissed his face.

"I belong to two worlds these days, Phenmal. There are two of me. One that wants to be here with Taneth, one that needs to be at Miranne, and leading the Araki people with you at my side. I am about to leave the world that Taneth belongs to and expect him to leave it and to take the lead as an Artreth, possibly higher," She said. "I know we joke about the concubine thing, but it isn't a joke,"

Phenmal rolled off of her and propped himself up on an arm, his face a picture of puzzlement.

"I have discussed this with Taneth." Phenmal's brow creased and his eyes widened.

"You what?"

"I talked about it with Taneth; after our kiss the other day. After you left. I told him what I needed. I explained my feelings. He knows I love him and that will not change. Nothing really will except for some details. He knows he loses nothing." She said matter-of-factly.

"I don't understand..."

"I was going to talk to you about this after we got to Miranne. I know it's selfish, to ask Taneth to sacrifice and share." She paused. "Phenmal... will you marry me?" Tinna asked. "I think I realized I need you more than ever. I have always loved you, perhaps not so much in the beginning, but you grew on me. I need you, not just for practicality, but for your strength and for how crucial you are to our family. Avria needs you, Istvan needs you. I don't want to go to Miranne without you.

"Taneth's attitude towards the palace is ambivalent at best. He wants to focus on his duties as Artreth and he, like me refuses to give Thamatoc up completely, however *I* will not get my way. His obligations are not so burdensome that he can actually keep a strong connection with Thamatoc..." she paused, her voice breaking. Phenmal knew this was painful for her. She loved Thamatoc like no other. "I asked Taneth what he thought; of my taking a second husband and his reaction, as always was pragmatic and rational. I gave him leave, if he wished, to take a lover, but he did not want that. He loves me, and wants no other. He said his work is his lover; and he feels less guilt focusing more on it knowing he is not leaving me without support. He even seemed relieved and he told me that if it had been anyone other than you, he might have been hurt, but you have always been part of our lives and so it changes things little."

"Except now I finally get the benefits of the title of concubine," Phenmal chuckled. Tinna rolled onto her side and propped her head on her arm. Her face looked so young and lovely. Phenmal could not help but let his admiring gaze slide down to her beautiful breasts. He could hardly believe he finally got her into bed.

"Not concubine... husband. You never answered my proposal."

"Of course, I will marry you, in so much as I can. Is it permitted under the laws? It is for men to take multiple wives, with the regional rule's approval. But this is progressive; and who would approve of it?"

"I *am* the law now, am I not?" Tinna grinned. Phenmal laughed heartily and pulled her to him, her small, tight frame felt so good against his body. She slid her thigh up his and arched her body against him.

"You *are* the most beautiful creature ever to grace the earth." Tinna sighed contentedly, and ran her hand along his strong jaw line.

"Why is it you never get old, old man?"

"It's a secret," he replied. Tinna sighed. Her eyes wandered down to his chest, and she noticed some strange little figures and letters drifting on it. They looked like they were partially submerged in milky water, buoyant but not entirely, rising up to clarity and then sinking down into the murk of his skin. It was the strangest thing she'd ever seen. They were sort of like the markings she'd seen on the Driva, but not quite. These moved; these drifted.

"What are these? I've never seen your chest before."

"They are my Chaiva markings," he replied, lifting his head and awkwardly gazing down his nose at them. "They sometimes are faint, other times, they ride the surface and are clear. If I am... excited they tend to surface. Most creatures of powers possess some manner of these letters or other. At least those that I know of." He seemed unimpressed by the letters. Tinna touched his skin where they seemed to float just beneath the surface. As he relaxed, the letters sank down into oblivion.

"I suppose I need to tidy this place up and finish packing everything."

"Where is Taneth anyway?"

"At Adremateen. The Keepers are keeping him busy."

"Yes. They do that," Phenmal grunted.

"They are demanding and suffocating, aren't they?"

"Controlling, sometimes yes," Phenmal agreed.

"It could be worse, I suppose. We can be grateful that they aren't completely mad like the Hevra," she said with a smirk. "If we must be controlled by some powerful faction or other, at least it's not a pack of lunatics. I'm glad of that."

"Who told you the Keepers aren't complete nutters?" he asked, but he paused for a moment. Something came to him. An inspiration. *Of course.* Phenmal rolled onto his back. He reflected for a moment and then returned to the moment at hand.

"Nobody tells me *anything* about the bloody Keepers," Tinna muttered. Phenmal turned his face towards her.

"I suppose I need to give you my answer about Miranne?"

"That would be helpful." Tinna raised her brows and smirked.

"Well, you *did* go through significant lengths to persuade me," he grinned. Tinna smiled and kissed him, a hot, sensual kiss that stirred his desires again. "My answer is yes, if you're wondering," he replied. "But on one condition; that you travel north without me." He had to put his finger on her lips because she was about to protest.

"Wait a moment. I will meet you at Miranne. I need to go northeast to Effring."

"What for?"

"The Hevra. Eleran belongs to them. I think I should go and see that they take some responsibility for their little boy." Her playful face had gone stone serious. Phenmal sighed heavily and groaned.

"What's that about?"

"That's about being away from you again; now that I've finally gotten you where I want you."

"Oh, is that so?" Tinna laughed. He nodded, and she smiled smugly. "So you think this is *your* doing?" Phenmal arched his brow and nodded again. In a quick move, he threw her onto her back and climbed over her again, a sinister smirk on his face. Tinna sighed contently and relaxed in his grasp; pleased he was happy to take control.

Chapter Ten – Fairy Tales

Igro dove down, and instead of the temperature climbing, it seemed to get colder. Phenmal frowned darkly, imagining himself back in Tinna's bed. The thought of it brought his core body temperature up and he smiled to himself. It was more than he could have hoped for. He thought of the idea of being a second husband and it made him laugh, but it was all silliness in the end. The conventions didn't matter—the root of it was he was able to love Tinna the way he had always wanted, from the moment she arrived at his old manor on that rainy night.

I HOPE YOU WILL NOT BE HERE LONG; IT IS ALMOST TOO COLD FOR ME HERE. AND THERE'S NOWHERE FOR ME TO GO

I won't be long, Igro. I suggest you drop let me hop off and then keep circling. I'll call you when I need you. The dragon nodded. Phenmal had one advantage that nobody else shared. He could speak to his dragon companions telepathically. Igro had gotten used to thinking his replies, and projecting deliberate discussions so Phenmal would hear it over other chatter if need be. There was also a much greater advantage of distance. It had served everyone well during the buildup to the One-Day-War. Dragons had scouted the enemy movements and informed Phenmal of them using simple flyovers.

Igro informed Phenmal they were near and he dropped into a plummet, picking up incredible speed before leveling out over a frozen lake, flying at an arrow's swiftness towards a large fortification on the shore. He climbed suddenly to a near stall so he could clear the parapet wall. Phenmal prepared to dismount and Igro managed to fly only a few inches above the ground and he leaned a bit so Phenmal could leap down in his usual fashion. The man landed on the snowy ground with a crunch of the boot heels, sliding a few feet forward in an agile, graceful move. The dragon pulled immediately up and flew vertically up the face of the main building, vanishing over the roof.

Phenmal barely straightened when three guards emerged from the large door carrying large voulges. Phenmal used something he rarely used anymore and he stunned their minds with a painful, searing din. The guards gripped their heads and fell to their knees. Phenmal stepped over one and walked up the steps to the old-style castle.

He entered a rather shabby looking hall flanked by fires. The rest of the guard was inside, gripping their heads and writhing on the floor. The only figures that weren't doing so were the tall, willowy forms of what Phenmal knew to be Hevra.

He wasn't sure how many there were in total, but five stood in this hall. They lived in a collective and rarely separated. They were beautiful creatures; the first of the soul-bearers, made immortal to watch over the world. Legend said they held whole souls, and it was too much for the physical body to bear… the soul drove them mad. It was only then that the gods realized their mistake and instead imbued humans and other creatures with only half-souls, and made them mortal.

Phenmal didn't quite swallow the legends like others did. He knew they were powerful, and old. The Hevra were the most ancient living creatures in the world. But he also knew they were not created by the gods, they were born to the earliest peoples. They were immortal, and they could not make new Hevra. Their branch of peoples had died out eons ago; he knew they could imbue magic into certain mortals, and they did so, creating their 'children' the Zshathri. The Zshathri were not born of magic as others were—and the Hevra were fiercely protective of their children; preventing any of them from falling under the control of the Keepers.

Many centuries ago, there had been a conflict between the human Keepers and the Hevra for control of their children. It was a war nobody could win; and there was a treaty signed that one would leave the other to do as they wished, as long as nothing adversely affected the path defined by the Keepers. A peace had reigned since, but the Keepers were not shy in sharing their low opinion of the Hevra, and did a great deal to undermine their creation of new magic bearers by the Hevra, or allowing the Zshathri from breeding with other magic bearers to produce born-Zsathris.

Phenmal was surprised to see them all dressed in the most modern of finery. He had heard of their strange quirks; their vanity, their preening self-absorption—but he didn't think it was quite so bad. Here they were with their ancient residence crumbling all around them, and they looked like perfection in the latest fashions from the human cities.

Each one looked impassively upon him while their guards suffered. They could have been effigies they were so still.

"Why have you come mind-reader?" asked towering woman with hair cut shorter than he'd ever seen on a woman before. She wore a sapphire blue gown and stood near the fireplace. The massive room was not cozy or comfortable by any means, but they collected there, on a worn rug, sitting on heavy old-fashioned furniture. An ancient tapestry on the far wall hung in moth-eaten tatters.

"I pass through here only to tell you a story. Then I am gone." The five heads tilted in interest, all in unison and he hid his satisfaction. Once during a gathering of the Keepers, he heard one of them mention the penchant the Hevra had for stories.

"Like little children they are, as soon as they hear 'once upon a time' you have their undivided attention. They do get angry if the story ends in tragedy however." he had said gravely, chuckling mockingly afterwards. "Old as the sky but as dense as a brick of lead." Taneth did not believe this was true—but it was worth a shot. But it was, for three more of the graceful creatures entered, soon followed by three more. Phenmal noted the fine wool of the flamboyant frock coats and the shining silks of their waistcoats. The women rustled in silks too precious for ordinary day use... but here they all were, dressed as if about to go to a ball, trimmed in diamonds and gems, feathers and dancing slippers. It was a stark contrast to see these richly; fashionably dressed figures against a backdrop so dilapidated and ragged.

"Not so long ago, there was a Zsathri. A Zsathri who broke the laws of bearers; a Zsathri so besotted, so filled with love and dedication for his chosen woman, he sacrificed his own essence to protect her from danger; casting spells that took lives. The powers punished him, and cut the tether between his being and his body and held it fast in the prisons of the voids." As Phenmal spoke, four more of the willowy creatures sailed in. Perhaps they were planning to have a ball. There was not a single plain one among them. They were all riveted, their strange, beautiful faces almost like dolls. One more and then five more gathered from another archway.

"The Zsathri slept and was lost to those who watched over him. And one afternoon, a handsome pair of Hevra appeared and they carried him away in their coach. His loved one mourned his loss, knowing she would never see him again." One particular woman, with immaculate skeins of raven hair as smooth as silk, dabbed a tear from her emerald eye. Phenmal took a dooming tone, and continued.

"But somehow, the essence of the Zsathri escaped the voids, and returned tainted and twisted. He returned to his world in search of his loved one, but his love was tainted and twisted, and instead he harmed her and caused her terrible pain and he hunts her. He is no longer bound by the laws of the bearers and he can take lives with his magic with no consequence. He runs free, searching for his love, seeking only to harm her." Phenmal stopped abruptly.

The dark haired woman's huge eyes blinked. "Is that the end of the tale?"

"The tale has not ended. He hunts still. He will harm her. He will continue to harm. It is up to the Hevra to bring this story to an end."

"The story is of Eleran," a male uttered. "Our dear child, Eleran." Phenmal stepped back.

"I will release your guard. My dragon comes. I hope you enjoyed my tale." A woman with white hair suddenly intoned in a singsong voice:

"But when does the dancing begin? We must celebrate the comings and goings, the beginnings and the endings," her hand lifted, bound in a white calfskin glove that wrapped her whole arm, circlets of diamond glittering on her wrists. She snapped open a tatty fan in her hand and made it flutter to indicate her excitement. Phenmal heard the approach of his mount and exited the still-open door. The dragon was not about to land, so he simply flew low enough to grasp him with his talons and lift him off the stairs.

Phenmal climbed the leg to the shoulder and managed to get onto the back of the neck.

WERE YOU SUCCESSFUL?

Who is to say? It's like speaking to a mob of half-wits. But since they like stories so much, I left them one they can attempt to conclude on their own. Happy endings are always preferable in stories, I'll wager. I don't know if it will help; but it was worth a try.

I DON'T LIKE THE WAY THIS PLACE FEELS OR SMELLS.

Neither do I. Let's go to Miranne. There's a warm barn and some fresh mutton in it for you. You certainly have earned it. The dragon's head rose and fell, and Phenmal settled in for the long flight. Phenmal, who was always so grumpy about dragons and flying, was grateful for his friend today. He sat down against his head and patted the soft skin on the back of his skull, scratching it. Igro made a pleasant sound; like a great cat, purring.

He could not read Hevra. They could not read him. He had no idea if this silly venture was worth the effort and the time away from Tinna, especially now; but he had to try. Avria would be safe as long as the Drathar remained with her; but what would happen to Eleran still remained in question; even the Drathar was bound by the rules of the bearer. Would he sacrifice his essence for Avria as Eleran once had if the situation called for it? There was no way to know. If the Hevra came to assist, perhaps there was a chance Eleran could be neutralized forever without requiring such a sacrifice from anyone.

MIRANDA MAYER

CHAPTER ELEVEN – ATTACHMENT

Her charm was almost magic; almost as powerful as a spell. He watched her toss and turn; his glassy eyes never leaving her fevered sleep. In the middle of the night, her eyes opened and they locked on the dark shape hunkered on a chair by her bed. It was a direct and cutting gaze directly into eyes she could not see. It surprised him.

"You don't sleep?" she asked in a groggy whisper.

"I am not like you. I can go without."

"What do you look like, beneath all that black? I haven't seen you leave me once except when I want to use the chamber pot; which you haven't done as of yet. You haven't eaten, you don't sleep, you don't bathe, but you don't smell... what are you?"

"I am not quite the same as you. I am something other than human."

"Or Araki," she surmised.

"We are more ancient than that."

"But born of humans?"

"Humans were born of us; we are remnants of the old kind. We are born different..."

"Let me see you."

"I cannot show you my face, girl."

"Then cover your eyes; let me see who sits by me day and night." It was never done; not even for the Keepers. It was their secret, their mystery. As children they still had remnants of their humanity; but that faded with age, and now he was something akin to human but not quite. He could not resist her; he did not wish to. He wanted her to see him and to know him. What compelled him to comply with her wishes, he did not know, but he suspected it was her hold over him.

He reached up and shoved back his cowl. "Close your eyes until I say," he instructed her. Avria obeyed. He unwrapped the sheer fabric through which his world was filtered every day, slightly shocked by the brightness of the dark room. He then lifted off his tunic for her to see the markings and then carefully tore a strip off of the sheer fabric, tying it around his head like a blindfold.

"What happens when someone looks into your gaze directly?" she asked while waiting.

"A thrall that does not abate. I empty the mind when I look into the eyes. I steal what's in there. It becomes mine. It is why we have so many abilities." She was silent, her eyes still closed. He could see through his mask and he stared at her in her vulnerable state, innocent and distracted by curiosity. "You may open your eyes."

Avria sat up on the bed and scooted closer to the edge. Her eyes took a moment to adjust; it was dark, but the fire was still shedding a bit of light into the room. She first saw the preternaturally pale glow of his chest, and a shock of snow-white hair that grew long down his back, as straight and as silken as the web of a spider. His face was beautiful, a white marble, with a square, defined jaw and lips like those of an expertly hewn statue. He wore a black blindfold that cut into his pale colours like a knife; his entire torso and arms and hands were covered in text, it wound all the way up to his neck. He reminded her of the Driva, another mysterious creature, but they lacked hair and the text wound around their faces and head. His face and head were clear of markings, and his hair was lush and beautiful. She could not resist and reached out to touch it. She grasped a skein of it, brushing his back with her fingers. He started. It was something he didn't expect and it was the first time in an incredibly long time anyone had ever touched his skin.

"You're too spare, there's not an ounce of fat on you... you should be eating more," she noted casually. "You are beautiful though. Not what I expected," she admitted.

"You expected massive deformities?"

"No. I expected you to be less human looking. Your skin is just skin, but you have the look of one of the old statues, of the old gods. Just a bit more than normal... the text, what does it mean?"

"I don't know. None of us do. The text is unknown and indecipherable. But we are all born with it, and it sometimes changes, words move about, appear, disappear." He felt her fingers touching the letters on his side and he froze, his eyes closing and his lips parting with a small gasp of hot breath; she took back her hand and looked embarrassed.

"I'm sorry. I let my curiosity get the best of me," she smiled timidly. She thought he was beautiful, as Eleran had once been to her—his body was lithe and elegant, wide shoulders, narrow hips, a chest and stomach defined and attractive. His hair was also striking, down to the nape of his back, cut into a perfect straight line across the bottom. His face was almost too perfect in shape; when he didn't move, he was a sculpture. He was like the opposite of everything Eleran had become, yet his presence reminded her of him; the real Eleran. Something deep inside her tugged at her heart and she started to feel the burn of tears.

"I wish I could see your eyes," she suddenly said, her voice tight. She slumped back into her bed. He shook his head, and then began to reassemble his clothing. He put the wrap on his head before removing the strip he'd used, putting it in her hand. She toyed with it, her mind temporarily elsewhere. He put on his tunic and his cowl.

"The light does not like my skin. It burns me sometimes. I must be covered," he said. He paused and looked at her. "I've never done this for anyone before. Nobody sees us as we are after a certain age. Our bodies are our secrets. The text starts to appear in greater and greater volume; we grow paler, our eyes become weapons. It is a difficult life for someone who cannot cope with being alone."

"I imagine," Avria said distantly. She was looking the other way, lying on her back, her fingers twisting around the skein of fabric. He could see, with his mind's eye, the silent tears dripping from her eyes on to her cheeks, pooling on the bridge of her nose before overflowing onto the pillow. He was unsure what to do.

"It isn't unusual for one of my kind to take his life." Avria's head rolled over to look at him, her eyes just watery glints of the meager light in the darkness. Her skin shone where the tears had fallen.

"Have you considered it?"

"A few times," he admitted.

"Me too," she whispered.

I know.

"Much since I've been here. But I cannot help to think of all the people who would be hurt by such a deed…"

"It is good you keep those you love in consideration. It is good you have them to consider. I don't have that to keep me grounded. I have nobody." There was a deeply pained silence that lasted a good long while. Then Avria stirred.

"Drathar… do you have a name?"

"No."

"Drathar," she paused, and then reached out her hand, opening it. He responded by laying his bare hand on it. Avria clasped her fingers around his and he felt her tears give way in earnest. It wasn't loud sobbing, just sniffing and the occasional gasp. Her mind was filled with memories; of moments with the man she had loved with all her soul; of kisses and of making love in a bed too small; making such noise that it roused the owner of the home where they were guests. He saw images of this Zshathri; bathed in the light of her love, short passionate moments, and then he felt her loss at his absence. He relived the rape with her, experiencing the gaping void left behind by the loss and betrayal; her confusion and humiliation that she clung stubbornly to hope that Eleran could still be what he once was-but she knew also that she could not forgive him. Her misery was profound.

She tugged on his hand—she did not ask him with words; only with images.

Without hesitation, the Drathar climbed into the bed next to Avria and lowered himself onto his back. Avria rolled up to his side, and rested her head on his arm. He gently placed his hand on her waist and reveled in the sensation of someone so close. He knew it was selfish what he was doing; providing her comfort was only secondary to his desire to feel her close to him. She toyed with the fingers of his other hand while she sorted through her thoughts. His head bent back, he reveled in the sensation of her skin touching his, her breath stirring the thin veil over his face. His heart raced. She sighed deeply and the movement was like ecstasy, her warmth radiating into him. She talked about her irrational desire to stop feeling as she felt, and she talked about how she wanted things to be normal again. He closed his eyes and focused only on her words. He listened until her sentences faded, and she slipped into a heavy slumber, her head growing a bit heavier on his arm. He reached up and touched her face. He wanted to know what a kiss would feel like; to know it from this broken bird. Instead he turned onto his side and gazed at her through his dark veil, his preternatural eyes seeing her as brightly as he would see her in the day. He arranged her frizzed curls around her face, and traced the line of her jaw and eyebrows with his finger.

He clamped his eyes shut and chewed his mandibles. He *could* do it…as easily as a game. He toyed with the temptation, to deceive her; to manipulate her. He could transform himself to appear as the man that occupied her mind; to become Eleran; the gentle, loving Eleran she wanted. The Eleran she wanted to forgive. He *could* make love to her, kiss her, and take on the guise of the man with the shining black hair who captivated her so. To heal her somehow by bringing the man she loved and not the one who pursued her now. The desire to do so was so powerful, the Drathar had to withdraw.

He slid away from her without waking her, and nearly stumbled onto the floor. He stood there for a moment, confused by his feelings. There was some power there, in the attraction, it had to be, for in his two hundred years never once did he succumb to the wiles of any woman as he had with her. He'd never wanted anyone so badly. He straightened himself, and carefully readjusted the state of his clothing until he was tidy and in order again.

He then sat down in the chair and faced forward, mouthing the words of concentration and meditation that he used to hone his powers. By the time morning came 'round, he was back to himself. Avria awoke, and turned to look at him, stiff and stoic in his chair by the bed, his eyes hard and forward. When Avria tried to take his hand, he simply let it fall slack on his leg. Avria's brow furrowed and she first looked confused. She then she glowered. The servant girl appeared with a decanter of hot water and deposited it on the side of the bath-tub. She left to fetch some more. Avria rose wordlessly and padded into the bathing chamber, and with no consideration for her companion, or likely too much consideration of him, she lifted her night gown off of her body and climbed into the tub. The Drathar was immediately aware of not only her body, but the bruises and scrapes that still marked it.

She knelt down and poured a little bit of the hot water over herself and bathed right before him. The Drathar did not turn his eyes away. The servant girl returned several times with urns of heated water and Avria bathed at a leisurely pace, her baleful eyes fixed on the Drathar.

He sat in his chair and bore witness to a woman who seemed to be hanging on the precipice. He had no idea what to do.

Avria was pale and despondent. Her silent companion had gone cold on her, and she knew deep down it was probably for the best, but she could not help but feel completely abandoned. She hardly ate. Even the ever-distant Drathar told her she should eat, that she had not only her own welfare to consider. He liked to remind her apparently, that he was without people to care for *him* and that she was so fortunate. He never left her side, but he had also remained aloof and silent. After touching the person behind the veil, it was difficult for Avria to cope with his silence and distance. It hurt her. She needed comfort, friendship; to be held and to be heard. Her project of transcribing books sat untouched on the desk, and Avria spent the better part of each day either curled up on the bed or sitting by the window in the chair with her knees drawn up to her chin, lost in her thoughts.

She thought of Eleran. Of his crime against her; of his forceful, willful pursuit. She thought of the man he once was, and she tried to erase the pain he caused her. She tried to think of all of the guidance and caring from figures like Phenmal and Master Gavorre that got her through his vanishing.

The Drathar was in no doubt of Avria's emotional decline. He was at a loss. This was too personal a need, too much to ask of someone whose entire sense of control had been shaken by simply by the nearness of this girl. He watched her as she sat, all day, every day in her chair, or curled in the bed. He listened to her silence, and amused himself by sorting through the memories she wasn't touching; the ones of her childhood, of her brother, of the group of her closest friends, including the now lost Jestin. He observed her memories of playing in the river on a steaming summer day, of idling about on horseback, without saddles, all wearing nothing but short leggings and cool tops—forging across shallow waterways on atop their horses to cool off. She had crisp, untapped memories of hanging about in the deep grass under the sun at Kettle Hill, just talking about nothing while their mounts grazed; tails switching. The Drathar often saw moments like these, moments of what was normality—of what most young people in her world did to occupy their free time and he was envious of her. She was so separated from that part of her now; she could not appreciate the gift of it. He thought it was a terrible shame.

She was dwelling. He could hear it all in her head; the confusion, the memories of her own distress and sadness—her betrayal and her sense of being completely abandoned by everyone who supposedly loved her.

And then he sensed the dangerous thought the moment it appeared; the one where she realized that not everyone who loved her had abandoned her. *Not everyone.*

The Drathar, who was in the same chair he'd been in for days, rose to his feet and approached Avria. He had no idea what to do, but he had to do something. There was nobody here close to her to guide him.

"That is ridiculous," the Drathar intoned, the hint of disgust coloring his words. Avria was startled from her reverie and she twisted in her chair to glare at him, her brow creased; her chapped lips a heavy frown. Her hair was a frizzy disarray of raven curls, piled into a messy bun on her head. Her nightgown hadn't come off for two days.

"Pardon?"

"To interpret the obsessive, mad pursuit of someone who means only harm to you as something other than what it is; to call it 'caring' or to give him undue credit for being the only one not to abandon you. No matter how alone you feel; do you not see how selfish and self-destructive this thought is? To erase his actions for the sake of feeling loved?" Avria's face blanched and she became furious.

"*Stay out of my head!*" She screamed, her eyes glossing instantly with tears, her fingers gripping the hair at the sides of her head. "Stay out of my head you bloody savage, how dare you?" She leapt to her feet, sobbing. She stalked to the dresser, and she pulled on her riding breeches and overskirt, throwing her nightgown to the floor and pulling on a thick woolen tunic directly over her bare skin. Still weeping, she pulled on her boots and ran for the door. "*Get away from me!*" she cried, slamming it in front of him. The Drathar followed at leisure, sure by the misdirection in her head that she would lose herself in the labyrinthine passages of this old place.

True to form, she did get lost. She took the wrong stairwell and the wrong landing, and ended up in a place where the Drathar easily found her. She entered a dark library of low ceilings and shelves that seemed to be holding up the entire room. There was row upon row of them, all filled to capacity with books, paper stacks, scrolls and even jars containing odd looking things suspended in strange fluids. She came to a halt, and frowned through her snot and tears.

The Drathar simply moved from one place to where she was. His transition there was a smooth, subtle thing; his form disappeared from one place in a curling cloud of black smoke, and he reappeared directly in her path the same way. The sight of him appearing invoked her wrath, and she attacked him.

"Get away!" she shrieked, tears still flowing. She grappled at his clothing and in a desperate move, she tore away his veil. The Drathar immediately clamped his eyes shut even in the dimness of the library, and took a step back from the glare of the distant window light. Avria had no notion of the danger she'd subjected herself to by exposing his eyes. She ran away sobbing. Blind, the Drathar used his powers to guide him. The unrest created by Avria's outburst had stirred the core. The sisters were responding at last to her pain.

He found Avria again kneeling on the floor of an old conservatory. Avria had seen part of it on her arrival on the dragon, a faceted glass jewel embedded in the back of the large building. Once upon a time, this construct had surely been impressive. Now it was a sorrowful-looking place. Its age and state of disrepair gave it a sagging, derelict feel. Piles of snow had accumulated on the glass roof. Many panes were cracked, and all of them had years of accumulated dirt etched on the surface, making what should have been a bright, white snowy day seem yellowed and tainted. The wild-growth of plants in the conservatory were osteal, wretched and spare; growing crooked, or spindly, with tendrils and vines shooting out from the rusted, crumbling containers. There was the sign of someone tending to the greenery, but they were doing a dreadful job of it.

Avria had run in and was blinded by the sudden glare of dirty light cast in from the snowy panes. She fell to her knees, shielding her tearful eyes with her arm and wept. She shrugged off the hands that touched her shoulder, only to be grasped by another set of hands and then another. A circle of black wool rustled about her trembling form. Pale faces surrounded her. Small, reassuring whispers calmed her hysterics, and she found herself being lifted off of her feet, the hard chest of her insensitive, cruel guard coming against her side. He hoisted her into his arms and cradled her. The sisters, who continued to appear in whispers of black smoke, gathered around them. Hands fell upon her like gentle snow while the Drathar carried her in his iron-hard arms. His face was exposed, his eyes pinched tightly closed, his skin showing signs of burns from the cold light. A sister draped her shawl around his beautiful, hard stone face and shielded him from the day as the rest of the sisters soothed Avria's pain.

"Fair and Ancient Gods, she is not alone," someone whispered in sheer wonder.

"No, indeed; have you ever touched such power?" another agreed.

"Shh," the Drathar hushed from beneath his facial covering. The sisters obeyed, their whispers of wonder subsided.

"I will tell the Mother Superior," someone said in a rich, velvety voice. "Return her to her chambers. Others will follow." Drathar nodded, and left the conservatory with Avria in his arms. She did not feel or sense the transition except to see the searing dirty light suddenly trade itself into the cave-like darkness of her assigned sitting room. The room then accepted three more forms of concerned sisters. Candles were lit.

"You did not tell us she was this far gone," one of them chastised the Drathar.

"It is not my task to assess her state; I am here to protect her. It's your job to care for her emotional wellbeing," he grunted. "Not a single one of you has visited..."

"We have been distracted by some unrest in some of the local villages. They are acting against those that are not entirely human or that bear powers," the sister explained. "We have been tasked with instilling peace. We cannot leave this place en masse without shrinking her protection in the core, so we must spread our efforts to calm the locals."

The Drathar hadn't been paying attention to his sisters' thoughts or their activities. He'd been too preoccupied with Avria to notice. "It is good you roused her ire when you did. She was in a dark place. You might not have tasked yourself with her emotional wellbeing but you surely must be aware of it on some level to have interceded when you did."

"Stop talking about me like I'm not here," Avria muttered through her tears, her runny nose making all her words sound staccato and child-like. She pushed the hands away as the sisters began to undress her.

"A hot bath will do you good. I've ordered to have the whole tub filled. Wouldn't that be nice?"

"Stop talking to me like I'm an idiot child..." Avria mumbled. She did however cease interfering with the sisters' efforts to disrobe her. The strange, seemingly useless valve on the side of the tub was opened, and hot water began to spill into it from mysterious origins. The water was fresh and scented, the tub filled quickly. She wondered if it was so simple to make the valve actually work, why they bothered making that poor servant girl carry urn after urn of hot water to her. She'd toyed with the strange metal valve before and nothing had come out. Now it was gushing like a spring, spilling steaming hot water into the marble basin. Avria was lowered in by the Drathar, who soaked his arms in doing so. He then shook his arms dry and pulled the veil from his pocket where he'd stuffed it after retrieving it from the floor of the library. He stood aside to cover his face.

Avria's anger was blunted. She sniffed and sat in the hot, soothing water while hands lifted her arms and washed away the last few days. She looked past the faces around her, she hardly heard their soft humming; she was somewhere else for a long moment. Her thoughts coalesced and she seemed to startle with realization.

"What did that sister mean I am not alone? Is he here?"

"No, he has not arrived yet. But he will soon. The core can feel his approach." Avria looked at the nearest face, and frowned.

"Then what did you mean?" She thought back to when the Drathar was worried about her refusal to eat—to what he had said to her. The lack of response provoked her.

"You should wait until the Mother Superior arrives and discuss it with her."

"I am with child, aren't I?" she asked. "I am with child and it's Eleran's child because it has great power." The sisters exchanged glances and two of them rose and vanished. The other one remained, rising to fetch a towel. She put it on the broad ledge of the marble tub.

"This is for when you are finished. You should soak for a while, it will do you good." In the wake of her exit, she left a whorl of inky mist. The Drathar was back in his chair, his face invisible behind his veil.

"You know, you answer me," Avria twisted in the tub, and clutched the ledge, her hair wet and clinging to her face. He stirred, the surface of his facial veil facing her.

"You are. It is a power I have never felt before."

"He told me so, you know. Long ago. He told me that a child of magic could only be born of two halves of the same soul," she whispered. "He told that when we shared our very first kiss." She twisted herself back onto her bum and leaned onto the side of the tub, propping up her knees.

"The Zsathri and their Hevra have always been infuriatingly prosaic in their interpretation of things; half souls, whole souls, those are all legends created by the Hevra—story-tellers all. The immortal beings are mad because they have lived unimaginably long lives. They were present before the first historical records. They are not mad because their souls are too great for their vessels. That is nonsense. It is well known by almost all magic bearers that power is passed through the blood. You were already imbued with power, Avria, from the moment you were born. Whether it manifests itself or not during your life, you have always possessed it. It was likely passed down from your mother. Her bloodline comes from a likely source. I'm afraid your father's line is ordinary."

"My father is not ordinary," Avria snapped defensively. "He is brilliant." The Drathar remained silent. She paused, and her irritation faded to curiosity. "So my mother could be a bearer?"

"Very likely. And she passed it onto you. Some people are born with power but it never quite surfaces or makes itself useable to them in a practical way. They would have more passive manifestations. But if your power is great, your child's power is great; and it is overt, for we can all feel it; those of us that possess the gift. So early in the formation of the child and the power of the tiny infant is already quite marked. If it were hidden power, like yours, like your mother's, we would not have sensed it." Avria's hand slid down to her tummy and she frowned. What would Offrin think of this child inside her; this product of Eleran's aggression? Would he love it? Hate it? Fear

119

it? She swallowed and sank down into the water until it reached her lips. She remained there until the bath became tepid.

Chapter Twelve – Grave Matters

Tinna did not take a coach. The coaches were consigned to the material goods and dogs, and were slowly making their way north, past the busy city of Loshan, around the great lake, following the ancient roads. Tinna was not patient for that sort of travel any more, not when she had Ledroran, for she could not turn down any chance to spend time with her old friend.

The massive dragon's crown shield could cover a small cottage and no longer had any large side openings, so it was like standing in a cave of sorts, with the view of the back and pumping wings. The cold snow blew like a funnel outside the shelter creating a dizzying tunnel effect she could scarce tear her eyes from. The dragon's body heat and the block of the wind made it comfortable enough for her to carry Istvan with her, swaddled in layers upon layers of warm coverings.

Taneth was still at Adremateen. Tinna worried that perhaps he was secretly angry about her decision to involve Phenmal in their marriage. She was careful however, to let him be the final deciding vote. She would not force it on him; she would be willing to let Phenmal remain as he was; a close family friend, if Taneth had decided against it. She guaranteed him she would not hold it against him, or make him feel bad for expecting a traditional marriage with his wife. She gave her husband the chance to tell her he did not like this idea. She knew it was selfish and she knew it was asking something difficult to a man she had been married to exclusively for twenty years.

There was no history of rifts; no cracks or fissures in their relationship to excuse her desire for Phenmal. They did not fight to speak of, except for silly things. Their relationship was harmonious most of the time. They spent a lot of time in different places these days; Taneth with his projects building and rebuilding; academies, archives, dragon rookeries. She was at Klatna, or embroiled in some political ridiculousness or other. Their marriage was not falling apart, it was... *broadening.*

Each one acknowledged these things during their long, forthright discussion of the matter. They were able to withstand the distances, the time apart as if it was not a matter to consider. They reunited into the natural rhythm of their lives and were happy when they were together—rare as it was. They still remained vastly passionate in their lovemaking. None of that would change, and as long as it didn't, Taneth did not seem to mind. Phenmal had been such a fixture in their lives, from the moment he first visited Thamatoc to find them after the burnings, and it was just natural to have him there, part of their most intimate discussions, mediating their disagreements sometimes.

Taneth had always been open minded and pragmatic. He saw this as adding a support system he regretted that he wasn't able to provide, and he did genuinely love Phenmal. There was one stipulation only; "Never the three of us", he told her. Tinna laughed and agreed wholeheartedly. Phenmal was definitely more dominant than Taneth. It was a refreshing change.

Of course, due to her close relationship with Ledroran, Tinna naturally discussed these things with him on this leisurely flight. She rarely had a chance to talk to him, except through a third-party summoner, which was like speaking through an interpreter; Summoners were naturally connected to the conduits through which Dragons spoke to one another, and could tap into them to relay messages.

Ledroran's size made him less bothered by the cold winter air. Because he loved Tinna, and enjoyed time with her, he took his time, his wings pumping slowly, often just gliding; his impossible size slipping through the crisp air with a languid grace.

SUFFICE IT TO SAY, AITINNA (he was the only one of Tinna's friends who used her traditional Thran appellation any more, and often, he dropped it these days), IF I WERE FORTUNATE AS TO BE TRANSFORMED INTO THE TINY FORM OF A MAN, SO I COULD STAND BESIDE YOU ON TWO GANGLY PINK LEGS, I WOULD HOPE YOU WOULD

MAKE ME A HUSBAND AS WELL, he said, the words vibrating through his whole skull and shield, the bass reaching her bones.

"I'm not sure about the pink legs..." she shouted back. The dragon snorted.

I AM NO JUDGE OF BEAUTY BY HUMAN STANDARDS, I CAN SORT OF SEE IT IN SOME WAY; MUCH IN THE SAME WAY AN ARAKI CAN ADMIRE THE BEAUTY IN ONE OF HIS HORSES. Tinna laughed loudly and shook her head. *I CAN SEE THE BEAUTY IN A HUMAN OR A SIMILAR CREATURE—BUT TO LOOK AT YOU IS NOT WHAT MAKES ME LOVE YOU. I BELIEVE I BEST QUALIFY AS YOUR TRUE LOVE, FOR I LOVE YOU ENTIRELY FOR WHO YOU ARE. I BELIEVE IF I COULD SOMEHOW LIFT YOUR SOUL OUT AND PUT IT IN A COMELY LADY DRAGON, I WOULD SURELY BE THE HAPPIEST DRAGON ALIVE.*

"Oh, Ledroran, you're making me blush," she intoned loudly.

THAT, I VERY MUCH DOUBT, he said with good humor. She laughed again. The dragon paused for a while, sighing deeply and pumping his wings to gain a bit of altitude so he could glide again. When he'd reached his desired spot in the sky, and let his wings ride the winds, the membranes of skin holding them aloft trembled on the hard gusts of air. His body remained perfectly still and level. He seemed to ponder things for a while, taking in all the things Tinna had told him in the last few hours.

ALLOW ME TO ASSUAGE YOUR CONCERNS, MY DEAREST, SWEETEST LADY. YOU FEEL SELFISH FOR ASKING TANETH TO SHARE YOU WITH ANOTHER MAN. TRUTH BE TOLD, MY LOVE, IS THAT OVER THE PAST TWENTY YEARS, YOU HAVE FORCED YOUR HUSBAND TO SHARE YOU WITH COUNTLESS THINGS, PHENMAL ASIDE; LIKE YOUR RISE TO POWER FOR ONE; YOUR RELATIONSHIP WITH ME AND WITH MY KIND; YOUR PART IN THE END OF THE BURNINGS, YOUR IMPORTANCE TO THE PEOPLE OF THAMATOC AND THE ARAKI. OF ALL THE THINGS THAT PULL YOU FROM TANETH, THERE IS AT LEAST ONE THAT HE CAN GRASP AND SEE AND IN SOME ESSENCE, CONTROL. AT LEAST PHENMAL IS A KNOWN QUANTITY; AN ACTUAL, MALLEABLE, ACCOUNTABLE THING. THE OTHERS THINGS ARE MOSTLY UNSEEN COMPETITORS AND MUCH BIGGER THREATS TO YOUR RELATIONSHIP THAN SOMEONE WHO'S ALWAYS BEEN THERE—SOMEONE HE ALREADY KNOWS LIKE A BROTHER.

TANETH, OF WHAT I'VE LEARNED OF THE SQUIRRELY FELLOW, IS A MAN IN SEARCH OF RATIONALITY AND FACT. HE FINDS THAT BY

INSURING HE KNOWS AS MUCH AS HE CAN ABOUT HIS WORLD, HE CAN GAIN CONTROL OVER IT TO SOME DEGREE. IF HE FINDS EXPLANATIONS FOR THE INEXPLICABLE, HE GIVES HIMSELF POWER OVER IT. PHENMAL, OF ALL THE ELEMENTS THAT DRAW YOU AWAY FROM HIM, IS THE EASIEST ONE TO IDENTIFY AND DECIPHER. HE IS NO THREAT. I BELIEVE, IF TANETH IS ANGRY AT YOU ABOUT ANYTHING, IF AT ALL, IT IS HOW YOUR LIFE HAS SEPARATED SO MUCH FROM WHAT IT WAS WHEN YOU WERE BOTH YOUNGER, AND YOU'D JUST MET. HE DOESN'T FEAR THAT PHENMAL WILL TAKE YOU AWAY, TINNA. HE PROBABLY FEARS THAT YOUR LIFE WILL DIVERGE FROM HIS BECAUSE YOU HAVE BECOME SO IMPORTANT. HOW COULD HE KEEP UP?

"My goodness, dragon, who knew you were so insightful?" Tinna's eyes watched the swirling tunnel of snow beyond the arched opening. The wind did not pull hard. If he'd been moving faster, it might, but it was oddly comfortable inside his shield.

YOU DID. YOU'VE ALWAYS KNOWN. Tinna sighed and nodded, checking on her son, who slept comfortably in his bassinette, wedged against the warmth of Ledroran's head. She gazed down at him, and touched his warm, flushed cheeks.

BESIDES, WHAT CHANGES? A THIRD PERSON IN YOUR MARRIAGE; WELL, THAT'S BEEN GOING ON FOR YEARS. YOU SHARE YOUR BED WITH HIM? SEEMS A MINOR ADJUSTMENT. AS LONG AS TANETH IS NOT EVENTUALLY EXCLUDED FROM THOSE PRIVILEGES AND SET ASIDE, I CAN'T IMAGINE HE HAS MUCH TO LOSE.

Tinna laughed a bit uncomfortably, unsure how to respond to the dragon talking about intimate subjects. She finally said in a loud voice:

"I am glad I have such a friend who would help me justify such a thing." The dragon laughed in the way dragons do, a snorting wheeze that the wind mostly carried away.

YOU ARE TO BE QUEEN ARE YOU NOT? YOU CAN DO WHATEVER YOU LIKE, AND THE ARAKI PEOPLE WILL FOLLOW SUIT, BECAUSE YOU HAVE PROVEN TO THEM YOU ARE THEIR LEADER. THE ADREI RESPECT YOU, EVEN YOUR OWN PEOPLE RESPECT YOU. I'LL WAGER, IF YOU SHOWED UP AT MIRANNE WITH A HAREM OF MEN, NOBODY WOULD EVEN BAT AN EYE.

ALL THIS PROVES TO ME IS THAT YOU ARE MORE DRAGON THAN ANYTHING ELSE, MY LOVELY TINNA. BECAUSE WE DRAGONS ALL

HAVE MULTIPLE MATES THROUGHOUT OUR LIVES. WE ARE LIBERAL-THINKERS, I SUPPOSE, LIKE YOU.

Tinna's laughter rang out in delight at the image her friend Ledroran painted. She reached down and patted the base of his skull. How she adored this dragon.

"Oh, Ledroran, you make me laugh. You are such a good friend."

LIKEWISE MY PRECIOUS QUEEN. He banked a bit and then leveled out. *I RECOMMEND YOU HUDDLE IN; WE'RE ABOUT TO HIT A ROUGH PATCH OF AIR. IT WILL BE IMPOSSIBLE TO HEAR YOU UNTIL WE ARE THROUGH IT.* Tinna sat down and scooted back against his head, wrapping herself up in her blankets, and snugging herself against the baby's bassinette. The dragon's wings hit the first streams of turbulent air and pitched rather powerfully. The air gusted in from behind, and threw her hair about. A few times, the dragon fell by several feet, lifting Tinna off of his neck. She put her hand up and braced herself on the top of the shield, and held Istvan tightly to her. For a moment there was a lull in the turbulence.

HAVE YOU HEARD OF THE GOINGS ON IN THE NORTHERLY AND WESTERLY COUNTRIES? I'VE HEARD OF SOME SKIRMISHES WHERE TOWNS AND VILLAGES ARE CASTING OUT THE GYPSIES AND NON-HUMANS. A GROUP OF ADREI SOLDIERS RIDING BACK FROM TRAINING WEST OF LEVRA WERE PELTED WITH ROCKS.

"No, I did not know this, Ledroran," Tinna said in shock.

I WAS JUST INFORMED OF THIS BY MY DAUGHTER AS SHE MADE HER WAY HERE FROM THE COASTAL CLIFFS OF OUR HOME. THERE SEEMS TO BE SOME ISSUES RISING UP WITH THE REMAINING HUMAN COMMUNITIES. IT LOOKS LIKE THE HIGH THRONE HAS BEEN BUSY UNDERMINING YOUR RULE ALREADY. IT DOESN'T BODE WELL, AND I WONDER HOW LONG BEFORE IT ERUPTS INTO SOMETHING SERIOUS. HAYNA TELLS ME THERE ARE TRAVELING TROUBADOURS SENT OUT TO TELL THE HUMAN CITIES TALES OF YOU IN A NEGATIVE LIGHT; TO PAINT YOU AS DARKLY AS THE THRAN THEMSELVES, AND TO MAKE IT SEEM LIKE YOU ARE NO MORE THAN ANOTHER, LESS EVIDENT ATTEMPT AT AN INVASION.

"Gods..." The air grew rocky again and the dragon concentrated on that for a while, until he hit a smoother patch.

YOUR RULE WILL PROVE ITSELF TO THEM. THEY HAVE NOTHING TO FEAR.

"I know that, you know that; but if the King has sent out hordes of tale tellers to rouse up the human communities, I'm not sure what I can do."

SPEAK TO HIM I SUPPOSE, IS THE FIRST COURSE OF ACTION. PERHAPS THIS CAN ALL BE TURNED AROUND BEFORE IT IS TOO LATE. Tinna could not believe what she was hearing. Was it really getting that bad out there? Everything looked so peaceful from high up. The sky became turbulent again and she felt the whole dragon lurch violently.

"How far do we have to go?"

NOT FAR, TINNA. ANOTHER HOUR PERHAPS. She held on, hoping this bad air didn't accompany them the rest of the way.

The Keepers had sent a welcoming party to receive Tinna upon her arrival. She was shaken from the last hour of the flight, and in spite of her enjoyment of the special time with Ledroran, she was actually delighted to feel firm ground beneath her feet and she needed more information on what Ledroran had shared. She climbed down with the baby, and found two gentlemen awaiting her. Both of them bowed deeply at the sight of her and waited patiently as she moved towards Ledroran's eye so she could lay her hand on his cheek-plate and bid him farewell for now. Her residence at Miranne did offer her one advantage that she could not rebuke, and that was she would be able to see Ledroran more often. It was a better place for large dragons to land.

The gentlemen, as most humans were, seemed still a bit leery of the great beasts. Their memories were long, of the time when dragons had burned and destroyed the better part of their civilization, leaving humanity to languish against the growing power of the other races. There was much to resent; however Tinna had managed to help the dragons redeem themselves in some ways by involving them in the one day war to save Oromoii from invasion.

They stepped back warily when the massive creature lumbered over the thick curtain wall to find space to take flight again. Tinna called farewell to him and watched his form recede into the sky.

The representatives of the Keepers had been careful to remind these gentlemen, who introduced themselves to Tinna as ministers that they would be best served if they welcomed Tinna with open arms. And they did.

"Of course it's not quite... uh, considerate to the King to put you at residence in the palace proper, quite yet," one of the gentlemen declared, "however for now, we have secured you some lodgings at the Vedri House, which is more than suitable for someone of your stature; at least as a temporary residence." The one who spoke was a tall, lanky, boyish figure with thick sideburns that melded into a manicured beard. He wore fine garments, Taneth and Phenmal had pieces much like them for formal events, and over those, he wore a deep scarlet open robe, as did his companion. These were apparently the ministerial robes. The one on his friend had more intricate decoration in gold cording woven along the front panels and tall collar, giving Tinna the notion that the young fellow was junior to the other. "I am Minister Belval and this is Minister Dranai," the young man said. Tinna bowed her head to both, and heaved her son's bassinette onto her hip. She began to walk beside them as they led the way across the spacious bailey facing the palace.

"I confess, Ashru," the elder Minister Dranai intoned, "that I have heard much of your exploits already. Not simply by the talk in general that has been prolific since the war, but from a more direct source; a mutual acquaintance. The Duke of Zadrudas, in particular."

"Ah, Adracoor," Tinna smiled. She last saw him at Avria's wedding. The undercurrent of guilt in Tinna's head became heavier for a moment, as she thought of Avria, and she thought of Offrin. She frowned, and shook her head, trying to come back to the conversation. She'd become good at compartmentalizing things in the past years of her life; of taking all her worries about personal matters and putting them aside in a mental box to examine later, after she'd contended with pressing issues of great importance. With a slightly forced smile, she replied; "He is a good friend."

"His lady in particular, the Duchess Rhoa is as well."

"That she is," Tinna could not hide her smirk, the idea of Rhoa with such a title made her want to laugh out loud. No matter how many years had passed and no matter how much Rhoa had changed, Tinna always saw her as the gawky, silly, whining girl she first knew. *The one who complained constantly, the one who fell in love with an invisible creature.* It was difficult to envision her afterwards, a quiet, serious, grieving young mother whose perspective had lost its vibrancy and colour and whose soul seemed trapped and lost somewhere else part of the time. But a little part of the old Rhoa returned during the war, when she met her Duke; a grizzled, scarred, hideous man and Rhoa fell in love that day. She needed only a quick thought to decide to return to Zadrudas with him, and they were inseparable since. He called her his little red devil.

Adracoor was a rough character these days, but what she heard from him and from others that once upon a time, he was a part of the royal family, and quite the dandy. She knew what had changed him into the gruff warrior today and his face still bore the heavy scars of his suffering. Rhoa had never seen his days as a fop. She'd only known the hardened, rough-edged soul who could not believe any woman could ever love him with a face like his. His visage was riddled with terrible bad scarring and he was missing an eye. "I do hope to see them," Tinna smiled, her heart warming. She missed Rhoa.

"Oh, you most certainly will, most shortly. They await you at the Vedri house. The Duchess is most eager to see you again. They made the trip from the great isle the moment they got word you were confirmed to arrive her at Miranne."

"That's wonderful," Tinna exclaimed. They walked in silence for a while, still slowly making their way across the vast, empty cobbled bailey to one of the less prominent edifices surrounding this massive square. Istvan seemed to be getting heavier by the step. She wanted to rest. The ministers were kind enough to carry her other bags. She sighed and kept walking.

"I must say, my Lady, that I take it as a great recommendation that you have such respect from my old friend, Adracoor. He is an honorable and brave man."

"I know. I've seen his bravery first-hand."

"Yes, we all know the tale," the Minister laughed heartily, and paused, puffing out his chest and lifting his finger. "He tells it often; of how he stood near the rise, watching the Thran army thunder towards his scant army. He'd already resigned himself to dying an honorable death in battle. He told of how your army all but materialized from behind him, and poured through his front line and flattened the Thran before his men could reach them. He recounted that at your command; dragons rained from the sky and burned the archery lines to a crisp."

"It didn't *quite* happen that way," Tinna chuckled. "His men fought among the Araki cavalry as bravely as any other. We certainly did not materialize. We nearly arrived too late. Thankfully the dragons were watching from above; veiled under cover of cloud, and urged us to move quickly. We flattened the camp as we rode through it, and came over the hill just in time to see the armies about to collide. Had we delayed only a few moments, there would have been many more losses on our side.

"And the dragons, well, they were there and they were many, but the ground dragons were as deadly as their flying brethren. The sky borne dragons were limited in what they could do. They could not bathe the melee in flames without harming their allies, so they focused on the lines of archers and also the berzerkers. Their columns of fire caused great chaos on the Thran side of the valley. Their infamous organized ranks and their time-tested strategies went up in flames."

"It is your intimate knowledge of those strategies that saved us, I am sure," he replied proudly. Tinna was highly animated as she spoke of the battle. It was a memory she cherished. No matter how reluctant she had been to lead the army that day, she was proud of how powerful a throttling they'd given to the Thran; an people whose entire culture revolved around war. It had humbled the arrogant women so tremendously; they'd offered Tinna their fealty in the end. She could see the appreciative smile on the Minister's face.

No matter how much she resisted what the Keepers were doing to her, she could not deny the satisfaction of knowing that she brought peace to this world twice, reunited the polarized races, and gave people like Adracoor and Dranai a second chance. She knew not all humans would look at her with the same reverence, but she would have to endure that. Humanity was still flailing for a foothold among the races again; and their best bet was not the leadership of their present King, who existed for self-indulgence alone. Because the Humans had become the minority of the races, it was logical that the dominant group's representative take the throne. Tinna was of both worlds. She was born human and gypsy, but now lived as an Araki. She represented all. Their best choice was her. She knew this. It was the only reason why she didn't fight Phenmal more when he came to tell her to go to Miranne.

The group got underway again. "Tell me ministers, my companion and friend Ledroran mentioned some rather disturbing things to me today. He tells me the High King has sent out an army of people to misinform the human settlements about me and the people I represent. I understand human groups have been acting out, granted, in rather benign ways right now, against the Araki and the Adrei. Do the dragons have something to fear as well? Has the goodwill from the war somehow been undermined?" She paused and hiked the child up onto her hip. The ministers looked strained the moment she brought it up and they exchanged a worried look before the elder minister replied.

"Yes, there have been some rather disturbing actions made by the High King in his effort to hold onto power. His methods have been less than savory, and many in the ministry have been vocal about it. But since the war, the High King has been incensed by the improving attitude towards the dragons. He is not about to accept that humanity has become a minority. When he was crowned, what many do not know is that one of his first statements was one where he promised to put things back where they ought to be." he muttered. "We weren't sure what that meant, but when the first messages of the Keepers arrived declaring the appointment of a new High Ruler and demanding he step down, he redoubled his efforts to stop them by any means necessary."

"It doesn't mean everyone supports him by any means," the younger minister added almost frenetically, waving his hand. "Almost all viceroys support you; including the most difficult man, the Viceroy of Gheraine. Almost the entire ministry is in support of you; we all know what happened at Chrotrioth, we all know who you are. But the High King is a young and obstinate boy, who was handed the crown far sooner than he should have gotten it. His father was tired, and perhaps he already knew a new bloodline would be appointed soon anyway."

"I should be concerned then, that humanity might not be receptive of me now as their leader?"

"I don't know yet, Ashru, I speak to you in all honesty. I cannot speak for everyone anymore. Things have been changing so rapidly. But you can be assured that all of us that support your ascension to the High Throne will be working as hard as possible to smooth everything out and settle any misgivings the people we represent may have," Minister Belval assured her. Dranai nodded. Istvan woke up at last and started fussing. They made their way the rest of the distance to the house.

Tinna was never more relieved to see Rhoa appear at the door of this particular building; looking a contradiction in a gown so fine with her freckled nose and strawberry blonde hair. She looked divine, Tinna had to admit it. But far more importantly, she looked so happy. *Finally.* It took a moment for Tinna to realize she was not only glowing with happiness, but there was a rather telltale little lump forming underneath her flowing, columnar gown; it was still small, but it was there nonetheless. Rhoa was thoughtful enough to rush up and to take the crying toddler from her arms before even uttering her first word of greeting. Her eyes smiled and she kissed Tinna's cheek, and took her hand.

"Gods it's good to see you. You ground me. You remind me where I came from. Come, Adracoor is so excited to see you and we've had every fireplace stoked so it's warm and cozy. Little Ishty here can toddle about, I brought him some new toys and we can catch up," she rattled. "We also poured out some stiff apple brandy that the Keepers sent to you as a welcoming gift. They sent several cases!"

"Ah, they also bestowed some of the rare and delicious libation upon our ministry as well. Everyone took a bottle home last night!" Belval declared. Tinna smiled, she did like apple brandy. She wondered how the Keepers knew this, but then she realized that was a silly question. They seemed to know everything.

"When did this happen?" Tinna asked, pointing to Rhoa's little baby bump. Rhoa glanced down and blushed. She was only about two years Tinna's junior and like Tinna, she was having a second child later in life. Drashun would be shocked, Tinna thought. Avria was thrilled herself when she found out about the arrival of a new baby sibling.

"I realized I was with child shortly after the wedding. It was actually the formation of this lump that clued me in. I haven't had any of the other symptoms."

"Congratulations, Rhoa," Tinna smiled. Her joy was subdued and Rhoa noticed it.

"Is everything alright Tinna?" Rhoa asked, furrowing her brow and tilting her head. She hiked the child more snugly onto her hip and gazed at her dearest friend. Tinna, relieved of her burden, gestured for Rhoa to go inside and then followed with ease, nearly forgetting the two ministers who lugged her bags behind her.

They all entered the huge formal parlor and the ministers set the items down on the floor. The men politely took their leave with deep respectful bows to Tinna, and then wandered off to find the Duke, who was somewhere else in the house.

Tinna knew Rhoa's exuberance would be extinguished when Tinna would sit down, and in earnest, tell her what transpired since the wedding. She did not look forward to discussing it or bringing down Rhoa's happiness.

Rhoa's expression of shock and incredulity was one Tinna would have to work hard to forget. Rhoa's eyes glassed up and she pressed her hand to her stomach, which was swelling with the Duke's child. All she could do was croak out Avria's name before submitting to a flurry of sobs and hunching forward into them, her shoulders shaking. Her sobs were heard by her husband, who was in the adjacent room smoking from his pipe and talking to the ministers, and he appeared, the grizzled bear, his brow creased in concern. He knelt beside his wife, looking at Tinna in both confusion and accusation.

"What have you told her to upset her so?" he growled. Tinna hugged Istvan closer to her and opened her mouth to speak but Rhoa shook her head and accepted the handkerchief he offered her. She dabbed her eyes delicately, which still seemed so strange to Tinna, and then clasped her husband's hand.

"Avria's been violated," she blurted, "by her mage."

"What?" Tinna had to explain it all over again, and the pain of it was taking its toll. Rhoa rose and took the child again and rocked him as if he required comforting for this unsettling news. Tinna sat back and sighed shakily.

"And now you're here. As it always is—timely and convenient for everyone but you and yours," Rhoa said acidly. "Bloody Keepers," she finished with a snarl. She bounced the baby almost too hard in her frustrated state. Adracoor sat, his scarred face fallen and distant, trying to process what had happened to the girl Rhoa called her niece.

Tinna studied her old friend Rhoa. She had grown leaner in the last year. The gowns of the north suited her, but her freckled skin and reddish hair just seemed so un-duchess like. Her mannerisms were also still casual and easygoing as well. Tinna had managed to teach herself some refinement in the past two years, knowing it was necessary to deal with the politicians and advisors she often saw down at Klatna. Rhoa didn't have any political obligations to speak of; she was the wife of a Duke who no longer took interest in the entitlements of his rank. He ruled over his little Duchy isle country of Zadrudas in a much more connected manner than he had before the burnings. He knew his people, he cared for them, and they embraced his commoner wife with great aplomb, bringing him even closer to them. It wasn't unheard of nowadays to find him out in the field in the autumn, forking hay into the drays alongside the farmers. Tinna had heard lots of anecdotes that painted him as a man of the people. He was beloved.

Rhoa's husband had no designs on the throne or any more responsibility than he already had. His connection to the present King, a young nephew of his was tenuous at best. He was finished with the sedentary and indulgent ways of the old nobles and sovereigns. He'd seen too much, suffered too much to ignore his responsibility to his people. He was with Tinna now, only too glad to promise his loyalty to a Queen who stood to rule with fairness; and certainly for saving the rest of humanity from extinction by dragons.

In the past two years, Rhoa's family had become his. Thamatoc and its people, the greater people of Arak, who had come out in force to stop an invasion and to rescue the small human force that had been sent to stop it, they were his people as much as the Zadrudans were. He was incensed by the news of the beautiful Avria so egregiously violated. He turned and looked at Tinna. She looked exhausted and drawn. He thought perhaps few people had noticed her weariness, including his angered wife. He walked to her and looked down from his lofty height. Tinna found his one good eye so soulful and sweet, the expression of concern plain on his ruined face. He picked up the glass Rhoa had poured for her and gave it to her. It was a rich amber-colored brandy with the pungent aroma of apples emanating from the glass. Smelling it brought her to the lingering golden days of early autumn. Tinna drank it down in three swallows and then handed it back to Adracoor who raised his brows at her.

"You should rest," he recommended. Rhoa turned from her absent gaze out the window and nodded in agreement.

"I have to send a letter to Gavorre and Offrin, letting them know where we are and where things stand. I'm not even sure where they are, I'm hoping they'll be back at Thamat..."

"Tinna, you should rest," he said more forcefully. He offered his hand and pulled her to her feet.

"It's barely into the late afternoon..."

"Go sleep, you look exhausted. Red will take care of the little one." Tinna glanced at Rhoa and smirked feebly at her.

Rhoa laughed and shook her head.

"Go on, I'll have a servant show you where your apartments are," some shadow-like figures had already scooped up Tinna's bags and ferretted them away somewhere. She'd scarce seen a glimpse of them as they flitted about the place, but they were there; and evidence of it appeared in the form of a young man of about eighteen wearing some fine footmen's clothes who came when Adracoor pulled the cord.

He bowed deeply to Tinna, his eyes wide and curious about her. "Take the Ashru to her apartments. The child will remain here with us. See to it she gets something warm to eat before she retires," Adracoor instructed him. The boy nodded and backed out of the room, and gestured silently for Tinna to follow.

She climbed the stairs at his heels, feeling all of a sudden the weight of everything that had happened, and where things were. Her life was changing in so many ways. She was thankful for Adracoor, and *Red*, and for Ledroran, Phenmal and Taneth who were always at her side when she needed them. She missed Hanru and the dogs but most of all, she missed Avria's bright face. With a hard swallow she crested the first set of stairs and followed the boy down a long corridor. The dogs would be arriving with the rest of her things. She'd barely paid them any heed of late, and thought of Reega and her arthritic hips. For some reason that thought put her over the edge, and she started to cry. The boy remained tightlipped and uncomfortable as he led the sniffing Tinna down to her apartments. He pushed open the double doors to the palatial space within, and then bowed shortly.

"Evra will help you from here," he said. "I will see to it that some dinner is started for you." He ducked out and closed the door behind him. Hunched by the elegant fireplace was a slip of a girl who looked like Rhoa when she was seventeen; awkward and wide-eyed. She straightened and curtsied to Tinna.

"My lady," she said. Tinna frowned. She did not want to be anyone's lady. With a sigh, she told the girl she wished to retire for the evening. The girl assisted Tinna into her night clothes and stayed to finish unpacking her belongings while the exhausted mistress drifted off to sleep in the center of the frigate of a bed, as if marooned on an isle alone.

MIRANDA MAYER

Chapter Thirteen – Assassin

It had been a long time since Tinna felt that shiver of wrongness. The tiny hairs on the back of her neck rose up and a frisson washed over her skin, bristling into goose bumps. Instinctively her hand slid soundlessly underneath her pillow. She was gratified to feel the familiar shape of the hilt of her poignard slipping comfortably and neatly into the palm of her hand, but her mind was instantly ablaze and she could barely think around it. The little knife never left her side; it traveled with her tucked into its little scabbard underneath her skirts in reach of her open pocket, and at night it rested underneath her pillow. This was a remnant of her assassin days and it wasn't going to go away.

She could hear the short, quick breaths of her baby son sleeping in his cradle at the foot of her bed, which she was able to make out as her instincts kicked in. She shut out the sound of her own heart and the rush of her own blood in her ears. She made an effort to relax away the tenseness this sense had created, to regulate her breathing and to appear at all costs, asleep. But her senses focused on the room around her. With her ears and her mind's eye, she listened.

She heard the breathing and she could tell where it was located in the room. She took a deep breath and rolled over, making a contrived sound of sleepiness as she turned. She turned her back to her intruder and then relaxed herself out, bringing her breathing back to the heavy, languid breaths of sleep while her hand tightened around the knife underneath her head. With nary a whisper the radiant heat of the figure closed in on her, her arsenal of senses focused on every little sound the person made. They approached warily, but also a tad recklessly. She wasn't impressed with their stealth by any means.

This was not a good assassin. This person also smelled quite distinctive—there was nothing familiar in their subtle scent. This was a stranger.

She clearly heard the sound of metal being drawn ever-so-carefully from a hard leather sheath. As soon as her mind confirmed that this was the case, something else seemed to take over. She moved imperceptibly to pull her knife down in front of her without giving any clue her body even stirred in the slightest from the observer behind her. In the darkness of the room, she had many advantages over her would-be assassin. She closed her eyes and focused.

With a speed and precision almost impossible to believe, her arm jerked up and the knife was released. A grisly thunk was followed by the stomp and stagger of the person the knife just imbedded itself into; then a faint grunt before the noise of agonizing gagging. Tinna rose at her leisure. She pulled the covers aside and slid her legs off the side of the bed. Barefoot, in her long and elegant nightdress, she circled 'round towards the figure on the floor still writhing.

The darkness was momentarily obliterated by a blinding flare of a fire-twig being cracked in two, the flame flaring up before settling into a steadier yellow burn. She touched it to a lantern and then carried it to her attacker. Stricken and still struggling to breathe, a woman lay on the ground, her hair fanned out on the carpet in skeins of gold. She was wide-eyed and her feet were kicking as her hands wrapped around the hilt of Tinna's poignard, which was firmly embedded in the attacker's throat, the blade's tip protruding out the back of her neck, just left of her spinal cord.

"Hello there," Tinna said in a strange smiling whisper. Tinna's usually warm and sweet eyes were blank and hollow. Her black irises were bottomless and seemed to lack the presence of any light or soul. Her amusement was empty and therefore even more chilling and haunting. She knelt, holding the lantern out in front of her to get a better look at her assailant, sweeping her boundless gaze over the face of her attacker. The wide, frightened, light-colored eyes of the golden-haired assassin locked on Tinna and she kicked, struggling to breathe still. Tinna reached down and twisted the knife. The woman's breath gurgled as she aspirated her own blood. "I'm sorry I'm laughing but this is just ridiculous. They send *you* to kill a Kanindra?" she chuckled again, keeping quiet as not to wake the baby. "Did they tell you that? That I was once a Kanindra? A Thran assassin? I certainly possessed a greater proficiency at this work than you, dear clumsy, noisy girl," Tinna pulled the knife out and immediately put her hand on the wound, holding it shut. The woman gurgled and struggled, in shock; weakening by the second. She was drowning in her own blood.

"It's safe to assume you were sent by beloved King? In some roundabout way of course," Tinna asked. The woman nodded and blinked her pale eyes, coughing up blood that belched out onto her lips, flowed onto her cheek and then trickled onto the rug. "So this is the way it's going to be..." Tinna sighed. With a purse of her lips and a strange little shake of the head, she grasped her poignard and lifted it high above the girl's body. "I'll make it quick," she said with cool assurance, her empty, cold gaze on the girl. Her hand fell; knife and all burying the blade deep into the chest and cutting into the woman's heart. Her struggle ceased almost immediately, except for a few twitches and a final gurgling rattle of air escaping her lungs.

Adracoor stared at the body in disbelief. He'd seen Tinna in action, in a sword fight with a few opponents at once, but he didn't know this tiny woman had the strength and skill to plunge a knife into someone's chest, angled just perfectly so that it avoided the sternum and bury it between two ribs just enough to cut into the woman's heart. He was impressed and a little afraid. When she described how she'd lobbed the knife at the assassin from the position she was in, he had to sit down. All of this happened with such quiet that not even the child was awoken. He was utterly shaken and his skin tingled when he set his eyes on the woman standing barefoot in a night dress and dressing-gown, with blood caked on one of her hands. Rhoa simply raised her brow and nodded at him as if to say: *See? I told you so.* He still couldn't believe it.

The representatives of the Keepers sent a group of four guards to the site and they were busily managing the scene. Tinna was adamant that she wanted Araki soldiers at Miranne immediately and she commanded that Adracoor see to it the moment morning came. Rhoa was standing nearby, clutching her elbows and looking horrified at the dead woman on Tinna's floor. With perfect timing, they heard the familiar sound of dragon's wings passing overhead and Tinna suspired.

"Phenmal's here." She dropped her hands and then realized they were covered in blood. A strange, evocative expression crossed Tinna's face when she looked down at them. She went into the bathing chamber and poured water into the bowl from the decanter, scrubbing her hands clean.

Adracoor looked at his wife. "You were right; she certainly didn't need too much protection. I knew she was able, but I had no idea she was capable of this."

"She's capable of much more, mark my words," Rhoa said with a bit of a laugh. Tinna returned from the wash chamber. Her expression was peculiar.

"I want to meet this King first thing tomorrow morning," she whispered. "Do you think you can make it happen?" Adracoor shrugged,

"I can try. He isn't being receptive to any of the nobles and ministers who have been supportive of the Ashru," Adracoor replied. He shook his head once more at the body as the guards fumbled with it. He was bewildered that this tiny woman could make so much damage with so little fuss.

Phenmal entered a few moments later, already well-apprised on the goings-on. He'd known the moment he came into range of the house. His hand fell immediately onto Tinna's shoulder and she reached up and clasped his fingers.

"Seems you had a visitor?"

"A laughable one at that. Clumsy and unskilled," Tinna replied in a muted voice. Phenmal nodded. The guards finally were able to roll the assassin onto the sheet and they grasped corners and lifted her up. All that remained were the dark spots where her blood was absorbed into the carpet. "I wonder who she was."

They watched as the guards hefted her through the doorway. Tinna then turned and stood on her tip-toes to plant a kiss on Phenmal's lips. "I'm so glad you're here," she sighed. He kissed her again, more deeply this time. Rhoa gasped audibly and her eyes darted about in utter confusion. Phenmal smirked playfully and even a bit smugly and pulled off his frock coat, hung it on a chair and then reached up and untied his cravat. He tugged the long strip of fabric off his throat and tossed it over the chair, pausing to look into the cradle where Istvan slept peacefully. He then removed his waistcoat, loosened the cuffs of his shirt, undid the loop that closed the stiff collar under his chin and pulled the end of his long shirt out from under his fall-front trousers.

"Come now, you two going to stand about gawking all night or can I get into bed with my wife to be? I've been in the air for hours and I've been looking forward to this all the while," he asked, highly amused by the look of shock on Rhoa's face and the smirk on Adracoor's.

"Tinna, You and Taneth... You're not..."

"Everything's fine. I'll explain tomorrow," Tinna muttered, finding her expression amusing as well.

"Don't you want different a room, Tinna on account of the blood?" Adracoor managed to ask, guiding his wife to the door.

"It's just a little blood. Someone will be up soon enough to scrub it up as best they can. Off you go," she replied. They exited and the door latch closed behind them, Rhoa's shocked voice bombarding her husband with questions and speculation.

Tinna looked at Phenmal and her amusement melted away. "If this is the sort of thing I can look forward to in the next few weeks, I'm not sure I want to do this anymore. It's not that I can't handle the attacks, but I am already emotionally dead. My daughter is alone with a demon, her husband is goodness-knows-where getting into goodness-knows-what sort of trouble with the Adrei mage, Taneth is forgetting about me completely, the humans are starting to rebel against all of us, and you... well I don't have to be a Chaiva to know that you are just thinking about all the wrong things right now. Now the High King is trying to kill me. Wonderful," she threw her arms out.

"Get into bed," Phenmal ordered. She arched her brow dubiously and he marched over to her and put his hands on her waist, lifting her up and tossing her into the mattress. Tinna could not help but smirk to herself in delight as she watched his hungry eyes devour her and his legs kicking off his breeches. He was exactly what she needed, so she abandoned herself to him.

* * * *

Avria stared quietly into nowhere, her hands fallen still from her writing. The Drathar watched her intently with his white eyes. She sat in the general reading room copying books for her father. She'd taken up this task again with aplomb, her mind focused on the idea that she had a life inside her that needed her more than anyone. She'd come out of her shell and started paying attention to things again. She was comforted by the presence of the Drathar. He could feel her emotions towards him and her quiet admiration of him because he reminded her of Eleran on some level. He was happy with even a proxy admiration; for he admired her as well.

He knew her power was latent and passive, but he knew that like her mother, the magnetism was almost unnatural. Not that she was not worthy of great attention, she was a beautiful girl, all of her features seemed to be the epitome of what was desirable in a woman; the plump pink of her lips, the sweep of her brow, the smooth line of her neck, the press of her breasts against the fabric of her gown, the shape of her hips and the way her back curved out into a fine posterior that was impossible not to admire in its beautiful dance when she walked. Her mother was the same way; stamped from almost every man's idea of womanly perfection it seemed. But Avria and her mother also inspired less than rational attractions. Tinna somehow unconsciously kept her power under control, but it was there. Avria's was out of control and it had driven more than one man mad in their attempts to have her.

The Drathar was fairly certain he was genuine in his attraction to her and not under her spell, so to speak; but even if the latter were true, he could not object to it for now. She was filling his days with something he had never tasted before and he wasn't about to just ignore it. He did not feel obsessive about his regard for her. It was more natural than that. He watched her with a fervent affection behind his veil and guarded her with his soul. He was growing to love Avria just like every other man who took a moment to look at her.

"Endrin bloom," she said in a scratchy voice. She'd shaken herself out of her reverie and started writing again. She did this sometimes; she read things aloud to him as she went along. "...found mainly on the western shores of Oromoii and south to Gheraine, this coastal blooming beach-grass can be rendered into a powerful poultice that can draw out infection and pus from festered wounds or abscesses. That is disgusting," she wrinkled her nose. The Drathar was charmed. "Dry in conventional fashion, and then pluck the leaves from the base. In the mortar you should powder them and add a bit of water and the milk of the Hadram weed to bind the powder... Working it will create a malleable, clay-like paste. Make a little patty to cover the affected area and bind to the patient with a bandage. The poultice will absorb a good deal of the infection and pus and will swell with it, so it should be replaced at least within a day or if it has doubled in size," she mumbled, her hand moving.

"Does it even grow anywhere near where you live, Avria?" the Drathar asked. "Your father may have knowledge of it from what you copied, but it does him little good if this endrin bloom is not available to him locally."

"He can send away for some. He has friends everywhere now. And his schools, they educate people from all over. It could serve to..." she trailed off as the Drathar suddenly stood and turned to the window. Her hand stopped moving, eyes wide, mouth partly open. The Drathar's shoulders squared and his chest seemed to widen.

"He's here, isn't he?"

"Something just tried to pierce the core. Either he isn't especially sharp or he is more conniving than I imagined,"

"He's a lot of things, Drathar, but Eleran is not stupid," Avria said. The Drathar's veiled face turned to her and he studied her for a moment.

"Get into your sitting room and close the doors to the archway," he said. A sister appeared out of nowhere, startling Avria. She looked at the Drathar and frowned darkly.

"He's attempting to cast a Kavarnoth spell. Arrogant thing. I'm taking her to the keep; he might get in," she said to the Drathar. The core has shrunk by at least a meter just with those two attacks."

"Where she goes, I go." The sister nodded and took his hand and then Avria's. With that, they were gone.

MIRANDA MAYER

CHAPTER FOURTEEN – OFFRIN'S RETURN

Offrin and Master Gavorre arrived at Miranne with a small mounted military contingent of Adrei. It was late afternoon and the bevy of mounted soldiers rode into the quiet bailey of the palace towards one of the visiting dignitary barracks. They wore the red and white of the Ashru's army, Tinna's symbols emblazoned on the surcoats. Master Gavorre was not in saddle but riding in a rather small-sized caravan being pulled by two heavy ponies behind the twenty or so riders that entered the square. The contingent of Adrei was mounted mostly on showy black Hale ponies, which looked like small versions of the heavy-breed draught horses that were bred to carry ancient knights and their heavy amours. The large destriers that these ponies were bred to resemble were still used by the Kanreth Knights, a dying breed of mounted warrior that used two tremendously long swords to fight in saddle. These ponies, like the much larger horses they resembled were powerful creatures, raven black with rippling muscles, thick crested necks, feathered hoofs and dense, long manes and tails. Draped in the red and white colours of the army, they were a sight to behold.

Taneth, who'd arrived only the night before, smiled at the sight of them. Tinna's power had given the Adrei many resources to create a sizable military force and to equip themselves with this special breed of pony among other things. They were loyal to Tinna. The Adrei were a group of people made up of throngs of little people born to the Humans; sent as infants to live among their own 'kind' in communities called Auberges scattered about the same forestlands that the Araki occupied. Like the Araki, nobody paid too much heed to these hidden communities, so nobody really understood how large, spread out and powerful the Adrei had grown over the centuries. The secret came out about both peoples after the One Day War, when the Araki made it known just how much of a power they wielded when united.

The Adrei joined the Araki, small perhaps in size, but great in courage and numbers, they rode into battle against the Thran at the side of the Araki riders. Tinna had given them the official distinction of their own identity as a people after the war, and she had honored them and asked them to become a brotherhood of sorts with their Araki friends. The Adrei summarily agreed, and because Master Gavorre had already established a close relationship with the Ashru and her family, he was named as the representative for their people. The marriage of the Adrei man Offrin to the Ashru's daughter only further cemented the bond between these two groups of people.

Tinna had been called out to meet them when they arrived. A runner from the gatehouse had announced their approach. She, Phenmal and Taneth had walked out the main door and met the group as they clattered into the mostly empty square. It was a beautiful day, ice-cold but sunny, the sky a pristine blue with only a smattering of cirrus clouds. The wind was sharp. Tinna wore a large woolen cloak of deep navy blue with a fur-trimmed hood, over one of her more casual gowns from home, made of a soft burgundy wool trimmed in thin bands of gold silk. Offrin rode in front and they met almost smack in the middle of the square. A few ministers were scurrying across the cold space to meet somewhere and here and there a palace compound resident or servant ran quickly against the edge of the icy wind. Tinna held her hood on and waved to Offrin, who drew his mount to a stop.

Offrin looked quite furious for a moment, but his stiffness softened when he saw Tinna's drawn and exhausted face up close. She approached his mounting side, putting her hand on the mount's neck. On his pony, he was taller than Tinna. He was wrapped in a thick cloak of red as were most of the others, their hands bound in fur-lined black gloves. His feathered helm was tied in front of his right knee on his saddle. An emblem on the front of his helm indicated his rank of sergeant. He smiled wanly at her. "I came as you wished."

"I'm sorry for everything Offrin..." Tinna intoned. He lifted his hand to stop her.

"I know why you pushed me out of the way and I can't say I am pleased by the idea, but I understand. But you cannot deny me the right to protect her too. She is my wife, and I love her. But I know now the logic of it," he said, "My place is here." Tinna sighed in relief and stepped forward to embrace him. He leaned down and wrapped his powerful arms around her, hugging the tired woman tightly, his armor and mail ringing pleasantly together with his movements. His pony shifted on his feet. He withdrew, gathering his reins for second, taking a moment to drink in the features that reminded him of Avria so much.

"What's the situation?"

"I'm waiting on our Araki guards to arrive," she said.

"They left only shortly after we did. Lejreth Asnan told me he would be a half day or at most a day behind us. We did not stop for long; for us it was eight days of hard riding from Thamatoc. They should be arriving shortly depending on how long their rest stops were. In the meantime, Temret and I will stand in as watch until your men get here," he said. "Gavorre is sleeping. He picked up a right beast of flu several days ago and was suffering so much that I think he might have over-medicated himself. He's been knocked out most of the journey. This isn't the sort of weather for an elderly fellow to be out and about in."

"He *was* offered a quick ride on the dragon," Taneth interjected.

"He's like the old man over there," Offrin glanced at Phenmal, "he doesn't care for flying."

"Well, our hosts have provided him with comfortable lodging right next door to our residence. I'll wake him and get him inside," Taneth said. The scholar made his way to the back of the procession and started talking to the man who drove the coach. The assemblage then rumbled off towards the residential buildings.

"You on the other hand are to stay with us," Tinna said. Offrin nodded and dismounted, handing his reins to another of the mounted Adrei soldiers. He sent them off to the barracks with a nod and then followed the three back to the house. They were met by Rhoa and the child at the door. He greeted her with a nod and they all entered the vestibule. He shrugged off his cloak, which a servant immediately took. Rhoa led the group to the parlor, her face also stressed and anxious.

"Did Cennik make it alright?"

"Yes," Tinna told Offrin. He nodded, his face unreadable. "That red-haired woman was asking after him back at Thamatoc. I am tasked by her to relay him a message."

"He wasn't happy to come, but he's settled in nearby. He keeps in constant contact with the dragons these days. I'll direct you to his residence after you've settled in. I'm afraid that red-haired woman is going to be disappointed. He's already taken up with someone here. He's quite the roving wolf, that one. His reluctance to leave Thamatoc was quickly forgotten once he got here and spied some of the ladies that serve the palace." Offrin laughed through his nose, and then sighed wearily, scratching the back of his neck.

"I suppose it didn't take long for the King to act out against you," Offrin shook his head. "We departed the moment we got your message. In truth we were going to come north anyway the moment we heard you'd been sent to Miranne. The Master thought it advisable that he be present here as a representative of the Adrei and he imagined that a small showing of our militia wouldn't hurt," Offrin said. "He had an idea where the Chaiva might have sent Avria, but he realized it would be a waste of time for us to go. He convinced me of that as well after working hard to get through my furious determination." He pulled off his surcoat and his mail, and sat down by the fire, opening his hands to it for warmth. "I've heard some rumours that things are starting to grow uncomfortable between Arakis and humans in some areas. A large fight broke out at Ivridorp two weeks ago between some of the royal guard and a group of Araki horsemen who'd ridden up to provide training for some of the new Kanreth plebes."

"The King has been creating some tension among his subordinates. He certainly has been trying to influence his court and the ministry. He refuses to see me. I've been trying for more than a week. I'm not sure what the Keepers expect me to do; they said they'd take care of it, that's what they told Phenmal, so I'm just waiting. In the meantime, I remain here. I'm not sure how long he can continue to ignore me, but I thought if I brought some muscle into the palace grounds, he might take notice."

"Tinna, you must know that the Kanreth have declared their service to the Ashru. They have renounced their connection to the present Throne. In fact, we heard the rumour of the fight from them. We came upon them just leaving Loshan. They are on their way here as well. They heard why we were coming and decided to join us. They will arrive only after stopping at a training school in Vyanne to collect some of their friends. They will want to don your colours when they arrive." Tinna suppressed the urge to sigh in relief and smile. That meant something; an old and trusted institution; the trust and fealty of the Kanreth Knights would surely give those who doubted the Ashru peace of mind.

Tinna wished for the thousandth time that day that she was not the Ashru, and she was not stuck in this frozen city, in a noble house in its large, cool rooms, awaiting the condescension of a King who wanted her dead. Instead she thought of being at Thamatoc, spending a snowy day in her apartments with Phenmal in his chair by her fire smoking his pipe, speaking with Taneth in a low voice while she patted the dog's head. She wanted that back again more than anything. She certainly did not want laughable assassination attempts and an obstinate twenty-four-year-old king with tremendous skill for manipulation. *Has he not learned anything from his father's reign, when the dragons had nearly destroyed everything the Throne exacted power over? His guard is small and ineffectual against my own militia alone, let alone with the addition of the Adrei and the Kanreth.* The total population of his people numbered less than an twentieth of the Araki alone. *What did he hope to accomplish by riling up what was left of humanity? Having them all killed?* Tinna shook her head and sighed, utterly bewildered by the monarch's determination to remain in power when he had nothing left to rule.

Tinna's frustration was reaching a limit. The assassination in and of itself, she took care of quickly. It was a physical response more than anything. She reacted as she had been trained. Tinna had vowed to herself years ago that she would do whatever she could to avoid living a life even remotely like the one she lived before she came north. She did not want to see blood on her hands ever again. The reaction and defense against the attacker had been so ingrained and practiced; she'd done it before she really knew what she'd done. The knife had flown as if of its own volition. She'd killed the woman before she had a chance to think of other ways to deal with her. She hated that. She hated that she'd been trained so well she couldn't even control her own actions once things were set in motion.

The last time Tinna had killed, it was in a battle orchestrated by her own mother and she had taken the lives of most of her mother's personal guard. She almost allowed the beast within her to exact that same fate on her own mother, but Avria's voice had pierced through the specter of her inner monster and had stopped her before she'd lost her entire soul that day. She was so grateful that her daughter was a creature of such goodness and thoughtfulness, that she could recognize the danger of falling into the cycle of revenge. She was so grateful that this child of her heart could penetrate the shadow of death that had been programmed so well into Tinna.

She was furious at the boy King for unknowingly taking her back to a place she did not want to revisit for the rest of her life. And a part of her feared that *she* would have to be the instrument to rid the world of him for good. She had enough pressure in her life; she did not want to be an assassin for anyone any more. Enough was enough.

She looked at her son-in-law, who so carefully avoided asking the questions she knew he wanted to ask and she sat down across from him. Phenmal knew the moment she set her eyes on Offrin that she wanted to speak to him in private. He gestured subtly to Taneth with his chin to leave the room; "Join me for a smoke, Taneth," he said. He then grasped Rhoa's shoulders and ushered her out as well. Offrin and Tinna were not blind to the lack of subtlety of the exit and they both smirked at one another knowingly. Offrin's smile faded and he sighed.

"How is she?" he asked softly, still looking at his hands.

"I don't know," Tinna's voice cracked and she cleared her throat.

Offrin lowered his face and stared at his hands. He had no idea how to even talk to Tinna about what was going through his mind. All he could feel was the intolerable pain he had felt for all this time, from the moment she'd been hurt. He wanted so to go to her, and show her he loved her and would always love her, and that he in no way could blame her for anything. He wanted to show her that he could wait with her indefinitely until she healed, as long as he was *with* her. He wanted to hold her while she wept and to comfort and love her. He finally allowed himself to dwell on his emotions enough that he became overcome with them. His shoulders shook as he began to weep, thinking only of his wife's pain and her humiliation and of how alone she must feel.

"I always want to fix things; it's who I am. How will I ever fix this?" he said hopelessly. "She does not deserve even a shade of this unhappiness beset upon her; her sweet soul is not fit for this pain. How she must be suffering alone," he said through his tears. Tinna remained in her seat, gazing at him with her own tears barely under control.

"She will come through, Offrin. And her love for you has never wavered. Her greatest fear was that you would no longer love her." These words made him weep harder, and then he remembered himself and tried to collect his wits about him. He'd been holding onto this sadness for a while now, keeping it locked away as best he could. He had hope in his eyes when he finally met Tinna's. Her words had bolstered him.

"Then I shall show her that I love her no matter what happens. I only wish I could kill that... whatever he is, myself," Offrin growled, his ire barely contained.

"That whatever-he-is will meet the fate he deserves, mark my words. If not by the means Phenmal has offered, then at my hands. I have vowed never to let these hands see blood again, but for that, I would take his life without hesitation. I must have faith that the measures Phenmal has put into place will insure her safety. She has the guardianship of a Drathar, and that fact alone has given me leave to focus on all these other things."

"A Drathar? Really? I didn't think those were actual creatures. I thought they were myth."

"I'd never heard of them until I came north. A book Taneth brought me of Oromoii lore mentioned them. The creature seems quite unlike the book described; he seems almost human, but I could not see any part of him; he was covered from head to toe in black, and he had his face wrapped in black muslin. I could see in certain light, his eyes glistening behind the sheer fabric, his skin so pale; but his eyes looked white, with but a dot of a pupil. It reminded me of the wolves. I miss the wolves. I hope they arrive soon," she added distractedly. She stood and stepped over to the young man, putting her hand on his shoulder reassuringly.

"She is in the most excellent hands, Offrin. She will be fine and on her way here soon."

MIRANDA MAYER

CHAPTER FIFTEEN - DRATHAR

"I don't understand. How could a mere Zsathri do this?" the mother superior asked. She folded over again in pain as did the six other women with her. The Drathar flinched and his presence seemed to darken. All of them surrounded Avria in what they called the Keep. It was a windowless, doorless chamber. Anyone who wanted to enter it had to have powers. The tall wooden paneled walls covered a stone one many feet thick, and around them the soil of the earth pressed in from all directions. The room was appointed rather comfortably, decorated like any common sitting room complete with a shelf of books. The lamps were lit, but no hearth offered warmth of a fire. She wondered how they even managed to get air in here.

Avria was sitting in a chair, her hands pressed together and resting on her lap. She was wearing a simple day-gown of the style she wore when in Loshan. It was white and the tiny bodice hugging her upper chest was ruched and thickly gathered. Below that, her skirts fell over her traditional pantalettes, shift, two layers of plain petticoats and snow-white thigh-length light woolen stockings. She wore a pair of plain black slippers. In the rush to get her to safety, one of the ribbons had come undone and lay twisted around her foot. She noticed it and bent down, lifting up her hem just enough to tie it around her ankle and secure it with a bow. Even at this moment of strain and physical discomfort as the Zshathri somehow managed to attack the core itself, the Drathar had to stop and admire the gracefulness of her movements and her astounding beauty of the sight of her dressed so delicately. That morning, he had enjoyed seeing her exit her chambers wearing the nice garments for a change.

She'd been so shabby and tousled these past days. The thought of that creature harming her filled him with rage. The memory of her violation burned through his mind like molten rock. Another pang of pain passed through him and he felt something unusual in it. He paused.

"This is not the Zshathri alone..." he muttered. The Dreff sisters straightened and their six faces turned to him with expressions of confusion. Another pang of pain, and he lifted his face, talking through gritted teeth. "He has help. Do you not feel it? No Zshathri could do this—even one as tainted and unconstrained as he. No one has the power to undermine the core. It is the magic of a collective of four hundred at least. Who could? I can think of only a few creatures in this world that have the capacity or the power to even scratch the surface of the collective spell. Most of those most powerful creatures are... *hobbled* by the Keepers. But there is one being that can and has no controls in place; one being that can pull someone from the voids; one being that can wield so much power: the Hevra. They are helping him," he muttered in a dooming tone. The sisters peered at one another as they reflected on this and again they felt a wash of pain as another attack was cast upon their core.

"Yes. There is a taste of the ancient in these attacks. You are right brother. What do we do?"

"I am hobbled. But with help, we can prevent this. We must do a summoning to bring all the Drathar here. It might divert your power from the whole of the core and weaken it, but with all eleven of us here, even the Hevra would be challenged to get through to the girl. Even with our restraints, together we are powerful. But we must get them here now, and for that I need all the magic of all the Dreff," the Drathar said. The mother superior nodded and closed her eyes for a long moment. When she opened them, her eyes were marbled eerily in white, as Eleran's had done when he petitioned the voids for answers and power in meditation. The mother superior however was neither meditating nor in any way incapacitated by this connection. She turned her white eyes to the Drathar.

"It will be done. The sisters are prepared. Join the summoning. We must be quick. We will restore the core in a smaller area around us when we are finished. It will slow them down," she held out her hand and the Drathar reached for it. Avria watched as physical manifestations of their powers arced across the hidden space in misted flares of pale blue.

Then the room began to fill. One by one, new forms began to appear, the language of their bodies defensive and confused; ripped from wherever they were to this new place without explanation. One by one, Drathar appeared, all like Avria's guardian, swathed in black, some taller, some shorter all veiled and grave. The eleventh Drathar materialized and Avria's guardian let go of the mother-superior's hand; turning to his brothers he showed them in silence the answers they needed. The sisters worked to communicate with the rest of the Dreff to refocus their magic on restoring the core, their eyes all turned white.

"The Hevra are strong. They now attack the sisters outside of the core to weaken it. I have ordered a retreat to those who still stand outside of its defenses. Their powers are ineffectual against the ancients," the Mother Superior said.

"We cannot kill them, what do we do?" one of the women asked in desperation. "They are killing my sisters!"

"We will remedy this. Concentrate everything you have on the girl. Keep her protected at all costs, and keep that core wrapped around her so nobody with power can see her or find her," the Drathar told her. She nodded. Avria watched them all vanish in their telltale puffs of black mist that dissipated so quickly. Her stomach iced over in fear. The sisters surrounded her in her chair and linked hands, throwing their heads back, their eyes all ghostly white. Twelve more sisters appeared in the room and made a circle 'round them. Avria lifted her feet up onto the chair and lowered her face into her knees, her arms clutching her legs and her hands tightly clamped together. She was terrified with the Drathar gone. All she could do was visualize the horror of Eleran harming her again. He was probably already well within the building, powerless, but searching; biding his time until his friends broke down the dampener that made him ordinary.

"Get out!" the Drathar shouted to his sisters. The nave where Avria had first entered the abbey filled by eleven people in a matter of seconds and the sisters that stood against the assaults were facing the doorway, hands aloft creating shields against which a collection of people pushed just inside the gaping doorway. The core had been pushed all the way back to the main edifice, and the attackers were now fully in view, no longer hidden by the forest.

Outside the shrinking core, the bodies of dreff sorceresses lay prone on the ground of the courtyard, their clothes and cloaks rippling in the wind. The first line of defense had fallen. The tear-streaked faces of their sisters protecting the inner core pivoted in shock at the appearance of the Drathar. Their hands dropped; they retreated, some by magic, others on foot, vanishing into the variety of corridors behind the rows of massive columns. The Hevra proceeded forward unhindered; Eleran leading the pack. He had remained with his protectors, biding his time while they undermined the core, hoping he could act quickly when they'd weakened it sufficiently. He would find Avria and take her out of here the moment the magical veil was torn down. The Drathar were fortunate. Eleran could have run ahead and gotten lost in the building, searching with naught but his eyes, but he was thinking this through, and he knew that separating himself from them gained him nothing, especially inside the labyrinthine building.

The Drathar had a clear image from Avria what the man looked like, but Eleran somehow grown a sinister air to him over the past weeks since he attacked the girl. His long black hair was loose and hanging heavily down the sides of his head, fanning out along his back and in front of his shoulders. His gaze was dour, his eyes upturned, sunken in deep sockets that were a reddish purple. His eyes were cold and menacing.

Behind him, the collection of beautiful, ethereal people followed; all with guileless expressions and wide, curious eyes; all had their hands up like claws, which they cut into the core with, piercing its invisible skin like the talons of a raptor. They halted when they saw the Drathar brothers before them, their hands dropping as curiosity filled their faces. They sensed their ancient roots, and immediately knew these were not simple creatures.

The air was thick with electricity, and the smell of ozone washed the space. Splashes of magical energy surged forth from their beings as they fought against the core from within, fighting to collapse it for the Zsathri. Eleran stopped too, looking bemused by the presence of the eleven black figures standing before them in a neat arc. Nobody really knew what a Drathar looked like anymore. Lore had made them into hideous demons. These eleven figures were a mystery to the intruders, but they did not miss the undercurrent of power emanating from these darkly clad figures as they drew closer together before them. They realized this power was present in spite of their being inside the core. It had no effect on them.

"Who are you?" Eleran asked. The figures remained deathly silent, waiting until every set of eyes was fast upon them. When the intruders all gazed in puzzlement at the ones inside the core, in an act of synergy, the Drathar tore off their veils and threw them aside. The veils drifted gracefully to the floor. Their cold gazes seemed to suck the colour from the world; drawing everything into them. The vortexes that drew the energies were merging into a violent maelstrom that spread out over the area before them and enveloped the sixteen people standing there, riveted to this spectacle and now trapped irrevocably by it.

There were horrified cries from the Hevra; two of them thought quickly enough to cover their eyes with their arms and turn away, but the rest were instantly rapt, gazing directly into the vortex and strands of misty light began to bleed out of their faces, from their eyes, ears and mouths, floating outwards, where the it stretched out into tendrils that merged into larger ones that undulated and extended like tentacles towards the Drathar. The Drathars' eyes absorbed them. The Drathar stood in wide stances, strong against the power of their magic, their shoulders hunched and their fingers clenched. The cries became piercing screams of horror as the essence of these ancient creatures was being sucked out of them in beautiful layered streams of luminous mist. They collapsed to their knees.

The devastation of the combined Drathar gazes spread, extracting the lingering souls and essences from the open eyes of even the dead and dying Dreff resting on the cobbles of the courtyard; shriveling up and making grey and lifeless the evergreens that hugged the edge of the square, bringing birds down from the sky to fall twitching onto the earth.

When the screams faded into silence, they relented, closing their eyes and stooping to pick up the veils they'd thrown down. They pushed back their hoods and quietly and methodically draped their faces. Only two of the Hevra were left with any sense or consciousness. Both were on their backs on the hard stone floor, weeping behind their forearms. Eleran himself knelt on the floor, staring blankly into nothingness. The essence of who Eleran was, of who he had ever been now resided inside the eleven souls of the Drathars; including the sum of his power. Tingling and surging now with the power of Hevra and Eleran and some of their Dreff sisters, the Drathar began to leave, one at a time until all that remained was the first. As they each vanished, the clouds of smoke they left behind were peppered with tiny figures and glyphs that spun and floated momentarily before vanishing along with the mist.

The remaining Drathar walked to Eleran. He reached out his gloved hand and tilted the Zshathri's chin up to see his face. He looked down into the empty eyes. Nothing remained.

"This is not how the story should end," one of the two remaining Hevra whispered through her tears, her flaxen hair tousled and her eyes red. "It was supposed to be happy. It was supposed to end happily," she insisted. The Drathar stood staring at her and her weeping dark-haired sister. They could harm nothing just the two. They no longer had reason to. Their story had ended.

Avria was huddled in her chair. Around her, the sisters dropped their hands to their sides and the mother superior nodded. The others vanished from the room, seemingly taking some of the limited air with them. Avria felt weak and wanted to breathe fresh air. The mother superior reached out her hand. Avria's knees dropped down and her feet touched the floor. She took the mother-superior's hand and stood.

"It's over," the mother said. Avria was suddenly blinded by powerful daylight. Unexpectedly, she was standing in front of the entranceway to the great abbey, the sunlight bright and white and pouring in from the open doorway. She shielded her eyes for a moment, squinting against it. And then her focus came back, and she saw Eleran kneeling in front of a scattering of unbelievably beautiful bodies, two of which wept and rocked on their knees, hands reaching out to touch the still forms of the others around them. Eleran was staring forward to the top of the nave where the three great windows cast their colored light onto the floor. He paid no heed to Avria. The Drathar stood nearby, his face pointed to the floor, his arms crossed.

Avria clutched the mother superior's hand at first, instantly filled with terror at the sight of the man she once loved. When she realized he was in a trance, she let go and padded forward on her little slippers. She came to stand in front of him, her head tilting sideways in puzzlement. She waved her hand in front of his blank gaze. "Eleran?" she asked weakly. He did not flinch. He stared steadily forward. When she tore her eyes from his beautiful, peaceful face, she noticed all of the people save two were in the same quiet trance, some lying on their sides, others flat on their backs, others sitting or kneeling like Eleran, all staring blankly at nothing. She turned her gaze back on Eleran.

"What's wrong with him?" she asked. The Drathar shook his head.

"It's what happens when a person's eyes meets our gaze. He is not in there anymore. Not the good Eleran, nor the bad one. There remains nothing but basic instincts like chewing and swallowing and breathing. He will no longer be of threat to you Avria. You may go home," the Drathar said, the regret at bidding her farewell well hidden in his words. Avria began to cry, her hands gripping each side of the Zshathri's finely hewn jaw.

She stood before him, peering searchingly into his empty gaze, which did not even lock onto her face but looked somewhere beyond. He was so beautiful. The evil in his eyes was gone, as was the love that had once filled them. He was a facsimile of what she remembered, a painted image. His face, the one she'd come to dream about and so secretly hoped to see again even when she accepted Offrin's offer of marriage was there, but he was not in it. Avria's grief overwhelmed her and she knelt in front of him, weeping and crying his name, "Eleran, Eleran," wrapping her arms around him and hugging him close; shaking his shoulders and calling his name again and again. Impassive and hollow, he allowed her to do this, sitting on his knees still, stiff and unyielding, vacant and hapless. "Say something," she whispered to him. "Say you are sorry. Say you are sorry for what you have done to us." But he remained silent. His gaze looked through her as if she didn't exist. She wanted to hit him, to claw at his face, to kiss him, but he wasn't there. This thing before her was innocent of crime, and incapable of love. She knelt weeping in front of him for a long time.

When her tears had run dry, she stood and wiped her eyes with the ball of her hand, hiccupping still from her sobbing. She couldn't even bid him farewell. Not to this thing. The Mother Superior came to her and put a cloak on her shoulders.

"Could we just *walk* back to my rooms?" Avria asked in a soft whisper through her hiccups. The mother nodded, and they made their way towards the corridor, the tall woman holding Avria's shoulders as they walked. The Drathar vanished without a goodbye, leaving only a cloud of mist and glyphs which too vanished as if he'd never been. The two remaining Hevra hovered over their brethren in confusion, trying also to draw them out of their stupors to no avail. The sisters then began to file out of the corridors into the nave to clean up the mess. There was a strange bristling sensation as the core began to wash outwards again like a great wave; unhindered now. Its size was only reduced marginally by the deaths of the eight sisters. The arrival of so many power-bearers into the nave sent the two remaining Hevra packing. Avria did not put a single thought into what would be done with the empty people now.

Chapter Sixteen – Homecoming

Phenmal was filled with a strange sense of apprehension when the Drathar arrived. Something oozed from his being, something barely controlled. He appeared without invitation in Phenmal's private chamber where the older gentleman was about to go to bed for the night. Their powers were unbelievably strong, but he felt even more powerful this time, like it was straining against the seams of his loose, draped clothing.

"What are you doing here?"

"The mother has cast you out of her bed for the first husband I see," the Drathar mumbled sardonically. He took the liberty of sitting down in one of the chairs and stretched out his legs. Phenmal did not answer him, and simply continued unbuttoning his waistcoat and loosening his cravat. "The girl is safe. The Zshathri has been neutralized." Phenmal's hands dropped and he smiled, nodding.

"Well done," he said.

"Your actions put her in greater danger. The Hevra took your intervention as incentive to assist the Soothsayer. The ancient idiots wanted to help him finish the story with a happy ending; to reunite their lost child with his beloved. Lives were lost," he said icily. Phenmal's smile faded and he bent his head down, his fingers rubbing along his forehead in frustration.

"It was a stupid idea. I thought they would stop him..."

"You were wrong. I cannot say you are to blame; you are not familiar with the ways of the ancient ones. They are mad and old and stupid from ten thousand years of idleness. They are mostly gone. There remains only a few now. Their power—the essence of the others resides in me and in my brothers; additional power that will probably cause the Keepers to attempt to impose even more controls upon us." The Chaiva nodded knowingly and sat down, his shoulders dropped in hopelessness.

"You killed the Hevra?"

"My brothers and I did not kill a single soul. We consumed them," he replied. "Our combined powers were able to overcome their resistance and to draw out their essence. No one of us could have done it alone. We broke one of our most stringent rules to save the girl; we gathered together in one place." Phenmal shook his head and sighed.

"You will likely see repercussions for uniting against the Hevra," Phenmal muttered, "for absorbing new power. I am sorry I put you all into that position with my recklessness," he said. "I merely wished to save the girl from more suffering." The Drathar visibly softened at the mention of Avria. Phenmal immediately knew she'd drawn his soul in and took ownership of it as aptly as the Drathar did to others with his gaze.

"In that, you were successful. She will no longer suffer at the hands of the Zsathri. He is nothing more than a drooling idiot now. As for my brothers and I, we will manage. She will leave the Abbey soon and she will need her family to make her whole again; her husband..."

"Yes, of course."

"I will go. I must go to the Citadel. Make an explanation. I have already been summoned."

"Drathar..."

"Yes, Chaiva..."

"Tell them your actions were inevitable and they were performed with the intent of saving the Ashru's daughter. They are protective of the Ashru. They see her as the salvation from a future they cannot see. Tinna will be happy now that Avria is safe. She can concentrate on the issues before her with peace of mind. Knowing this, they will surely understand your determination to keep Avria safe. I will send them a message of the like, with my gratitude for their allowing me to have your services." The two stared at one another for a long, pregnant moment, and then the Drathar nodded and disappeared. Phenmal's eyes widened at the sight of the lingering figures and letters left in the Drathar's wake. His skin rose into bumps as he realized what implications this seemingly benign little detail meant.

The knock on the door roused Taneth and he was irritated to be pulled from being notched against his wife underneath a pile of warm blankets. He padded barefoot to the door, his long loose-legged pants waving against his legs and he tugged open the door to the bedroom. He found Phenmal in a state of partial undress in front of him. He rubbed the goo from the corner of his eye with his finger and squinted at Phenmal's candlelight.

"It's my night, go away."

"I have news of Avria," Phenmal retorted, shouldering his way into the room. Taneth shut the door, his fingers rasping through his beard, hiding his emotional response as best he could, but his breath was short and shallow. Tinna was just lifting her head up and blinking the sleep out of her eyes.

"What's going on?" she asked groggily.

"Avria is safe. The Soothsayer has been neutralized. The Drathar just came to me to inform me of this," he said. Tinna sat up, her face a shock. She then dropped back onto the bed and she released a sigh as if she'd been holding it in for weeks, her arms splayed out at her sides.

"Good, Phenmal. I thank you. For everything."

"She's as much family to me as she is to you."

"You kept her from being hurt again, and I love you for that," she said, her voice heavy with emotion. He could barely see her past the glare of his candle, but he knew her eyes were glassy with tears. He wished he could just crawl in there with her. Tinna sighed again, and rolled onto her side. "Phen, call on Cennik first thing. Get her here; and can you let Offrin know?"

"Of course my sweet beloved soon to be wife," he said, smirking at Taneth. The scholar rolled his eyes and crawled into bed, pulling the heavy blankets over his legs. Tinna laughed quietly and turned onto her side with her back to them both.

"Your message is delivered, now go away," Taneth replied with a grin. The older man nodded and waved his hand dismissively at them both, exiting the room. What an arrangement he'd gotten himself into. He shook his head at the thought. But at least there was honesty now; and freedom to speak one's thoughts.

He wandered down the corridor and crossed the central part of the house. Offrin was not consigned to stay in the guest barracks with the rest of his men. He was family, and he stayed with Tinna. The Araki guard had arrived the day before and four of them sat at a table in the large vestibule playing cards to pass the night. They glanced up as Phenmal crossed the mezzanine and the stairway into the wing where Offrin slept. Only one face was a familiar one from Thamatoc. The rest were people from other clans. The soldiers were serious now. Two years since the One Day War, and the Araki had started forming a true army, and training them alike. This was no longer the group of volunteer horsemen that had ridden into battle with little experience and a sword in their hands; these were true, experienced warriors.

Offrin was still awake, a book clutched in his hand when he answered the door. The news of Avria's safety filled his face with relief and he bowed his head for a moment to contain himself. He lifted his hand and laid it flat over the Chaiva's heart. He thought his gratitude loudly and clearly to the older man. Without another word he withdrew and closed his door. Phenmal felt good. In spite of his error in judgment with the Hevra, he had been for a rare moment the instrument of good news for a change. He was regretful he was not the one next to Tinna this night, but he had at last that satisfaction to take to his sheets at least. He made his way back to his rooms, in the morning he would order a dragon to fetch the girl he thought of as his own little daughter.

Avria watched Wye pass soundlessly beneath her; she knew it was Wye because it was the only town on that coast that was in view of the Isle of Gales. It was strange to see an Araki town that was not in the style of the clan villages. This town was of individual houses made in the human style, the angled rooftops all square and white with snow. Somewhere, her brother was down there with his wife Skye, and they were happy and ignorant of what had transpired for the rest of the family. Her heart hurt she wanted to see Hanru so badly, but instead she was told she would be going to the palace at Miranne. Before her, the forests of the Araki people spread vast and endless. The dragon banked to the right, and cast itself north. The cold had abated a bit, but not enough to melt the dry snow. It was a beautiful, clear day without a cloud for miles. It was not so frigid that Avria could not occasionally peer out and watch the landscape fly by. It astounded her that what would take days of foot or horse travel took only hours for the dragons.

Avria, in spite of the weight of her sorrow, could not deny she was pleased to see Eretrix swooping elegantly into the bailey. She could scarce hide her relief at departing the old abbey. Her bag was made heavier by a stack of papers she had managed to copy for her father—for that she was grateful; but the heavy ceilings and hunkering weight of the building and its shrouded core had made her feel uneasy. She regretted that the Drathar was not there to say goodbye, but she appreciatively bid the sisters farewell and did not look back. Instead she huddled against the back of Eretrix's warm head and tried hard to act out in her head her imagined reunion with Offrin and not a single of her performances ended without her succumbing to the tears of humiliation and culpability. Her guilt was profound.

She had admitted to herself that she had wanted Eleran back even when she had committed herself to Offrin. She felt shame for wanting to kiss his blank face, but she knew the man who had harmed her was not the man she longed for still. But her guilt for loving Eleran still was strong. Now she carried a child that was not Offrin's. A child conceived of an unwilling union; a child with unknowable power. She was without idea of what to say to him. Even though she felt lighter in leaving the Abbey, her stomach started to feel heavier and heavier the closer she got to Miranne. She hoped Offrin was not there so she could have some more time to prepare.

Avria's hopes were in vain. Eretrix found footing in the empty square at Miranne only to be greeted most gleefully by Igro who happened to be out stretching his wings when they arrived. It was late evening and everyone was preparing for bed; the royal city was quiet and settled. The light cast from the windows from the town circling the square glowed like a wreath of candles. Miranne's ancient moat still glimmered against the curtain wall, buffering the main square and bailey from the sleepy town that hugged up against it. The main palace dominated the center of the back wall of the square across from the main gate, wings stretching out like arms to meet the buildings on each side that were built up against the curtain wall. Pillars of fragrant wood-smoke rose up in amorphous columns through which Eretrix slalomed as she made her way to the destination.

A dark shape had slipped up beside them soundlessly in the air just before they landed, and then snorted. Eretrix barely acknowledged him, probably aware of Igro for a while now. Eretrix was markedly smaller than Igro, but both were formidable sights. The larger dragon sped up and landed before Eretrix, and he waited with barely contained exuberance until Avria stepped down before trouncing Eretrix playfully and rolling with her across the square. They made little mewling growls, their delight in this encounter most evident. Avria took a moment to observe this rare sight, using it as a perfectly acceptable excuse to avoid finding the people she loved. She was filled with dread. The playful dragons offered a brief respite, until someone shouted from their window at the dragons when their tousle took itself too close to their walls. The dragons ceased and greeted one another affectionately. Igro nipped at Eretrix demonstratively as he led her to the byre that had been set aside for visiting dragons. Avria smiled wanly and turned to find herself face to face with Phenmal.

She immediately dropped her bag and jumped up to wrap her arms around his neck, her sobs instantly soaking him. He hugged her to him and rocked her back and forth. "I've never been so happy to see you," she said through her tears.

"I don't know how I should take that..." he said with a touch of humor. She let go of her tight embrace and let him straighten again. She laughed and then wiped her tears.

"You felt my arrival?"

"Of course. And the dragons' as well. Igro likes the little red one very much. It was his abject joy I felt first when he sensed her approach. Then I felt you. You have nothing to dread my dear, come..."

"Please Phen don't read my mind," she sighed.

"It's too late. I know everything. I guarantee you there will be nothing more than pure happiness at the sight of you. What other burdens and secrets you may carry can wait until morning if you prefer. Offrin's heart is so open..."

"He's here?" she asked, her voice rising in pitch.

"He is. Master Gavorre is here as well, but he is incredibly ill. I think you need to set aside your personal reservations, Avria and keep an open heart too. He is your husband and he loves you inside and out. His forgiveness isn't needed for he holds nothing against you. He wants only for you to look at him with love, Avria." She began to cry again, hating that she's done little else but weep of late. Phenmal simply put his hand on her cheek and said:

"In your case, Avria, all the tears are utterly forgivable and justified. Come inside now. Nobody knows you're home yet, I thought it would be best if you had a moment to collect yourself first, rather than beset a horde of worried family upon you the moment of your landing."

"That is thoughtful of you, Phenmal," she smiled through her tears. He stepped aside and gestured her forth with his arm. With a shaky sigh, she walked ahead of him. He caught up and took her bag from her. She looked up at him gratefully and slid her hand into his.

Avria was almost suffocating between her two parents. Tinna covered her face in kisses and hugged her hard again, with Taneth clinging to her all the while. They were both teary-eyed and overjoyed to see her; trying hard to somehow absorb her shame and her sorrow into themselves so they could see happiness in her face again. She scarce got the bleary-eyed baby into her arms when Offrin burst into the room and then froze as if afraid. She felt little Istvan's hands tugging at her frizzed curls but all she could do was stagger a bit into a turn to see Offrin's face. Her soft smile melted away into something else. Istvan was carefully pried from her arm, and she let her hands fall to her sides. Offrin approached, gazing up at her searchingly. When he came before her she fell to her knees and wrapped her arms around his chest, her head pressed against his shoulder. He bent down and kissed the top of her head.

"Offrin..." she sobbed, "forgive me!" she cried.

"There's nothing to forgive, Avria," he replied, which only made her weep harder. All she could think of was her hope that Eleran could be saved, that he could be the Eleran she once knew, the Eleran she loved, and all she could feel was the wash of guilt for holding on to that hope even with Offrin's heart in her hands. Now she would have to tell him that she carried a child by Eleran, a child created when her most horrid memory of her life was created. She could not stop the tears as Offrin wrapped her in love that she was sure she was unworthy of.

Even after she'd been scooped up by her family and guided to her room, even after her mother tenderly helped her into some night clothes, promising a hot bath in the morning, even after Offrin had lay beside her, never once touching her in any way other than pure affection, and gazing at her until he finally succumbed to sleep, Avria could not shake her sense of guilt. She did not want to tell Offrin about the baby. She did not want to tell him that even though Eleran had done what he had done, that when she saw him kneeling there in the abbey, that all she wanted to do was to kiss him and find a way to bring the man she loved back. She felt like an awful person. In the light of the slow-burning fire, she studied Offrin. She loved him, she knew that. If she didn't, she would not be so worried about hurting him.

She realized that her guilt would be something she'd have to learn to live with; because she needed him as much as he needed her. She would not tell him what she thought and felt after Eleran hurt her. She would only tell him what she could not avoid telling him. In the morning, she would sit down with Offrin and reveal the existence of the child. With a glance at Offrin's peaceful, handsome face, she turned over and finally fell asleep.

CHAPTER SEVENTEEN – PLAGUE

In the darkness of the room, the Drathar was invisible. His quiet form watched Avria in her fitful sleep. He ignored the person beside her who huddled close to himself, even in his slumber, careful not to trespass too closely to her body. The Drathar stooped by the bed so that his face was level with hers. His eyes studied her as she slept. Gently, he leaned forward and kissed her through his veil. Her eyes opened, and she neither withdrew nor objected. He felt her lips go soft, and press against his. She then slipped her hand out and lifted his veil so that their lips touched. The Drathar's soul melted as he kissed her. When her lips withdrew from his, he heard her whisper: "Thank you." He used his thumb to wipe away the tear shimmering at the corner of her eye, and he vanished leaving only his earthy scent behind.

* * * *

Avria awoke to the sound of shouting. It was muffled and the words were difficult to make out. Offrin was not present. Instead, a young girl entered and smiled shyly at Avria. She couldn't have been more than twelve years old. She was a willowy, reedy girl with long straight brown hair loose on her shoulders, and a small navy-colored gown with an apron bib pinned to the bodice, the wide front tied around her high waist.

She wordlessly gestured Avria through to the adjoining bathing chamber and discovered a hot bath awaiting her. She soaked for a while, still listening intently to the angered voices below her rooms. Offrin was there, as was Tinna and Taneth. Phenmal was probably there but he was not a shouting sort of person. He was probably hunched in a chair, looking on to the noise and chaos while occasionally calmly chiming in his opinion.

The girl, whose name was revealed to be Teya could barely find it within herself to speak, she was so shy. She wanted to simply help Avria and flee. Avria was put into her white dress again. Her mother had always frowned on having to wear the more formal northern garments. Northern women almost always wore long gowns, although the styles had changed significantly since Tinna's youth, and the gowns were infinitely more comfortable and free flowing and as far as Avria was concerned, much prettier. But her mother was a southern woman born from a matriarchal culture, and the woman there were infinitely more daring in their choice of clothing, including short little skirts and breeches like men wore. They believed in the power of the woman's body and flaunted it quite brazenly. Tinna however did not believe in flaunting; she believed in complete comfort. She did not want what she was wearing to come into her mind at all through the day, and so she wanted simple things. She was still resisting the new fashions she would invariably have to wear daily, remembering the common woolen gown she was wearing last night.

It didn't take Avria too long to get ready. She didn't bother much with her hair. It was still wet, so she combed it through, parted it down the center pulled it back tightly and rolled the rest up into a tight bun on the back of her head. No jewelry, no adornments, she got up and smiled at the girl and decided to investigate the sound of the discord below floors.

She slid quietly into the formal receiving room when she got downstairs and everyone fell silent when she came in, including a huge man of about thirty years who literally looked like a larger version of Offrin. He was shaved bald with a thin beard edging his jaws, his moustache trimmed close to his face. He had green eyes and an angry scowl which melted the moment he saw Avria, his mouth hanging partly open and his eyes locked on her pretty figure as she moved through the doorway and closed it behind her. Her spell was powerful and it brought the discussion to a halt. Offrin did not miss the man's reaction and he became visibly irritated by it, rising to greet to his wife.

"Avria, good morning," Tinna muttered in surprise.

"Hello mother. I wanted to know what the hullabaloo was about."

"This gentleman is sent by the King. He is the Sheerchai of the guard, and has been told to deliver us a message from his highness," she replied. "Come sit dear. Have you eaten anything?"

"No, not yet," she replied. She sat down next to her mother, and Offrin maneuvered himself into the space on her right. "It must be a long message, you've been shouting at one another for more than half an hour," Avria replied. The man snapped his mouth shut and looked a bit embarrassed for her observation.

"My pardons lady if our discussion has disturbed you," he said quickly, shaking his head.

"The gist of his message is that we are to ask the 'murdering scourge' dragons to leave the compound at once," Tinna said to Avria with an amused smirk.

"I don't understand; how is the King making such orders when you are to take his place?" Avria asked innocently.

"Our point exactly. It is the Keepers who choose the ruling family. They have appointed me to succeed this monarch. He is to step down and he is in no position to issue orders to me. I think it would solve many problems if the King would allow me to speak directly to him. Right now, I've been here almost three weeks and he hasn't said a word to me except through messengers. I will not accept his orders; nor will I accept his threat to send in dragon hunters if I do not comply. I have a contingent of men here from my army, from the Adrei army, and I have the Kanreth knights who are at my command. Also, I have mentioned this before, on the advice of the Keepers, I have the sum of the Araki mounted army standing by should I require their assistance, as well as a large fleet of the noble dragons and ground dragons. Do we truly want to end this in a scrap over something so arbitrary? Do we really want that? I ask this because if this is the case, the monarch will lose," Tinna said sharply, her laughter imbued with incredulity.

The messenger looked most frustrated, but he was now utterly distracted by the quiet presence of the girl. He sighed in frustration and shook his head. "I am here to deliver a message, I cannot provide you with any answers in the King's stead; I am neither his advisor nor his minister."

"Then as I said, your message to him in reply will be that I will only speak directly to him about these matters. The dragons are staying where they are, and I'm not going anywhere. I've said it before, and I say it now. I don't think I could be any clearer. Your lingering here and shouting at us is not going to change my answer. Unfortunately you will have to return to your monarch with an answer he will not be pleased with, but it is what it is, as they say. If your monarch has issue with our presence here, and those of our allies, he should take it up with the Keepers."

The man looked defeated. He was regretful he was the deliverer of this message, but he was still charged with service to the monarch. With a last lingering glance at Avria, who seemed distant and distracted, staring off into nowhere, he simply walked out without leave.

Tinna shot to her feet the moment the Captain left and made a sound of frustration. Avria was surprised to see her mother in a gown of the latest fashions. A gown of simple white gauzy muslin with mid-length straight sleeves, a ruffle on each cuff made of a fabric so sheer it was almost invisible, a V-neckline of heavily ruched panels coming together with an unpretentious wood-carved and gilded brooch underneath her bust-line. The skirts were gathered lightly up front as the ruched top ended and the gathers flared out, and in the back, a small train of heavily pleated fabric came up to a short, beautifully sewn bodice back. Her hair was up in a loose bun on the back of her head with a ribbon of gold wound around her head. It was a day gown with few embellishments. The white suited her, Avria thought. She sailed around the room to a sideboard and poured herself a stiff drink, downing it quite brusquely, a look of irritation plain on her face. It was from the several cases of fine apple brandy sent to her in congratulations for her arrival at Miranne; a gift from the Keepers. They had drunk most of one case already, it was delicious. It was the only thing the Keepers had sent at this point. Tinna had mentioned several times while imbibing this brandy that as good as it was, it was no substitute for the actual presence of someone from the Citadel.

"That damned fool of a King. What is his problem? Pride? I'll fix his pride..." she growled. "And where are those idiot Keepers? They pushed, pushed, pushed for me to come to Miranne, 'You must come at once! We need the Ashru there!' they said. Well I'm here! I came at the cost of everything dear to me! I'm here and I've been here and *nothing* has come of it! This is ridiculous!" she ranted, slamming down the glass goblet. "Phenmal I want answers! And I want to see that ____ King!" her expletive made all the brows in the room arch up in astonishment, even Phenmal's. He barked out in laughter and scooted forward to the edge of his tall wingback chair, where he propped his hands on his knees and looked at Tinna with amusement.

"Laugh all you want old fellow, I'm not staying here another day unless something is done. We make to leave in the morning. Pack up our things!"

"What?" Adracoor asked, finally chiming in. He also moved forward to the edge of his chair angled by Phenmal's side and put his mug of hot grog down on the table between them. "You can't just leave..."

"Why am I here? There's no reason at all for me to be here. The King refuses to step down; he refuses even to just speak to me; the Keepers promised he'd be taken care of, I haven't seen anything of these mysterious Keepers and yet I am to feel compelled to follow their orders. Meanwhile the longer they delay, the longer the King succeeds in spreading his lies and vitriol to the human settlements! I'm starting to lose my patience. I won't sit about anymore; I won't be threatened by a nineteen year old fool..."

"He's twenty four," Taneth corrected her.

"Whatever," Tinna waved her hand irritably at him.

There was a knock on the door and a face peered in, a worried face. It was Embri, an Adrei healer who'd come up at the behest of Tinna, who was worried about Gavorre. He seemed unable to pull himself out of his illness. The city Wiseman was too preoccupied with his work, and Taneth was about to leave again soon. So she called his local healer to assist. The healer had been there for several days, carried up on the back of Igro from Taruttee. He had been up to this point, isolated with Gavorre in his house where the old homeopath was still ailing quite terribly from his illness. She was surprised to see him.

"Your highness, I am sorry to interrupt." Tinna turned and her brows came together in puzzlement. "I'm quite concerned. I'd like to speak to you in private, if I may." Everyone including Avria vacated the room and filed out the door. Offrin tried to stay but the healer sent him packing as well, shutting the door behind him.

"I have a suspicion, your Highness, and it is a perhaps leaning more towards a certainty which I am not quite willing to accept myself," he said. He was a youngish fellow, perhaps within five years Offrin's age, about the same height as Offrin with long black hair tied back into a tail. He came to the height of Tinna's shoulder. She sat down to give them more of an equal footing. He seemed to appreciate it but did not move to sit down. He remained standing in the open area in front of the chairs, trying to formulate his words in an anxious way.

"Is Master Gavorre *that* ill, Embri?" The healer twisted his hands together and looked at her fearfully.

"He is showing some unusual symptoms, your highness," sweat began to bead on his brow. "I've never seen a case of it myself first-hand, but I come from a long line of healers who have passed this down from generation to generation. Ashru—" he sighed, his brow wrinkling, "I have reason to believe Master Gavorre has been infected with the wormskin plague."

* * * *

Tinna's stomach turned ice-cold and her skin grew waxen in a matter of seconds. She almost wanted to vomit. "*TANETH!*" she screamed at the top of her lungs, rising shakily to her feet. The man burst into the room wild-eyed and looked upon her with trepidation.

"What is it?"

"Taneth," she could barely speak. "Get Phen, get everyone... anyone who isn't Araki. Get them... Oh gods, get them out of here now... Fetch Cennik at once!" she lifted her violently trembling hand to the window. She turned to the Healer, eyes wide.

"I don't underst... what's wrong?" Taneth muttered in confusion.

"How many of the mounted contingent came into contact with him?" Tinna asked the healer.

"He only started to show the symptoms of contagion this morning. The pustules have started to open and he has the telltale serpentine rash forming all over his skin. Seeing that cemented my suspicions, and I came over right away. He's been infected long enough that others who would have been infected would show the early flu-like symptoms if they were infected. Those who came into contact with him before, I do not see symptoms yet. His isolation in the coach might have a bearing on that. Once he's gotten to this stage, it's likely it will spread and spread quickly. It has already probably spread. The servants of his residence, for instance, all came into contact with him at some point, assisting me with his care during his fevered stage. I would propose not moving him at this point. It's too risky. I have washed myself down with hevla simply to bring you this message in person, but I would hope that nobody with human blood would touch me, I am surely infected but not contagious as of yet, but you never know. You never know with Wormskin," he said through a tremulous voice. Tinna's hand clapped over her mouth and she bit back her sob.

"Gods," Taneth muttered, finally understanding. He turned "Wormskin! Get everyone out. Avria, you must leave at once! Phenmal, call the dragons!" he shouted, his voice edged in panic. "Tinna, you must go as well. Immediately!"

"I am gypsy, Taneth. Chai-Opse. Even part-bloods are safe. Avria and the Istvan are safe," she said stonily. "You are not. Phenmal is not. Offrin is not. The Kanreth, the humans in all those houses outside this square are not," she said in a hoarse, broken voice. "Hanru is safe, the Araki are safe. The Adrei are not. Cennik! He is human! How will we summon the dragons without him?" Taneth shook his head, for once, speechless and stunned.

Phenmal appeared in the doorway, the stricken look on his face was even more horrified than anything Tinna could muster, for he had come to an alarming epiphany as he heard all of their thoughts.

"*We* are not in danger," he said. He walked to the sideboard and picked up the bottle of brandy. "None of us who drank this are in danger. The Keepers said they'd take care of the human king and they said they'd prevent a war between the races for the throne. I think now I understand how." He looked gravely at Tinna, whose eyes widened in horror.

"Why would they do that?" she asked as the reality of this situation washed over her. "Why would they set loose a disease that could make the human race disappear? Why would they do that?" she started to hyperventilate into sobs. Tinna could feel the numbness spread over her body, starting at the pit of her stomach and growing outward until she felt like she was floating. She did not feel the muscles go weak in her knees; she did not feel them give way. Her body fell and she landed hard on her kneecaps, her skirts billowing out around her; her hands falling flat and open on the woven rug, pale against the dark tones. A tortured, horrid cry escaped her lips and she slumped forward, tears flowing hot and fast. She hunched in on herself and wept... crying out "oh by the gods, why?" again and again, her shoulders wracking with sobs. Everyone closed in around her, hands reaching out to grasp her weakened arms. They lifted her into a chair where she was given water to drink. She sipped, her hands barely able to hold the glass. The idea of the devastation this disease would cause filled her with dread and a ghastly sense of responsibility. She gathered her wits as best she could.

"Get the Adrei and Kanreth out of here. Send them south to the forests. Evacuate the town around here as well; send them, oh gods, if they're carrying it they'll just bring it with them. Do we have any of that brandy left? Give it to the Adrei and the Kanreth. I don't know if we should move the humans out of the town, we risk carrying the disease outwards..." she rambled. "You must send out a directive to the Araki—use the last relay to Klatna to the delegate office. Close down all relays from human settlements into the forests. You must direct all Adrei communities to shut down and be prepared to shoot an arrow into anyone who comes close to their communities from outside. Shut down the trade roads, shut down everything that moves people around. For at least four months." Tinna took another drink. Adracoor immediately rocketed out of the room with Rhoa at his heels. Rhoa had only made a late appearance to be confronted with this horror. Phenmal, Taneth, Avria remained while the Healer exited quietly and gingerly.

"The Thran! Warn the Thran! And the Gheraine... Oh Gods..." she fell into a whisper and sobbed again, grabbing Phenmal's hand.

"Can we not end it here by... I'd hate to say this... but if we disposed of the source..." Taneth spoke these words as if he couldn't believe they were coming out of his mouth.

"I highly doubt he's the only source, Taneth. How did Master Gavorre become infected? When?" Phenmal barked.

"He's been ill since he left Thamatoc, correct?"

"No, since we passed through Lemoram. He started getting sick in earnest the morning after we departed. He dined with a group of wisemen that night, and came home feeling quite unwell," Offrin said. "I wonder if all the wisemen are ill." Phenmal nodded knowingly and crossed his arms.

"Wisemen are largely from human settlements. They will carry it wherever they go. And Lemoram, with its host of visitors and students..." his voice trailed off.

"It's only a matter of time" Tinna replied, her voice breaking. She shook her head in disbelief.

"Four weeks for the disease to spread. That's what it took last time there was an outbreak," Taneth said matter-of-factly. "Four short weeks it cast itself across the continent and the isles and obliterated almost everyone that had human blood. The disease takes a while to fester, but in two months, this world could be nearly bereft of humankind."

"Indeed. It was the only solution," a new voice added.

An old man appeared at the door of the receiving room. Phenmal recognized him at once as Evankor, one of the younger of the Keepers. He was lowest ranked among them and therefore, subject to errands for the others. He stood in the doorway, his hands clasped, his clothing a bit dated against the newer fashions, his velvets looking garish, the gold-embroidered designs too fussy. He wore black slippers; dark green stockings, burgundy knee breeches that were loose around his legs, a gold waistcoat with elegant leafy whorls embroidered in ivory, and a burgundy frock coat of the old style. His white hair was carefully coifed into forward-sweeping whorls in a vain attempt to look stylish. He had dark brown eyes and a mouthful of perfect white teeth. His papery, wrinkled skin was marked with age spots. His eyes wandered about taking in everyone in the room, stopping abruptly again on Avria. They widened significantly and then they traveled down to her tummy where her hand unconsciously lay.

"Goodness gracious," he said absentmindedly. Avria's hand pressed onto her belly and she allowed herself to fade back behind the side of Phenmal's shoulder. The strange old man shook his head and tore his gaze from Avria, letting them fall on the horrified face of the new Queen.

"In three weeks we will all attend to your coronation, my dear. There was no avoiding this, we could not really foresee if the humans would revolt or not, but it seems there has been some success on the part of the young monarch in instilling a sense of righteous entitlement to power in his people. We were seeing rumblings of war and we did not want that for the Araki; to be humankind's death knell. It would be easier if we reduced their numbers one last time," he said openly.

Tinna thought about what she'd done to keep their secret all those years ago, and again she could feel her gorge rising. She sat back, glaring hatred at the old man.

"It will solve your problem with the King as well. It won't be long before they all start to show the symptoms. The servants that attended to the Adrei magician have done their job. No need to move anyone about, except of course to protect the Adrei," he added swiftly when peering at Offrin. "All known Adrei wells have been generously dosed with heeda, so your people will be safe. You can thank your loyalty to the Ashru for your people being spared, sir. We know how any of the Adrei being harmed would wound our beloved Queen." He turned his face back to Tinna. "Your knights can be easily protected with the remains of our gift of Heeda-laced Apple Brandy. Clever wasn't it?" He seemed genuinely proud of this exclamation, expecting nods and smiles in return. He looked disappointed when Tinna's eyes narrowed into two furious slits, and she gripped the arms of her chair, white-knuckled.

"What of the Thran? The Gheraine? They have no involvement with our throne!"

"They are human. They will be affected. It is inevitable. But like it has in prior outbreaks, they will be somewhat protected by the distance from Oromoii, with fewer losses, for certain. And those who are here, some will survive; the strong ones."

"And what dare I ask does the Trinity think of all this?" she asked acidly. They governed the Keepers—one representative from each of the three predominant races, "surely they could not sanction this mass murder yet again?"

"The Trinity no longer has a say on this matter, Ashru," the old man replied. "It became clear that there was an imbalance there many years ago," he said. "Our organization itself is a human effort with human leaders, and *we* understand this. We did not understand our priorities then; our responsibility to this world and the races of people that reside in it, but we *do* now.

"Thousands of years; humanity has not learnt its lesson. Not even recently, when they were dealt the most humiliating blow by the dragons, they still arrogantly believe themselves above other races. Perhaps the dragons never should have been stopped," he sighed lamentingly, "perhaps we would have been best served to let them finish the job," he said. Tinna's eyes widened in shock.

"Instead we saved what we could, and let the human leadership continue on. And in part we have had nothing but poverty and instability until the One Day War. We allowed our sacred lands to become vulnerable and weak—nearly invaded by the Thran. Now that the true peoples are given their chance to right the wrongs of humanity once and for all, the humans, even in their reduced numbers, are fighting it. Change must occur. It is inevitable. Our methods are drastic, but change *will* occur." He shook his head regretfully,

"Ashru, you must not be angry, this is not your doing. We are simply acting on what we must, to insure the survival of all races," he assured Tinna.

"You have made the people my responsibility, Keeper, now you tell me I should not feel responsible for what you are doing to them?" Tinna barked.

"Fear not, humankind will not be destroyed, Ashru. They will be humbled—which they should be. The plague has been a means of control for our troublesome race some time. It has worked in the past to make things right. The Chai-Opse have resurged and grown quietly and efficiently. Now it's their turn. It will give the world time to heal from the effects of humankind. You will understand in time. War would not be any solution, only a lot more work and pain and suffering to achieve what will ultimately be the same end. We are saving your armies the trouble." The entire complement of the room gazed at this old man with unadulterated hate and disbelief, faces aghast, unspoken rage hanging on their lips. He left them that way. He turned and exited.

"Wait just a moment!" Taneth shouted. He ran after him but when he reached the corridor, it was empty.

He returned to the room and looked at Tinna disbelievingly.

Tinna gazed at him and then at Phenmal, their eyes seemingly speaking a thousand words.

MIRANDA MAYER

Chapter Eighteen – The Fading King

Avria thought she was seeing things. It began shortly after the visit from the Keeper, and she was starting to think she was going a bit mad. But it was Phenmal who told her quietly that she was not suffering from delusions. The things she thought she saw did indeed exist. They were hovering. Shadows and watchers. At first she thought she was losing touch with reality. A slip of movement here, a flit of something there, always just out of the corner of her eye. She was stricken when she joined her family for a somber breakfast.

Nobody really knew what to do. They could not travel, lest they carry something out of Miranne, they could not think of anything else to do or anyplace else to go. So they stayed at Miranne until someone came up with a plan. It had been a week since the Keeper had come. Their household went oddly on as normal. They rose, they talked, they pondered, they slept, and they ate. It was a strange state of limbo as they waited for the next thing to happen; yet none of them knew what they were expecting.

But Avria, since the Keeper's visit, existed in a bizarre apprehensive state. Her instincts were prickling her, and these little nothings she saw were weighing her down. She stepped into the dining room, and Phenmal caught her darting gaze. Phenmal's searching eyes saw what she had seen, and he gave her a reassuring look and patted the seat beside him. Tinna, Taneth, Phenmal, Offrin, Avria, Rhoa, Adracoor and Istvan were seated around a large oval table, the baby on his mother's lap. Even Cennik was present— having partaken most generously of the brandy, he was in no danger. He was however, extremely morose, and he had come to join the others in this strange time. The center of the table was heaped with a variety of foods none of which anyone had touched yet. Everyone appeared to be slowed and made still by the idea of what was to come. They were horrified to be expected to go on with things like breakfast and dinner when the world around them was going to crumble at any given moment.

What was worse this particular day, was that Master Gavorre had succumbed to the disease only hours before. It was the news that woke the household. They rose all as a family and sat at the table staring at one another. Avria was beside herself. She loved the apothecary so much. She'd only just manage to stop crying, feeling hollow and drained, she sat, pale and wan, staring at nothing.

"I'm with child," Avria blurted. Even Phenmal looked startled by her sudden declaration, in spite of his knowledge of it. Offrin's face turned even paler but he did not say a word. Avria's eyes lowered to her empty plate and she sighed. "It isn't your child, Offrin." She looked at him and he was visibly having trouble containing his emotions. She was impassive. She was resigned to whatever the outcome. He could be angry at so many things, the injustice of having to raise a rapist's child, the fact that Avria chose to tell everyone at once rather than him in private; but he did not speak until he controlled all his anger. A part of him understood. Avria then reached for a bowl containing a clutch of shelled boiled eggs and spooned one onto her plate and watched it roll to the raised lip of the plate.

"It is not of your doing who fathered the child in your belly, Avria. It will have a loving home regardless," he choked out. Avria's waxen face gazed at her egg and her eyes misted up. Phenmal offered her a reassuring pat on the hand. Someone started eating; the sound of the silverware seemed to prompt the others. They ate in strained silence, the clatter of the forks and porcelain seemed almost deafening. Phenmal glanced at Avria and then and leaned in to her ear.

"You are not seeing things, Avria. I think they're watching you. Well, more accurately, watching your baby," he whispered. Her eyes met his and she furrowed her brow, but she did not speak.

"The Keepers have always been the controlling factor for almost every type of power-bearing creature in this world. Some do not fall under their dominion, the Zshathri Druidic Soothsayers, for instance; the Hevnelor, the Diviners and Thranic Sorceresses—but most do."

"What do you think they want by watching me?"

"There's no mistaking what's inside you, Avria. Anyone with even the smallest power can feel it. The most powerful creatures that I know of are the Drathar, and they require tremendous control to keep them in check. Without the harnessing spells, there's no telling what the Drathar are capable of; what anyone with powers is capable of. And that little baby already radiates something unequal to anything I've ever felt. The Keeper that came, he saw it at once. They will seek to harness your child, Avria. They will seek to control it and cover it with spells, as they do all of us." Avria remembered the Drathar for a moment, how he'd mentioned something about being hobbled. She hadn't understood what he meant until now.

"Each creature under the eye of the Keepers has figures etched into their skin. The more letters, the more power is required to contain them. I am certain that the Drathar must be covered—" he mused. He dwelled momentarily on the memory of the letters that had fallen away when the Drathar had left the room. Avria nodded. She knew the Drathar were indeed covered in letters.

"What would they do?" she asked, her hand falling protectively to her belly.

"They would take the child, Avria," he replied. "And hobble it with spells. They would raise it to serve them." Her dry, red eyes moistened instantly, and her lips tightened. Phenmal put his napkin on his lap and looked up.

"Tinna, I must say this to you. The Keepers; they are a danger to the child, to Avria," Phenmal blurted out. Tinna's eyes rose up and she looked at him in puzzlement. "The Keepers. They are a danger to this child. The child has powers; anyone with the ability can sense it. They will want to take it, as they do any child with powers, and use the child to their own ends, as they do me, and the others."

Tinna gazed at him blankly for a second and then put her tea-cup down. "Gods, I just want to go home to Thamatoc," she sighed, rubbing her temples for a moment.

She looked at Taneth, and then Phenmal, then her eyes swept over the rest, falling with an expression of tired, loving resignation on her daughter.

The woman then found her reserve of strength; she found it in her abject fury that was boiling just under her skin. She found it in her heart, and with it, she sat up straight and looked each and every person in the eye.

"I think we can all agree—the time of the Keepers must come to an end," she said with finality. She picked up her napkin from her lap and put it on her plate.

Tinna got up and walked out without uttering another word. It took only a moment for her to find her cloak and to don it, moving with quiet purpose to the door and exited the house.

There was less resistance to her arrival than she had imagined. The people of the palace were worried, some were already ill; some had simply abandoned Miranne at the first sign of the plague. Outside of the isolation of her household, Tinna was only marginally aware of the disease spreading around the palace grounds and beyond. She didn't want to know.

Tinna had walked into the great room to find nobody there. She turned into the next room, and the next, finding only one of the few remaining members of the court standing by a window in a great library, gazing out numbly. It was a great lady of one kind or other, a shawl tightly wrapped around her narrow shoulders, the folds of her gown tumbling out from its edge into a beautiful, rumpled silken train on the floor. She scarcely moved when Tinna approached.

"I am seeking the monarch," she said in her velvety voice. The woman's pale face turned to peer at Tinna, her drawn, wan features seemed sunken and hollow. She was sick, there was no doubt of it, her skin was waxen, her complexion pale and her eyes two dark hollows from which her golden brown eyes gazed out at Tinna. She was still dressed impeccably, as was expected of all of the royal court. Her hair, styled in a rather sizable heap on top of her head was all elegance with decorative ribbons and a several strings of glassy blue beads. She looked Tinna up and down and then sighed.

"He has fallen ill. As have many of us," she replied, "while your lot thrives in health and blush, how convenient," she said bitterly.

"This was not *our* doing," Tinna said uselessly. The woman turned back to the window where she watched some ravens pecking at a smattering of dried bread someone had thrown into the garden courtyard beyond.

"I don't care," she replied.

"I must speak to the King. Do you know where he keeps?" The woman turned to look at Tinna again, this time with accusation.

"They say you possess a cure to the plague. Is this so?"

"The Keepers gave us such a cure. We were unaware of it. But it can only prevent the wormskin, it cannot cure it. It is too late for everyone here who hasn't had this elixir." The woman's brow furrowed and her sunken eyes grew glossy with tears. She studied Tinna for a long silent moment.

"I never objected to the idea of your assumption of the throne. I welcomed it. I thought Oromoii could use some new blood, someone forward-thinking, someone strong and unselfish; someone who knew adversity and who knew pain as their subjects do," she hissed. "I looked forward to the day when the monarch would step down and you would come to live here. I looked forward to standing in your court," she muttered with anger, as if she regretted these feelings. "Come along, I'll take you to him." She turned and moved in a rustle of silk. Tinna followed, her lips tight, her brow furrowed.

The King was sitting in a chair, looking a lot more than his mere twenty-four years. He hadn't gotten quite ill enough to show the pustules or the rash, but he was well on his way. He sat in his chair by the window. Outside, it had started to snow again, and the sky was boulder-grey. His skin was almost the same value. The fire roared in the fireplace. The young man was wrapped up on two blankets, and his hand was clutching a thick clay goblet of something steaming. A spare girl was serving him, she did not appear ill. He turned to look at Tinna, and then his eyes seemed to smile at the realization of who she was. He ordered everyone out, and then pointed to a chair across from his. While she sat down, four people exited, the door clicking loudly as the latch fell into place.

He was a good-looking young man; younger than Hanru. His face was a bit long, but the jaw was strong and angled. His eyes had a liveliness to them. She knew he was charismatic and engaging to people. He was deathly ill. His face had a strange grayish tint to it, and his hands trembled. But his humor seemed intact, at least at the sight of the rival he'd worked so hard to discredit and avoid; even kill. "I suppose the people who were meant to keep you out are gone now?" he said with sardonic laughter. Tinna shrugged her brows and shucked the cloak off of her shoulders. He looked at her elegant garments and scoffed at her.

"You have thrown off the common linens and cheap wools I see..."

"Nothing less can be expected from any self-respecting usurper," Tinna replied dryly. He smirked and sipped his hot drink, grimacing at its taste.

"As if this concoction is going to stop the wormskin plague," he declared, putting it down on the small table by the arm of his chair. "If I'm going to die, I want to die drinking what I want to drink." Tinna nodded and looked out where he was looking, at the movement of a dragon crossing the great bailey, and slinking into one of the large livery barns.

"I hate them," he said. "I was small, barely old enough to hold onto memories, but I remember them. I remember the fear and the horror as news of each new city destroyed by dragon-fire was delivered to my father. I watched a vital man fade and shrivel at the terror of it all. I lost so many relatives—hundreds of people, killed. For no good reason. Why did they do it? Why did they render my race into the shambles it is today?" He paused. "But you know. I've been told that you know why."

"They were only instruments," Tinna replied, "nothing more. I used to think the culprit behind all that death was one man, but I suspect now, it was no mistake that he came upon the information that he had; it was no mistake that he had found enough to raise the ire of the Trinity and the Keepers, no mistake that the dragons were set to do what they had done."

"Yes, I was told of your great feat by the damnable Driva that have done nothing but haunt my father and I since I was but a small child. The great AiTinna, the Thran Gypsy who stopped the destruction of humankind. Nobody told us exactly how, or why, but we were told that we should be grateful to you. Here she is in the flesh, the magnificent savior, come to laugh at me," he said bitterly. "And worse, you bring dragons with you, to add insult to injury." Tinna shook her head and leaned forward, resting her elbows on her knees.

"The Keepers set this plague upon you. The Keepers decided that Humanity needed further humbling, that you must go in this fashion."

"I never would have stepped down. They *would* have to kill me."

"They have," Tinna replied. He shifted in his chair, and for a moment, he looked as if he was going to fall asleep, his lids drooped and he wavered. With the plague, there were no coughs, no sniffles, there was only the fever that burned from within, that made you sweat, but took your warmth. He was shining in beads of perspiration, but he clutched his blankets tightly around him. He came-to again, and then looked at Tinna, a strange smile on his face.

"Now, you serve them?"

"I do not. And I mean to never serve them."

"I do not like you, Gypsy. The idea of such impure blood taking the throne after a legacy of a thousand years of my family's royal blood makes me ill. But I admit that if anyone belongs here after me, it's you; especially now, with this plague destroying so many lives. I don't like to think well of you at all, but I cannot believe you would just walk away. Not you."

"I don't mean to abandon Oromoii, boy, I mean to save it."

"It's too late for that," he laughed. "Unless you mean the Oromoii without the human race living in it."

"It might be too late his time. But it can be the last time. I mean to stop this sort of thing from ever happening again." The King's pallid face turned to her; his eyes were bloodshot, watery and bleary. How pathetic he looked. He studied her.

"Why are you here?"

"I need something from you. Something I hope you are willing to give," she said; "Because if I do this, I will need your legacy to assure the remaining people that this was the right thing to do. The world has never known a time without them. The unknown may cause panic. The disease alone is something to fear, but if I am to step up after you, I will need their trust and your blessing. If they believe I've done something to harm them, they will not trust me."

"You mean to destroy the Keepers," he concluded with a bubbling, weak laugh. She stared at him in all seriousness. He then grinned and waved his hand;

"As if I could ever object! Look what they've done to me! To my promised one, to the children of my mistresses—they've killed us all!"

"I need you to order it. I need you to ask me to do it—to tell me that I must do it to avenge the people of this deed. I need you to declare that it was the Keepers that set this disease upon them; they must be exposed by the most credible means possible, and that is you! I need you give me freedom to act. I need you to will it as King." His brow furrowed and he struggled to sit up. Tinna stood and offered her hands. He looked up at her and nodded once. She slid her hands under his arms, and hoisted him up in his chair. He nodded subtly in thanks, and reached for the bell on his table. He rang it loudly.

"I'm dying. We all are. If I am to be replaced by anyone, it will *have* to be you," he said. "But you must vow to me you will do as you promised."

"If you know anything about me, young man, you would know that I do not break promises," Tinna hissed. His eyes burned into hers, testing her determination, trying to detect a wavering of her resolve. The lady who'd led Tinna to the King appeared.

"Fetch Rallnett if he can still move about," he said without breaking his gaze with Tinna, "Tell him I need him to scribe a royal order at once."

CHAPTER NINETEEN – TO END IT ALL

The family that surrounded Tinna sat in glum silence. Tinna stood in the center of the circle where they had all faced their chairs. The only sound for a few moments was that of the freshly applied wood popping loudly in the fireplace.

"I still don't understand why it has to be just you," Taneth mumbled, rubbing his temples. Phenmal shifted in his chair and frowned.

"I object to it as much as you, but not everyone can enter the citadel. We do not have time to fly an entire army there, nor can we send common assassins. Me, they know, and they will know my intentions at once. But Tinna, she is privileged. She is named and Keeper-appointed royalty now. She is not marked by the Keepers as I or the other magic bearers are. She will be able to pass through the gates with no resistance."

"What of the dragons? Can they not simply burn them where they sit?" Avria asked. Phenmal shook his head.

"As long as the old men are living inside the citadel, it cannot be destroyed."

"And nobody else can enter the gates besides Tinna?" Taneth reiterated.

"Maybe Avria. Or you Taneth. You are not King, but you are of the royal line now," Phenmal explained.

"I serve no purpose, I am no assassin," Taneth muttered.

"But I am," Tinna interrupted. "I am a Kanindra, after all. I cannot deny my heritage, my training. I am the best-qualified to do this task, in addition to being one of the only ones who can enter the citadel."

"How convenient," Offrin said sarcastically. Avria snorted through her nose, her brow furrowed in thought. Tinna shifted her weight onto her other foot, and clasped her elbows. The dogs seemed to sense her unease and they lifted their heads and made high-pitched whines from before the fire, both looking at her with their shining eyes. She looked back at them, her gaze softening, and a strange, whimsical look crossing her brow.

"When I get back, I want new puppies," Tinna declared. "Then I want to visit Hanru at Wye. And I want to spend the rest of the winter at Thamatoc, with occasional trips to Klatna. I will come here for the summer only. It is too high, too bleak, and too empty here. If I am to do this, to finally become what's been expected of me by the Keepers, I want these things.

"With the Keepers gone, nobody will argue with you."

"Why bother being Queen if you are getting rid of the Keepers?" Avria asked.

"Because the people look to me as Queen now, Avria. I am Ashru. I was chosen as Ashru by the Araki people. And what remains of humanity after the blight has passed will need someone to watch over them. I'm stuck with this role, with or without the Keepers. Only without them, I can rule by my own ethics, and not be guided by old men with none of their own." There was a long span of quiet.

"I suppose I should get Cennik then. He will need to call Ledroran," Phenmal blurted, standing. "I ask, as your husband to be, please don't get yourself killed. They are powerful men. I'm not even sure if they can be killed."

"There's one thing I'm good at, dearest Phenmal, and that is killing. I'll find a way. Sometimes the simplest means are the best ones. I will need a good, sharp sword."

"I can help you with that, Tinna," Offrin piped in. "The Kanreth are here and they are our friends. And they are equipped with some of the most deadly swords in the world." He said this grimly and stood. When he did, so did everyone else. Tinna watched them all leave and then followed. She donned her cloak and left the house, crossing to the great palace. She would sit with the King for a while, and keep him company.

Ledroran was quiet. Tinna, for a while, was worried for his silence. He mulled her words carefully. Cennik was not entirely cooperative when he called him, his messages to the dragons were tainted with his resentment for the loss of his people, and it was difficult to work around that—the dragons arrived reflecting his pain. They felt guilty, perhaps. Tinna feared she would lose one of the dearest friends of her life when the great dragon arrived. Bundled up in a woolen cloak, standing alone in the courtyard in front of the massive dragon, she waited. He seemed sullen and confused as he looked upon her.

THE TRINITY IS DEAD, he finally said. EJENAT HAS BEEN KILLED, OUR HIGHEST LEADER. THE LEADERSHIP OF DRAGON KIND NOW FALLS UPON ME. I AM NOT SURE IF I WANT THAT RESPONSIBILITY, the dragon uttered.

"I can relate to that feeling, my friend," Tinna replied. "But the truth is, you have been their leader all these years already, Ledroran. The dragon sitting for the Trinity did little else but focus on the Trinity. The others have always looked to you." The dragon dropped his head, his one eye studying Tinna intently.

NOW YOU WANT ME TO TAKE YOU TO THE CITADEL, FOR REASONS NOT GIVEN TO ME IN YOUR MESSAGE, BUT I CAN EASILY DEDUCE.

"They killed the Trinity," she replied matter-of-factly. "They have used you all extremely ill. They have all but erased the human race."

THERE ARE SOME WHO MIGHT THINK THAT WAS A HEROIC ACT.

"And there are some who believe that it should not be up to the Keepers to decide what should be the fate of an entire race." His great eye studied her some more, his hot breath steamed from his nostrils, and he tilted his head to look at her with his other eye. She loved the sight of him. She could not contain her adoration for this dragon, this creature that had carried her all these years. She reached out and put her hands on his muzzle.

"Ledroran, I have asked much of you. I have asked a great deal, I know. I understand this is against everything you are; the Keepers have always protected you. You have carried out their will without question because you, like everyone else, have always believed they had the welfare of all at heart. But with the murder of the Trinity's three leaders; this should show you that we have all been fooled— we've been deceived into believing that the Keepers were acting in our best interest. They have lost sight of everything. I need your help, Ledroran. After all this, we will need each other more than ever."

The dragon sighed wearily and groaned.

YOU DID NOT HAVE TO CONVINCE ME OF ANYTHING TINNA. I KNOW YOUR HONOR BETTER THAN ANYONE. I KNOW WHAT WE MUST DO. I AM MERELY CONCERNED. I AM FEARFUL OF WHAT IS TO COME. A WORLD WITHOUT THE KEEPERS IS A DANGEROUS WORLD, TINNA. EVERYTHING WILL CHANGE. OUR PEOPLES WILL REQUIRE A GREAT DEAL FROM US IN LEADERSHIP, AND YOUR RELUCTANCE TO REIGN, MY DEAREST TINNA, WORRIES ME, BECAUSE AFTER THIS, YOU WILL HAVE TO STAND IN THE STEAD OF THE KING, AND YOU WILL HAVE TO CONVINCE EVERYONE THAT THIS WAS WHAT YOU WANTED. YOU MUST COMMIT YOURSELF, AS I MUST COMMIT MYSELF, TO WHAT WILL COME OF ALL THIS.

She nodded. "I have resigned myself to what I am to do, Ledroran. I promised myself no more blood, but I am now left without a choice. If any of humanity is to survive, I am the only one left who will protect them from whatever is to come."

THEN TO THE CITADEL WE WILL GO. MANY OF MY BROTHERS AND SISTERS ARE TO JOIN US. THE CITADEL, ONCE YOU'VE DONE YOUR WORK, MUST BE DESTROYED. ITS SECRETS ARE TOO DANGEROUS TO BE PERMITTED TO FALL INTO UNWORTHY HANDS, ESPECIALLY WHEN ALL OF THE BEARERS OF THIS WORLD WILL BE AMOK.

Tinna didn't quite understand everything he spoke of, but she wasn't in disagreement. The Citadel would have to fall.

"Then we leave at first light," she declared. The dragon nodded and lumbered towards the byre. He was so large, he would touch the rafters and displace the other dragons in residence. She would have to order more space be provided for her dragon allies. She watched his huge form recede in the late afternoon light, and then turned back towards the residence.

Avria awaited her when she stepped through the door.

"Mother," the girl uttered quietly. "I am going to go with you."

"Absolutely not," Tinna snapped, gliding past her daughter. Avria grasped her mother's arm tightly and spun her to face her again. It surprised her to see her daughter do something so rash and forceful.

"They seek to harm my baby. I must go to ensure this threat is eliminated."

"I can handle it myself," her mother barked. Avria's grip tightened.

"NO!" she shouted. "I will go! I will go with you and stand beside you for once! I will go with you and I will share in the blood because everything should not only be your burden to bear! I will go!" she bristled, her voice raw and broken. She then calmed a bit, and her face softened. "Let me go, mother. My eyes are wide open now. I can be of help."

"I could not bear seeing you harmed, Avria. I could not bear that sort of grief."

"Then I will not be harmed," she replied. "Let me help," she said. "Let me take some of this onto me. Let me come so you are not alone in this." Tinna pursed her lips and nodded once before abandoning her daughter in the doorway. She did not want Avria to see her tears.

The sky was as blue as freshly bloomed forget-me-nots, and it was filled with dragons. Ledroran led the fleet of beasts westward, his passengers huddled behind his shield, mother and daughter. They held hands. Tinna's grasp was strong and steady, with no softness or warmth in it.

"It was important to have the approval of the monarch to do this," Tinna said out of nowhere. Avria looked at her questioningly, but did not have a reply. The girl, in breeches and the rust-colored sweater they both adored peeking out from her layers, gazed at her mother with a grim, straight line across the brow and a serious cast to her lips. On her belt she wore two basket-hilt daggers. These were the weapons she'd been trained to use for all these years. She'd never actually used them against someone else, but she knew she could manage well enough with them. She had no idea what her role was to be in all this, she didn't even think they'd survive, but she'd watched her mother take the brunt of everything these past years, and somehow, even with Taneth beside her, she was always alone with it. She wanted to take some of the burden from her mother's shoulders. She hoped she would not simply become yet one more burden for her to bear.

Tinna had a two-hand sword of mirror-smooth metal slung across her back. Her cloak and hood fluttered in the wind. She looked vibrant and young, but the look on her face was something Avria had only seen once before. Her expression was cool and distant. It was resolved and determined. It was cold. Avria had only experienced this once, at the conclusion of the war, when her own grandmother had challenged Tinna. She'd never seen her mother kill before that. She had no notion that her mother was capable of such darkness until then. Seeing it again chilled her.

Avria reached inside herself to see if she too could find that same stoic resignation, that single-minded purpose that would carry her through this. What she touched was the growing life inside her. It filled her with fire, thinking of the child being harmed. So tiny, so new, and it already had such great power. It was innocent. It was a part of Eleran that she could hold onto. It occurred to Avria why her mother was the way she was—so protective and determined. She knew her mother had always acted to shield Avria from the things that had hardened Tinna; the things that had taken some of her humanity away; to protect her from gaining the capacity to turn off her compassion and her kindness. She did not want Avria to become her. Avria finally understood. She wanted the same for her child. She wanted this child to live free of the pain she'd suffered, the loss, the fear wrought by people who were supposed to love her. She knew now. She finally truly understood. She wanted this child, who would be so powerful, to understand innocence and goodness, and to never be forced to do the things she was about to do. She wanted to protect it from the darkness as Tinna had hoped to do with Avria. She squeezed her mother's hand, and looked at her squarely.

"I love you, mother." Tinna's coldness flickered, and for a fleeting moment, she was warm again. She smiled wanly in response and squeezed Avria's hand in return.

"My treasure," she said, barely audible over the wind. And then she looked forward and her eyes grew icy again, and her brow dropped. Tinna was preparing herself for the kill.

There was no resistance because nobody had expected them. It surprised Tinna that they were not sensed as Phenmal said they would be. There wasn't even anyone to welcome them. Ledroran dropped the women off at the gates of the lone citadel, which was quietly nestled on snowy hilltop, surrounded by osteal, ice-covered oaks. The dragons retreated for now, allowing Tinna to do her work. They would wait until Tinna and Avria left the citadel. Eretrix was there to watch for them. Tinna instructed Ledroran to wait until the sun was about to set, and if they had not appeared, that they should do their work whether or not Tinna or Avria had escaped the citadel. Ledroran grimly nodded, saying in a low, gravely dragon-whisper, that this reminded him of a time long ago, when they had done something much like this. Tinna smiled and snorted through her nose and turned towards the gate, Avria at her heels.

They crossed under the gatehouse and across an old-fashioned courtyard. There were no guards. Tinna had no idea where they were going; she merely took the paths that seemed most prominent, where the stone flags were most-worn and shining from use, and they led them both directly to the doors of the main hall, where only a polearm stood on its butt, leaning on the wall by the door. The door was cracked open, and the mother and daughter crept up to it, Avria's hand gently pressing the door open, which widened silently.

Inside there was the collection of little old men that Phenmal described. Every last one of them was present. They were all huddled around a fire in their chairs, their backs to the women. They were quietly sipping some tea, eyes focused on the flames. One of the old men froze, his shoulders tightening, and then the rest did the same in turn, each twisting around. Their eyes went straight to Avria's tummy—every last one of them. It was bizarre. Only after they all had a good look at Avria's belly, then they looked up at the mother, and then finally, Tinna. There was a moment that they seemed to parse what they saw, when one of them finally said something:

"We did not sense you—how strange," someone muttered.

"You are an unexpected surprise ladies, unexpected indeed," one of the eldest of the old men said. "Where is Phenmal? He is not here."

"He has other responsibilities," Tinna replied. The old men began to stand in turn, some gazed upwards to the ceiling. Tinna's eyes followed, and to her astonishment, there she was, depicted in a somewhat stylized figure doing what appeared to be cutting through a tangle of vines with the sword she now had strapped over her back in its scabbard. Behind her effigy, images of her past two decades were displayed, the tail end of the events of the dragon-burnings among the earliest images; the figures moving the long band along the edge of the coffin-ceiling with languid grace. Tinna's eyes took in this wonder, studying her own face.

"What brings you here, honored Ashru? You and your beautiful, charmed daughter?" Tinna's gaze dropped, her look of bemusement quickly replaced by a blank expression. Her eyes darkened.

"I came because I have questions."

"Well, perhaps we have answers for you. Tea?"

"No thank you," Tinna replied, raising her hand. She stepped forward, approaching the old men, gazing into the eyes of each individual.

"Where are your guards?"

"We sent them away. We gave them Heeda, but in spite of our generosity towards them, they still acted with ingratitude towards us, angry perhaps that we had endangered their loved ones. We offered them a choice, to remain in service or to go. They chose to leave, so we sent them away."

"Can't say I blame them," Avria muttered bitterly.

"We are not entirely without assistance. Some of our servants have remained. You surely did not come all the way here to ask about the guards."

"We did not," Tinna retorted. She looked up at the moving mural again, unable to keep her eyes off of it. "Tell me, all of you were aware, all those years ago, who the perpetrator was that learned of the plagues that you beset upon this world. You knew where he was too, didn't you? You allowed him to continue." There was a pregnant pause, and then one of the old men walked to the tea urn, and poured himself a cup. Tinna wondered why the servants remained. Who would want to be around these murderous old bastards? He drank from the steaming cup and then said:

"Of course we knew where he was! Do you truly believe that we, who wield the most powerful creatures in this world, could be outfoxed by a mere mortal, an ordinary human? Of course not! We orchestrated it all. It was all destined to happen. All destined to take place," he pointed to the ceiling where the fresco with the depiction of Tinna hung heavily over their heads. Tinna's sword in the image hung heavily, blade down, the point moving slowly towards them.

"Do you not see what damage has been done?"

"We see only what benefits are reaped from the actions we take. We make the hard choices that must be made. This world is our ward, we must protect it; the races within it are our responsibility. It has always been so." Avria moved unhurriedly towards the side of the room where the windows looked out into the forests.

"What do you mean to accomplish, Ashru, coming here? You bring your daughter with you, endangering the life of the child within…"

"How would I be exposing her child to danger by coming here?" she asked, her brow rising in curiosity. "There is nothing here to fear, unless the danger of which you speak is you yourselves." There was a pall, a silence that lingered for a time and then one of the old men chimed in.

"It's odd that we did not sense your arrival Ashru. Odd indeed." Tinna dragged one of the chairs to face them, and sat in it, smiling with a touch cool smugness, her brow raised. Avria watched her from the side of the room, her fingers hovering over the cool hilts of her daggers.

"It's probably for the best. It's much better for us to arrive here without your being prepared to receive us."

"We would have been better hosts, for certain," the old man smirked—although she saw that each of them was beginning to show signs of alarm. They were finally realizing why Tinna had come. *How deluded they must be*, she thought, *to imagine I would come for any other reason—to take tea. With a sword on my back no less.*

She stood, and stretched. Her demeanor was changing right before their eyes; her cool reserve seemed to be barely holding back what seemed to be a boiling rage.

"My dear, I hope you do not intend on harming us," one of them finally uttered. "You do realize we possess great powers—and we have the protection of beings of great power as well."

"I don't see anyone else here, do you Avria?"

Avria shook her head, her face pale and drawn. Why she decided to come, she suddenly did not know. Why she thought she could do this alongside her mother, exact pain on old men—she felt irrational for even thinking so now. But then, as if sensing her doubt, a powerful surge of something radiated from her belly. She straightened and reached down to slide her daggers out of their sheaths. She watched her mother reach up to her shoulder and wrap her fingers around the hilt of her sword, drawing it out of the short scabbard and gracefully bringing it down in front of her.

"This will be the last time I will do something like this. I've been manipulated and toyed with enough. I am not your puppet. My family is not for you to control. I have accepted the future you have imposed upon me, to lead this land. But I will lead it without you. The time of the Keepers has come to an end." Her words were filled with ire, her eyes wide and empty.

The old men raised their hands up, and threw forth arcs of energy at both Avria and Tinna. Avria screamed and immediately covered her face with her arms, and hunched down into a defensive posture. Her body surged with power and she felt it radiate out from her chest. She was surprised to feel no effect of their attack. All she felt was a power radiating outwards. At first she thought it was her baby, but she realized it was not. It was coming from the center of her chest. She warily dropped her arms, and stood straight only to find the arcs of white energy colliding against a wall of nothing all around her, just as it had when Eleran had cast a protection spell on her long ago; only this time, it came from inside her. She looked over to her mother through the arcs of light, and saw them passing through her as if they were but beams of sunlight. Mother and daughter exchanged glances, and in tandem, the lifted their weapons for the kill.

CHAPTER TWENTY – ROYALTY

Avria could not deny that she was gratified to set eyes on the Drathar again. With the sorrow and pain of these past weeks laden upon her, all she felt a desire for familiarity and comfort, and he reminded her of these things for some strange reason. Her eyes took his form in warmly. She caught his appearance out of the corner of her eye, turned her head and looked at him. She realized there were several creatures in the room with them now. When they appeared, she did not know, she was too caught up in the mess she and her mother were making. She saw the Drathar, and she knew it was the one that was her friend by the way that he stood.

She just idled there among the carnage she and her mother had wrought, one pale hand gripping the top one of the chairs facing the doorway. On the chair below her hand, the bleeding form of an old man hunched forward, still twitching. Her other hand rested lightly on the flat of her belly. Her daggers were on the floor at her feet, both awash in an enamel of blood. Above, the mural was roiling; the tangle of vines twisting and writhing, wrapping itself around the past; consuming it. Tinna was haggard. Her darkness had yet to dissipate and the appearance of the Drathar made her spin around to face him, holding up the bloodied sword, her fingers and fist dripping with red.

"You have finished your killing, Gypsy Queen," he told her. She glared at the dark-robed figure and then dropped her hands and blade. "You have done more than enough," his voice had a smile in it. Avria looked on in strange, ambivalent silence. The Drathar's ghostly hand reached up and he threw back his hood. Carefully he removed his tunic and threw it aside, showing the full of his pale chest and arms to the women. The letters on his skin were flowing across his skin as if being carried by a current. One by one they were disappearing, sinking away inside him like leaves dropping down into the depths of the water. "You have freed us all," he said. As the last of the old men gurgled his final breath, his skin became completely clear of the spells that bound him. They watched as each of the ancient magicians began to dissolve like a lump of sugar in hot water, their blood drying up and flaking into ash. "We had nearly freed ourselves, but not quite. Not entirely. The Hevra's power had almost been enough to loosen our shackles, but not break them."

"But now, thanks to you, the Driva, the Chaiva, the Summoners, bearers of all kinds, the lot of us—nothing holds us back any more. Nothing." His words were edged with a manic joy, but his features were unseen behind his veil which was still wrapped around his head to protect the women.

The old man in the chair by Avria suddenly melted into sand the colour of ash, filtering down into sheets of tiny, glistening grains that piled onto the floor and in heaps on the chair, some remaining on the armrests as his hands fell apart into myriad grains. The blood on Tinna's sword and her hands also fell away, and Avria's daggers, once glistening red, were polished silvery steel again, the sand now resting on the beautiful rug beneath their feet.

"They are so ancient, nothing about them is real anymore. Magic held them together, and now they are dead, they've fallen apart," the Drathar observed. He stooped and scooped up a handful of the sand. "Reduced to the basic elements that made them what they were." Avria dusted off the beloved sweater, the blood that stained it was now a powdering of sand. She smiled. She realized she must have believed she was going to die when she dressed that morning, for she wore the sweater with the idea that stains wouldn't matter in the end.

"What you have done here is what will allow you to rule the common folk unhindered; it is what will solidify peace with the rest of us. Be warned; my bearer brothers will not withhold their enthusiasm for their freedom—they are unchecked now. The magic-bearers are now without laws, without restraint. They will wreak havoc," he explained. "Our power is why these old men kept a tight leash on us all. Because they knew *we* would be the end of order and peace. So they found ways to control us all. But now there are no more Keepers. No more Trinity governs. There is only you and it is your act of mercy that will keep us from destroying everything. We are in your debt. Yours…" he paused and his ace turned to Avria. "And hers." She in turn gazed upon him in quiet concern.

"Act of mercy?" Tinna scoffed, "you call this massacre an act of mercy?" The Drathar laughed quietly, and moved around the room, stepping over the piles of sand that were once old men, his face angled down to take in the scene in all its grisly beauty.

"If you had any knowledge of the sheer number of people who were in their grip for centuries, you would know how many people you have freed today; the thousands of beings that were muzzled by their spells, stifled, chained by their tyranny. We are free now. They can no longer control us; no longer harm us. The Drathar, we are the most powerful. The others below us will respect us. I speak for all." He paused in front of Avria and boldly placed his hand on her belly. She did not withdraw; she merely looked down at his hand. "Even for this one."

"They were threatened by the power in your daughter's belly. They were terrified of it. They were going to kill her and the child. I came as soon as I felt it," he looked up at Avria's beautiful face, and he caressed her cheek with the tips of his fingers. "But you had it all under control," he said softly to her, "beautiful creatures." He then turned and strode to Tinna, casting his gaze upwards to the moving ceiling.

"They could not see beyond you in the prophesies of the Founding Keeper. It was he who was the first to propose and implement the hobbling and binding of the bearers; to understand our power and to use it to exercise their own ends. But the founding Keeper was not all-powerful. His seeing eye could not see beyond you. His spells could not see beyond you, Tinna because none of them knew that your sword would kill them. They could not see even there, where your figure holds a sword that points down to where they sit, that their time on this world was at an end. They could not know that your power, Tinna, was to be immune to theirs. You were born to defeat these old codgers. Avria possesses the same power. You were the only ones who could ever do this," he spread his hands to encompass the room, "You are the only creature able to end their tyranny. That was your fate."

"Everything is going to change," Avria muttered.

"As long as the Ashru and her line rule this land, there will be some measure of peace. We can all promise you this," he gestured to the figures standing around the edges of the room. They seemed so still the women had almost forgotten they were there. "It is the gift we offer you for freeing the bearers. I cannot control everything that my kind will do, but I can assure you of our best effort to protect the common folk and most especially, your line, Ashru," he told them. He then took Avria's hand, and lifted it up to his veil, where he kissed her fingers through the fabric. She gazed up at him, her eyes wide and warm at the sight of him. She could see a glint of light catch his eyes beneath the veil. With a soft whisper that fluttered his veil he said.

"*You* and your child are especially dear Avria. I will be watching over the both of you." Once again, he vanished. Her hand was left poised in the air. One by one, the silent observers that had appeared only moments before stealthily followed Avria's Drathar and vanished in wisps of smoke. Tinna turned to her daughter, and shared a look of incredulity. They dusted themselves off, and walked through the silent citadel.

A young servant with dark wine-red hair and gold eyes appeared, drawn by the sound of their footfalls. Her face expressed severe alarm.

"I can't feel them..." she whispered in a strong Gheraine accent, her voice edged in panic. "Why can't I feel them?" The women stopped walking, and looked at her, their dark eyes taking her in. She was like a terrified mouse.

"They are dead. I recommend you run and find everyone else that still dwells here and urge them all to leave this place at once. In a little while, the citadel will be nothing but a burning ruin. Nobody will survive if they remain inside. The girl's frightened eyes flashed, and she scampered away, looking back at the women in fear.

Tinna and Avria made their way out of the citadel, happy to see Eretrix awaiting them at the edge of the trees, a shock of shining creamy red against the frozen, snowy landscape. Tinna and Avria climbed up onto the back of her neck and huddled up underneath her shallow shield. Up she went, into the sky, carrying them with her, her wings blowing clouds of snow-crystals with each pump until she finally got high enough to clear the tree tops. It wasn't long before the rest of the dragons had been summoned with their silent calls, and the women were delicately deposited on Ledroran's broad body. Dragons began to rise up from the forest like flocks of starlings.

Dragons of all sizes, gained altitude and spiraled higher and higher above the citadel, circling and circling until the sky was black with them.

WE ENTER A NEW AGE, Ledroran said. Behind them, a column of smoke rose up from where the citadel once stood, flocks of dragons still circling and blasting pillars of fire anywhere that was not already burning. It was a sight to see. Tinna and Avria sat against the back of Ledroran's skull. If they weren't it would be impossible to understand him in the wind. They watched the column of smoke recede, and the wildly careening dragons that continued to destroy everything that remained of the Keepers' home.

Tinna's hand slid over to her daughter's and they clasped onto each other. Her humanity had returned, and her eyes were glossed over with tears. She hadn't said a single word since they left the great temple that was now in ruins. Avria watched as Tinna's strength wavered and her grip tightened on her daughter's hand. It began with a tremor and then swallowed sobs. Tinna lost control. She lurched forward into the wind and began to weep. It was a sorrow that came from the depths of her soul. Her gut-wrenching sobs tugged at her daughter's heart. Avria was unsure what to do; she'd never seen her mother like this. She huddled onto her and gathered her close. Tinna crumpled onto her daughter's shoulder and then down onto Avria's lap where she cried and cried. Avria hunched over her mother, sitting her through her misery, fighting back the tears that threatened in her own eyes.

When her tears subsided she remained with her head on Avria's lap, hiccupping occasionally, staring out at nothing. Avria blankly rubbed her mother's back, touched and surprised that she was the one to give her mother comfort for once. She leaned forward and kissed her mother's cheek, and hugged her. She had no idea what awaited them when they returned to Miranne, but for the moment, they had some peace to simply be.

The coronation was a subdued occasion. The Magistrate, who was showing signs of illness, and several ministers who had been fortunate to have had the brandy were in attendance among a few others. The High King, looking old and frail, covered in lesions and rashes, had conceded his crown and handed it to Tinna from his deathbed. She was crowned in the company of only eighteen people; her husbands, her daughter, Offrin, the Duke and Duchess of Zadrudas and a smattering of other people. A message was dispatched across the countryside by Araki riders to inform the people of the coronation and to take an assessment of the damage caused by the virulent illness that ravaged the land.

The royal family moved into the main palace the day after the King died, but it was not long before the group headed south to Klatna, where Tinna insisted she would spend the rest of winter.

Taneth, being one of the few surviving human Wisemen, found himself falling into the role of leadership. The Keepers were no longer in control of the brotherhood, and the remnants of the organization turned to him for leadership. He accepted the mantle with sadness, for all his work to rebuild had been hampered by the decimation caused by the plague. There were fewer resources now, fewer people to continue the hard work rebuilding the academies. He would have to rely more on Araki and Adrei now.

Only one in a hundred humans in Oromoii survived the plague in the end. The isolated communities of Gheraine and Thran and the southerly countries suffered fewer losses thanks to their isolation and scattered communities, but they were stricken harshly nonetheless. At this point, it was impossible to know what the damage truly was, but one could see it in earnest riding through the cities nearly emptied of their residents, surrounded by large swaths of newly planted forests of trees where the Araki people had buried the dead.

Within months, the Araki communities began to emerge from the forests, branches of certain clans spreading into the old, nearly empty human settlements. A number of towns and cities were simply abandoned by the survivors. The remaining humans did not take long to gather into small, insular, jealously guarded communities where they were unwelcoming and suspicious of non-human races. Others moved south and west to join the less-affected communities around Thran, Gheraine and the xenophobic and scattered peoples of Kytrine.

Ledroran had been accurate in his prediction; it was a new age for the great lands. But nothing could fully prepare any of them for what was to come. The effects of unchecked magic-bearers was far-reaching and a growing problem. It wouldn't be long before the fragile peace would come undone, and the magic bearers would begin to rain chaos on the world. With no limits to their actions, no accountability or restrictions as they once possessed, they became increasingly violent and dangerous. The citadel and its secrets were destroyed. Tinna's peace would come to an end, in spite of the Drathar's promises—it was only a matter of time. She only hoped that the child Avria carried was truly blessed with the promise the Keepers had feared—and he or she could somehow bring peace and balance to the world once more when the time would come.

For the time being, the new Queen of Oromoii did what she could to rule the land and its people with a fair, but firm hand. With the support of the Dragon King, Ledroran, and her family, she was not alone. Avria, who had always been such a guileless creature had grown grave and hard like tempered steel. Tinna knew she would make an excellent Queen in her stead when the time came. For now, they all waited for the child to be born, and for the balanced future that this child might bring.